I0680499

The End

Book One
of the
Sanctuary Series

By

Roselle Graskey

and

Cheyne Curry

Bossy Pants Books

The End

DEDICATIONS

<u>From Roselle Graskey</u>:

A few years ago I was in dire financial straits, and my community helped me financially and emotionally. I said I would dedicate my next book to y'all. I meant it. I apologize for taking so long.

And to the women of the US Army Military Police Corps. Of the Troops and For the Troops.

<u>From Cheyne Curry</u>:

To the female soldiers who are never given enough praise and credit for the blood, sweat and tears they give to their daily missions. You will always be my heroes.

And, always, for Paladin

The End

**ALSO WRITTEN
BY CHEYNE CURRY AND
COMING SOON FROM BOSSY PANTS BOOKS:**

Clandestine
The Tropic of Hunter
Renegade

Permission To Recover
The Resistance (Book Two of The
Sanctuary Series)

The End

Book One
of the
Sanctuary Series

By

Roselle Graskey
and
Cheyne Curry

Bossy Pants Books

The End

THE END

Front and Back Cover design by Karen D. Badger

A Bossy Pants Book
Published by Bossy Pants Books
Columbus, Ohio 43229
bossypantsbooks@gmail.com

ISBN-10: 1-945124-03-2
ISBN-13: 978-1-945124-03-7

First Edition, February, 2017

Printed in the United States of America and in the United Kingdom

ACKNOWLEDGMENTS

Roselle would love to acknowledge the following people:

Cheyne Curry for being such a great writing partner. I still can't tell who wrote what parts. The first round is on me the next we're together.

Allison Mugnier, my wife - correction my long-suffering wife who takes amazing care of me so that I can do things like write with Cheyne. Tá tú mo bhaile.

Marie Logan, Nancy Bageanis Harrison, Sandy Thornton, Lynne Pierce and Jon Ryan Graves for reading and giving suggestions and generally making me laugh when I get too serious.

Cheyne would love to acknowledge the following people:

Roselle Graskey for having the same mindset and warped sense of humor.

Brenda Barton, my wife, my better half, my life. Your support and encouragement know no bounds. You are my champion and I love you with all my heart and soul.

Karen Badger and Bliss (Badger Bliss Books) for all their help, time and effort dedicated to making all this a possibility. And the wine.

Karen Badger for the cover/back cover art.

Day Peterson for her patience and mad skillz.

Barb Coles and Linda Daniels for always stepping up. You both will always have a special place in my heart.

Chris Westfield, M.E. Logan, Renae Hunt and Brenda for their proofreading, input and pep talks.

Chapter One

Warm. Smooth. The sensation of skin sliding along skin. Silence. Shaking.

Shaking?

Eyelids snapped open. "What was that?"

Branna Maguire sat up slowly, trying to orient her brain from dream state to the here-and-now. Her socked feet hit the floor with a quiet thud. When the blanket fell away, the chill of the air immediately raised rows of goosebumps. For a minute, she was distracted; she hated that sensation. It took a moment for the discomfort to ease. She was already moving away from the bed as she pulled on a sweatshirt.

Was it her imagination, or were the overhead lights just a bit dimmer than usual? She wasn't quite sure, but then again, she'd only had five hours sleep. Once upon a time that would not have bothered her; she would have known instantly if something were out of the ordinary.

"Soft living," she grumbled to herself.

She passed quickly out of her room and down the hallway. The door to the next room was open, and a half-second glance told her it was empty. The oddity of silence was getting on her nerves. Her temporary roommate was usually either chattering, playing music, or not watching a television that was constantly on. As often as Maguire complained about it, she always got the same answer. Her roommate needed the noise, could not sleep without it.

She passed the medium-sized galley kitchen, noting the lack of midnight snack remnants on the countertop that was the normal state of things. As she walked through the area styled as the living room, she began to worry. The television was off and a book was face up on the floor. As she pushed the far door open, she could hear tapping of a keyboard. Once she had cleared the doorjamb, she released a slow breath, relieved to see her roommate.

"What the hell is going on? Did we just have an earthquake?"

***

Jessica Baumer nearly jumped out of her skin, but to her credit she did not make a sound. Her light blue eyes glared evilly at her bunkmate.

"Jesus, Mags. You scared the daylights outta me."

She knew that her voice sounded like she'd smoked way too many cigarettes in her life. Privately she wished that were the case, as the truth of where the rasp came from was uncomfortable even to think about.

"Yeah, sorry." Maguire looked at the console. "What the hell are you doing?"

"Trying to figure out what the hell is going on." She felt a perverse thrill at tossing Maguire's words back at her. "I think the fracking messed us up again. The Richter reading was off the scale, which will happen if they drill too close to the post. It really screwed up our electronics this time. Power went out twenty minutes ago. Thirty seconds later the backup system kicked in, and fortunately it is still giving us juice."

Maguire scratched her head. "That's not supposed to happen."

Maguire's expression indicated that she knew that sounded stupid the second the words left her mouth. She looked around Baumer to the SecCom computer screen, but the only thing there was the cursor blinking in the instant message box.

"I'm trying to find out what's up, but no answers as of yet," Baumer responded. "The post commander is going to order heads to roll if they've knocked us off the grid again."

Maguire shook her head. "But when that has happened in the past, we have been up and running again in ten minutes at the longest. I mean, this whole station is pretty much a surge protector. You said the initial event was twenty minutes ago. What would cause the power to stay off and the backups to stay on?"

Baumer knew that Maguire was talking to herself, not

really expecting an answer. It was an annoying habit that Baumer had gotten used to, mostly. "There are five possible reasons listed in the manual."

"Five? Really? Makes me wish I'd read the damn thing."

Baumer glared, trying to figure out whether Maguire was being truthful or sarcastic. It was often hard to tell. As the silence stretched out between them, Baumer realized that she was being toyed with.

"You are deliberately being annoying, aren't you?"

"You Germans are stoic and serious; us mick types, we're smart arses." Maguire flashed a cocky grin. "What do you need me to do?"

Baumer considered for a moment. "Try to call up the surface cameras. With any luck, the terrestrial backup system is running them again, and before you ask—yes, I did try that earlier." She returned her focus to the display terminals in front of her before tossing over her shoulder, "And, I'm Austrian."

***

Sitting at the oversized monitor screens, Maguire sighed at the persistent fuzz running across them. She typed instructions into the system and mentally crossed her fingers. The screens flickered and then returned to fuzz.

"Feck," she muttered, and sat back. After two long minutes, the solution dropped into her brain, courtesy of the memory of an alluring audiovisual specialist she'd had the pleasure of dating for six months. She leaned forward and typed in a string of code commands. Hoping for success, at the same time she wondered if wishing for failure was actually the better option.

Baumer was correct that there were only five circumstances that would cause a system crash, the least disastrous of which was an epic earthquake. The movement that had awakened her from her bed had been minimal. They were close to the Barcones Fault, but that was inactive and had been for a few million years. A fracking disruption wasn't even on the list of potentially critical events. She hit the enter button and sat back.

Her attention was torn from the monitors by the sound of feet pounding the floor at a dead run. She turned to the door as

Baumer dashed in, nearly out of breath.

"Flash messages…emergency code…elevated DEFCON." She took in a deep breath. "They're still cycling in. Too many to read."

"From where?"

Baumer's voice was barely above a whisper. "Everywhere."

Cold sweat rose on Maguire's neck as she returned her gaze to the monitor. She blinked twice and wished to all the Irish Gods that she hadn't. "Holy Mother of Mercy."

Baumer peered at the monitors. Her knees gave out, and she sat awkwardly. "Unless this is a sick joke, or maybe a part of the experiment, we're most likely in a great deal of trouble. Please tell me I'm not seeing what I'm seeing."

For the first time in nearly five months, Maguire felt no desire to tease her roommate. Her voice raspy, she said, "I don't think I can."

Her gaze was locked on the grisly scene on every screen—bodies littering the ground, as far as the eye could see. She toggled the switch that operated the exterior pan, zoom, and tilt camera and pressed a few keys that called the image up to the largest screen. Some of the deceased looked almost peaceful in repose, while others showed evidence of having fought for every single second of life. Maguire's stomach turned, which surprised her, considering all the things she'd seen and done in her military career.

Baumer finally expelled a long breath. "What in the hell is happening?"

"I think the more accurate question is 'what the hell happened while we've been stuck down here like rats in a maze.'"

"Are these cameras set to record or are they real time?" Baumer asked, so clearly not wanting to.

Baumer outranked her, and so Maguire did as requested and checked the panel. "Record. Twenty-four, forty-eight, and seventy-two hour increments, depending on the camera."

Jessica Baumer swallowed audibly. "Call them up with each time wrap on a different monitor, if you can."

Feeling an edge of pain in her throat, Maguire typed in the

code string and was rewarded with a time frame. "They're in compressed data form. It will be three hours before we can see it."

"Three hours?" Baumer's voice was tight with anger.

"Kick the computer, not me. I just ask the questions," Maguire responded tersely.

Baumer took another deep breath. "I'm sorry. I know. It's just…"

"It's just fecked," Maguire added for her, knowing that her roommate would never resort to actual cursing.

Chapter Two

Baumer rubbed her tired eyes, then continued to read the backlog of messages. The news was of such scope and magnitude, that it was almost beyond the ability of her mind to take it in. Terrorists had launched a multi-pronged attack, which had, in turn, loosed the wrath and retaliation of nations that began turning on one another. Most of the world was now a quagmire of chaos and devastation. Most of the Middle East was melted glass; Europe, what had survived, was a toxic wasteland. Major American cities had been devastated by neutron bombs, while smaller cities had suffered from attacks of nerve agents and pulse waves. No country had been spared, and apparently only the most remote areas had survived total destruction.

Maguire sank into the chair beside Baumer's. "What's the report on Ireland?"

"Family?" Baumer almost regretted asking.

Maguire nodded sharply. "A very large one."

"Sarin gas in every major city and nerve agents that got caught up in the winds. Before RTE and the BBC went off line, they predicted ninety percent mortality rate." She watched Maguire's tears in silence. There wasn't much she could say other than "sorry," and that would be of no consolation in the wake of such a loss.

Maguire quickly composed herself, wiping away her tears. "What do we do now?"

Baumer thought for a very long moment. "Inventory what survival supplies and food and water we have left here, and ready them while we wait for word from anyone."

"Ready them for what?"

"For when we leave here. We can't stay here, and there is no guarantee that there is anyone left outside to rescue us."

"Or if anyone came, would they be friendly? And what does 'friendly' even mean anymore," Maguire observed.

"I have a friend who worked with a woman who runs a safe haven for women. For nearly two decades, she's planned for something just like this." Her laugh came out as a bark. "Hell, she warned her bosses for years that something like this could happen. I would like to think that she and her compound survived this."

"This woman, what makes her such an expert?"

Maguire's tone was more curious than suspicious, so Baumer provided additional information. "Noble used to work for think tanks that specialized in intelligence and analysis. The White House relied on her to unravel things their own analysts couldn't. She's one of the ones who early on said Noriega was a crook, and she advised that arming bin Laden and his group was not a good idea. When she got fed up with beating her head against the wall, she moved, bought a great deal of land, and created a sanctuary for women." She leaned back in her chair. "If she survived, at least we have a destination."

***

Baumer looked up from the monitor with a small grateful smile. Her stomach actually growled in anticipation of the food Maguire had brought.

"It's not much, but even I can't feck up grilled cheese," Maguire allowed as she set the plate down.

Baumer pushed the earphone off one ear. "You have no idea how much I love you right now."

Maguire flashed a rare sincere grin. "Oh sure, you say that now. But after I burn a cow or five, well then, it's back to grouse and complain." She sat down beside Baumer. "Getting anything?"

"A lot of static. Between listening to this and watching IM on MilCom, my brain is frying."

Baumer took a large bite of her sandwich, and for a while there was only the sound of food being devoured. Finally she said, with a hopeful lilt in her voice, "I'm confident we're going to make contact with someone."

Maguire talked around her mouthful. "Yeah, but which someone should we talk to?"

"I don't know." She thought for a long moment. "I could try NorCom. The trouble with that is, I don't have an ident code so they could just fry me off the net, or so I've been told."

Maguire cocked her head. "You don't have an ident code for NorCom?"

"You see these little baby bars? They don't rate a code at that level." Baumer scowled.

"But you're Intel, right?"

"Yeah, *now*. But my original clearance was Signal, enlisted at that. Hard to change those puppies." She shook her head. "My security clearance updates are still on delay because some camo wonder boy with zero deployments thinks I have a mental issue." She glanced at the sergeant. "And I don't have mental issues, believe me."

Maguire snorted. "Next lifetime, become an MP. You'll get all the cool toys."

Baumer looked at her over what was left of her sandwich. "You have a NorCom ID?"

"Yes." Maguire was not more forthcoming, and for a change, her face wore no smile of any kind.

"You can't just admit that you have clearance and then leave me hanging. You have to tell me." Baumer was all but pouting.

Maguire sighed and pointed to her shoulder patch. "Fianoglach. I'm Special Forces. I rate an ID, mostly so they can keep tabs on me," she added with a wry grin.

Baumer nearly choked on a bit of bread, and it took a couple of coughs to clear it before she could speak. "We've been stuck down here five months, and *now* you tell me what that damn flash means?"

"You never asked. And honestly, it came as a result of circumstances that I don't like to talk about," Maguire said. "I'd rather we not use my ident if we can help it."

Baumer's curiosity was piqued. "Want to tell me why?" When Maguire maintained her silence, she added, "I could make that an order."

"You could, but I'll save you the trouble. Remember when

Kim Jong-un decided to invade South Korea?" she asked almost casually.

"Remember it? My unit was getting ready to deploy when he was taken out by his ministers and the whole thing just...ended." Baumer exhaled sharply.

"I was there during it. Got shot there. After that..." Maguire took a moment, as if she was trying to decide what she could and should share. "I pissed off some brass decorations, if you will, and I'd hate to have to answer to them again if I can help it."

"How decorative, if I may ask?"

"Decorative enough to walk through the halls of the most hallowed of houses," Maguire answered honestly.

"Yeah. That would be decorative. You must have really pissed them off."

"You have no idea. In my defense, I do have to say that at the time, I was under the influence of the most wonderful painkillers." Maguire produced a roguish smile.

Baumer shook her head. "You must have nine lives, Mags." She suddenly bolted upright in her chair. "Holy shit! I have an IM hit." She slid her chair closer to the monitor and attacked the keyboard, her fingers flying over the keys as she fixed her gaze on the monitor.

AAGHuAZns5601: Moi drug is it you?

AAGHoTXjb1616: Szab it is.

AAGHuAZns5601: Prove it moi drug.

Baumer didn't hesitate.

AAGHoTXjb1616: Your father plays the cello, your mother makes the best gyros, and your brother Misha only wants to be a cosmonaut.

AAGHuAZns5601: I need more.

AAGHoTXjb1616: I was there when you needed a sister.

There was no answer for a long two minutes, just a blinking cursor.

"C'mon Szab, you know it's me," Baumer muttered.

AAGHuAZns5601: Stratzvitye moi drug. Sorry for the questions, but we have to be sure.

Baumer blew out a heavy breath of relief. "Thank God!"

AAGHoTXjb1616: We?

9

AAGHuAZns5601: Me and Pres. Yes, Prescott is here too. She is resting now. I think she will be happy to know that you have survived.

AAGHoTXjb1616: Szab, do you know what happened?

AAGHuAZns5601: Only that the world as we know it has ended. We don't know who or why, but we know a little of how. How did you survive?

AAGHoTXjb1616: I was down in a hole with a new friend, courtesy of the Army. Long story. I'll tell you when I see you, if I see you.

AAGHuAZns5601: Where are you?

AAGHoTXjb1616: Hood. Where are you two?

AAGHuAZns5601: Huachuca. Underground for now. Stay underground. Do not go up no matter what, at least one more week, possibly three, until the air clears. Remember what they used to say about the Soviet doctrine?

AAGHoTXjb1616: Yeah, it was beat into my head.

AAGHuAZns5601: They did not lie. Mid-level nukes, bio and nerve agents via air, but the fog will dissipate. They want the land intact.

AAGHoTXjb1616: Who, Szab?

AAGHuAZns5601: I don't know, but it was a Soviet doctrine attack.

AAGHoTXjb1616: Szab, the Soviets haven't existed for years.

AAGHuAZns5601: That does not change things. The initial attacks were classic Soviet, with allied response. Terrorist or country does not matter anymore, not now, only that it was done. Old Soviets could have sold the codes for money. Maybe Russian mafia, maybe the old KGB, maybe GRU, maybe anyone they sold to.

AAGHoTXjb1616: If they wanted that, they could have just hit with neutrons.

AAGHuAZns5601: Tell that to Tel Aviv. They were hit with neutrons. The only survivors in Israel were the deep-water miners. I think there are fifteen of them. Palestinians do not exist anymore, same bombs. There were not enough neutron bombs in existence to do all this.

AAGHoTXjb1616: Jesus.

AAGHuAZns5601: I do not think Jesus has anything to do with this.

AAGHoTXjb1616: Could China have done this?

AAGHuAZns5601: If they did, they do not exist anymore. It appears as though Japan and Russia nuked her with everything they had left. She is no longer a threat.

Baumer and Maguire both exhaled loudly. A potential enemy was dust.

AAGHoTXjb1616: China? Good God.

AAGHuAZns5601: I do not lie.

AAGHoTXjb1616: I'm not saying you do, it's just so damned hard to take in. Does anyone live?

AAGHuAZns5601: Australia is intact, but she has cut herself off from others. The poles are intact, but who wants to live in that cold? And some Far East pacific islands seem to be intact. Contact with them is intermittent at best, so we don't know for sure.

AAGHoTXjb1616: Who's in charge?

AAGHuAZns5601: Of what?

AAGHoTXjb1616: Of us, the United States of America.

There was a pause, which led Baumer to believe Szabo was trying to get information.

AAGHuAZns5601: Unknown at this time. We don't know who was caught where or who survived or who is hunkering down until the air clears. Information from NorCom is limited, and then only to those who can prove they have the clearance to receive the updates. Unfortunately, that does not include us.

AAGHoTXjb1616: So being surviving members of the military force doesn't count?

AAGHuAZns5601: Nope. Not in our case anyway.

AAGHoTXjb1616: What if one of us has—

When Maguire put her hand over Baumer's, the lieutenant stopped typing. "Don't. Something isn't right about no immediate chain of command being established, no orders being sent out, and especially about not allowing even limited information to go to established military checkpoints. You said they're at Huachuca?"

"Yes."

The screen blinked for their attention.

AAGHuAZns5601: What if one of us has what?

Maguire steepled her fingers. "Huachuca is where the Intelligence Center, NetCom, and one of the larger signal brigades are located. If NorCom isn't communicating with Military Intelligence there, just as it isn't communicating with battlefield surveillance and aerial, tactical, and MI ops here, something is terribly wrong. They're ignoring protocol. Before we give out information about my clearance, I think it's important to know who's running things. And until we know who is in charge, we don't know whether we're the cavalry or the enemy."

AAGHuAZns5601: LT? Jess? Lt. Baumer?

Baumer studied the screen as she absorbed Maguire's caution, then she began typing again.

AAGHoTXjb1616: I'm here. How secure is your communication?

AAGHuAZns5601: Unknown. We haven't been able to raise anyone else on post, so we can't be sure if there's any filtering. It's like the surviving elite just disappeared, which is odd. You'd think we'd be able to raise MI. It's just across the battalion HQ, and they were more protected than we were.

"See? That just doesn't make any sense," Maguire said.

"That almost sounds like they were prepared or forewarned and got outta Dodge with all speed," Baumer said.

"Which means we weren't expected to survive…at least not very long. We really need to get out of here ASAP."

"We need allies we can trust."

AAGHoTXjb1616: Is Noble still alive?

AAGHuAZns5601: She is. Sanctuary is still there. We had contact this morning. I have another contact coming in. I cannot tell how long this will take. Will you be on later?

AAGHoTXjb1616: I'll check back at 1500 hours my time. Kick Prescott out of bed by then.

AAGHuAZns5601: Roger. 1500 yours. Double AGHuAZns5601 clear.

Baumer waited for a message from any other source, but finally gave up. "Holy God."

Maguire nodded. "What the hell have we fallen into?"

"I'd say Hell about sums it up."

Chapter Three

For the first week after the catastrophe, Maguire and Baumer bunked down in the communications room. They tried to assess their immediate situation, as well as what might be surrounding them at Hood, internally and externally. They had eliminated most of the "what ifs" and "if onlys" from their conversation and focused on whatever realities they could glean from the information provided by their sporadic communications. It seemed miraculous that despite all that had happened, they still had a means to communicate through cyberspace with survivors in other states and countries.

Both soldiers were cautious with the information they gave out, speaking prudently only to anyone with the Active Army Garrison prefix on their screen name. The more they found out about the events that had caused the circumstances in which they now found themselves, the less they trusted anyone they could not personally verify. Eventually they stopped sending and receiving messages with anyone but Szabo and Prescott at Huachuca.

They took their nourishment from the provisions that remained in the cupboards and refrigerator of their small kitchenette. When those were gone, they lived on the heavily stocked Meals Ready to Eat or MREs in the attached supply room. They conserved as much water as possible, hoping that when they were able to leave, they would have enough extra to last them until they reached their next safe location—if such a thing existed anymore.

Once the shock began to wear off, although they seemed perfectly safe holed up in their underground home, they discovered that they had to rely more on their own instincts. Their sharpening sensory perceptions helped them know when it was safe for them to relax or, more often, made the little hairs on the backs of their necks stand at attention. Most of their time was spent waiting, watching their monitors for any signs of life, or more death, on the outside, any indication there were any other underground survivors like them.

So far, they had become aware of only one—a private first class named Davies, who had been in a walk-in freezer in one of the below ground storage units for the closest mess hall. He had put out a general SOS on a hand-held radio, which Maguire picked up on the second day. Davies was scared. He had entered a highly contaminated area after the initial attack, and even though he immediately retreated back underground, he had been exposed to moderate radiation. There was no one to treat his poisoning, and although it might take several weeks to ravage his systems, he knew his days were numbered. By week two, they could no longer raise him. Baumer guessed that his radio battery had died. Maguire believed that, knowing his future was bleak at best, he had ended his own life.

Both women had no doubt that others must have survived at Hood, but there was no way to confirm that, and no one else had yet been successful at establishing communications with them. As the weeks passed, Baumer and Maguire made preparations to leave their underground home, or prison, depending on one's point of view, when the backup system inevitably lost power. A second emergency generator kicked in, one that was specific to their building, but they knew it would not last long, so they used the power source sparingly. The fact that they were still friends after so much time being isolated with just the other as company was a testament to their mutual respect for how their different training and experience complemented one another's and made it all work. Still, that didn't keep touches of cabin fever and the occasional snappishness from overtaking them. When that did happen, each took to her own pursuits. Baumer took refuge in her books and intelligence analysis, while Maguire went to the weight room to work out her frustration.

Finally the day arrived when it was no longer an option to leave their subterranean quarters, and they faced the uncertain eventualities with equal parts apprehension and relief.

***

Maguire stood in front of the sealed door and pondered what they were about to do—open the door and step out into what was left of their world. She released out a slow breath and turned to Baumer. "You're sure about this?"

Baumer did not look up from the gear she was adjusting. "We don't have much choice. It's only luck that we haven't already been plunged into darkness. And, Prescott relayed Noble's information that neutron bombs and short life chemicals were responsible for the majority of the death toll in our region. We've been in here six weeks. The after-effects should mostly have worn off."

"It's the 'mostly' that bugs me, ya know? I really don't want to have survived that little boondoggle in Korea only to get zapped by something I can't see," Maguire griped.

"Did you see the guy that shot you?" Baumer asked, finally looking up.

Maguire grinned. "Oh yeah, I saw him. I got shot, then I blew his fecking head apart. By the way, there was cursing involved."

"Did you trust your instincts then?" Baumer asked, clearly ignoring the strained attempt at humor.

"Absolutely," Maguire answered without hesitation.

"Well, I trust my instinct to believe Noble and Prescott. We'll have the NBC suits, and the radiation and chemical alarms. We should have plenty of warning if we are about to run into anything nasty," Baumer reasoned.

"If we can get into all the nifty gear rooms," Maguire pointed out.

Baumer tapped her head. "While you were working out your muscles, I was working on my brains. I have access codes memorized, and I know where the base commander kept his all-access key."

Maguire nodded, not because she agreed, but because staying was simply not an option. It was either leave, or stay there and die—from insanity, heatstroke due to the lack of cool air, or eventual starvation and dehydration. She slid her chemical mask over her head, blew out excess air, covered the filter ports, and sucked in, sealing the mask. "All right. Let's move."

Baumer repeated Maguire's preparations and then tapped the code into the door pad. They could barely hear the door locks disengage. Baumer pushed the door open, then walked down the corridor and through another set of doors that led to the stairwell.

They walked up four flights to the ground level and stepped into something that was worse than anything Dante could have contrived. All around them were the decomposing bodies of fellow soldiers, with the carcasses of natural scavengers close by. Maguire tried not to focus on nametags or what was left of faces. She'd seen more than her fair share of combat and dead bodies, but it was never like this. At least then the corpses were policed up and either sent back home or buried.

Maguire led the way as they stepped out into the sun. Sweat instantly formed on her skin. Texas in summer was damn hot. She was very glad for the filters in her breathing mask; they cut down on the stench of rotting bodies. At that thought, her breathing became more rapid. Realizing her error, she slowed her respiration and looked back at Baumer, whose visor was beginning to fog.

Maguire's hand on Baumer's shoulder clearly startled the lieutenant, as Baumer stopped and pressed her hand against her chest. "Don't do that," Baumer shouted.

"Slow your breathing. I don't wanna haul you around if you pass out." Maguire shrugged, but there was a smile in her eyes.

"Sorry. This is just..." Baumer's voice failed her. When they began moving again, she said, "There are really no words to describe this horror."

"I know." Maguire surveilled the immediate area. "I say we hit the motor pool, grab some wheels, and get to the depots where we need to gather our gear. It'll be easier than walking." She glanced around at the carnage. "Plus, if we drive past the bodies, we won't have to see them as individuals."

Baumer nodded. "How far to the closest one?"

Maguire looked around and calculated their location in relation to the facilities on base that they would need to access.

"About a half klick west."

"Let's do it," Baumer said. "You lead, you know this place better than I do."

They turned west and resumed walking. It was not long before the eerie silence got to them. Baumer glanced at Maguire. "I've been meaning to ask you how you got chosen for the isolation experiment."

Maguire snorted. "Chosen," she mused. "Chosen is an odd word for it. Chosen suggests that I volunteered for selection. Basically I pissed off my CO and got tossed into the dungeon."

"Should I ask how?" Baumer's voice was muffled, but the humor in it was clear.

"I beat his car to death with a baseball bat," Maguire answered directly, with a grin that could not be seen. "I'm very good in the field, but apparently when in garrison, I have 'anger management' issues."

They walked for a short distance further before Baumer spoke again. "What'd he do?"

"He pulled passes from some Korea vets and gave them to his little suck ups. Those little 'chair borne' rangers had never been deployed anywhere. It pissed me off to no end. I guess that I should say those guys were never deployed until now."

"Sounds like he deserved to have his car beat."

"How'd you end up with the likes of me?" Maguire scanned the area in front of them.

"From what I was told, I have socialization issues. I can't stand to be isolated." Baumer took her time before she continued. "I got cut off from my unit. I spent one very long month and a half on my own outside Incirlik, when we were evacuating Kurds from Northern Iraq. I was listed as MIA the entire time. I finally made it to Adana, where I was able to contact the post."

"That would do it," Maguire agreed.

"Yeah."

When silence fell between them again, neither of them broke it.

***

Baumer pushed the last of the food and water into the back shell of the High Mobility Multipurpose Wheeled Vehicle, commonly known as the Humvee, and closed it with a latching click that sounded entirely too final. She could hear Maguire wrestling the new Squad Automatic Weapon, or SAW hybrid machine gun into place. "You sure you want to bring that puppy with us? We've got the M4s."

Maguire stuck her head out of the turret. She was sweating, and her face was red with exertion. "M4s are good, but a Hybrid is priceless. Nice to finally have a machine gun with the same 7.62 kick of the old M60 but as light as the SAW. This will justify all the extra ammo we're going to carry. Let's say we run into other survivors who do not have the best of intentions." She patted the weapon. "This baby can fire up to a thousand rounds a minute, depending on how I set up the ammo feed. Would you mess with it?"

"Good point. Sometimes I think I've spent too long behind a desk." Baumer sighed and pulled a topographical map from her pocket. "Okay, we're looking at least three maybe four days driving, depending on what we run into. That's the timeline I gave Prescott."

Maguire appeared to be calculating the distance in her head. "Depending on our speed, we should be good on gas. If we run low, I think we can forage for fuel."

"Siphoning?" Baumer made a particularly sour face. "Gas tastes awful."

"Siphoning? I don't think that will be necessary. If we find any abandoned vehicles, we can poke a hole in the gas tank and let it drain into a can. If that isn't an option, we can find an out of the way gas station where I can get us gas, even if the pumps are shut off." She grinned. "Don't ask, just chalk it up to a bored, misspent youth."

"I'll take your word for it. Okay, here to Fort Bliss is twelve to fifteen hours, give or take, depending on what we have to use for roads. I say we break for rest there, then move on."

She looked into the passenger compartment of the Hummer and blinked. The compartment was storing all the cans of ammo and jerry cans full of fuel. If they took a couple of serious rounds in the body of the vehicle, they would most likely feel the explosion for about a half a second.

"Hey, Maguire."

"Yeah?"

"Don't light a smoke anywhere inside the back compartment, okay?"

Maguire laughed. "What? You don't want to go out in a blaze of glory?"

"You could say that," Baumer agreed.

"Relax, L.T.," Maguire said, using the slang for Baumer's rank. "Those cans are designed to explode only after reaching a certain heat point, and the tops are rated as zero fume spill. If we roll over and are trapped inside, or some idiot pops us with armor piercing rounds, I'll worry, but a couple of Zippo flicks are not going to bother a thing."

"If you blow me to kingdom come, I'm going to be pissed," she grumbled.

Maguire laughed and turned her attention back to the gun mount. "Come on, you bitch." She wrestled the weapon onto a tight retaining pin. "Get in there."

Baumer grabbed two sets of night vision goggles along with extra batteries and stuffed them into a carry-all. Their essential gear would travel up front with them. Between the radio, food and water for the first day, personal weapons, ammo and body armor, it was going to be a tight fit.

I hope to God I'm making the right choice here. Baumer closed her eyes. The last time she'd made this kind of decision, she'd chosen badly, or so the military had decided. She added a pair of tactical binoculars and tried to quiet the doubting voices in her head.

Chapter Four

Behind the dark goggles, Maguire blinked her eyes several times to ease the tired burning. It didn't help. Twelve hours of standing, the last six hours staring at west Texas scrub and dirt while driving approximately parallel to what was once Highway 190 and Interstate 10 and the devastated small towns along those routes, was just not doing it for her. It was time for another short break from watching a whole lot of nothing.

She ducked into the interior of the vehicle and pulled the goggles down around her neck, then half shouted to be heard. "How you doing, L.T.?"

Baumer did not take her eyes off the road. "I'm good, but we're down to half a tank of fuel."

Reflexively, Maguire's gaze flicked to the gauges. "You want to pull over now or keep moving?"

"We can go a few more, I'm in the zone." The smile she flashed was confident and not at all tired.

"Roger that. I'm hungry. You want some MRE?"

"I'm good. I had some trail mix earlier." Baumer grabbed her water bottle, took a healthy drink, then set it back down.

Maguire reached down between her feet to grab the remaining food out of the brown plastic bag. She snagged the dessert with a smile, then ducked a little lower when the bag proved itself stubborn. She was pulling the brownie free when Baumer hit the brakes, hard.

Maguire dropped her dessert and her hand and elbow connected with the dash while she nearly went ass over head. Her helmet stopped her forward progress. Then all motion stopped. She was acutely aware of the smell of hot rubber. "Goddamn, Lieutenant," she grunted as she righted herself. "What the hell was that?"

Baumer did not look at her companion; she was staring out

the windshield. Her normally pale complexion was waxy. "That." She pointed to the road ahead.

Maguire turned her head and was struck speechless. In front of them the road was a ribbon of heaves and drops, *serious* heaves and drops. The areas to the left and right were just as damaged. Her stomach did a half roll and fear bled through her. As if what they had already witnessed on their short journey wasn't dystopian enough.

"I'm going to guess that's not normal," she finally managed.

"Definitely not normal." Baumer's voice was flat. "I almost drove us into the abyss."

"This sucks."

Baumer nodded. "That's an understatement."

Maguire looked down. "Aw, fuck." Her brownie was on the floorboard. "Reporting one casualty, Ma'am."

Despite their predicament, Baumer laughed.

Maguire glared at her. "I can't even invoke the five second rule."

Baumer rested her head back against the seat and continued to laugh. "Would you like to give it a proper burial? You should save it for later. Who knows when it will come in handy? In this existence, somehow I think a little dust and grime will be the least of our worries." She looked back at Maguire, who was still grieving the loss of her treat. "I'm sorry." She drew in a deep breath. "This is just all so unreal."

Maguire took one last longing look at her erstwhile dessert and shook her head. She unsnapped her Kevlar helmet and worked the straps free from her goggles. "While we're stopped, I'll fill the tank. I'd rather have the gas in and not need it, than the other way around."

***

Baumer listened as Maguire exited the Hummer and start digging out a fuel can. She closed her eyes for a moment and tried to think as the queasy feeling in her stomach began to lessen. Eventually she opened the stow, grabbed the road atlas and started flipping pages. Her advanced officer courses had outlined the different ways particular weapons would impact on terrain, but for the life of her she could not figure out what could have caused the earth to move to this extreme.

Her finger tracked west from their current position, having to flip the page to New Mexico, then Arizona, and finally California. Suddenly an answer from the Jeopardy game show popped into her head. She closed the atlas and exited the vehicle with her binoculars in hand. She scanned to the west as far as she could, decided she needed more altitude, and climbed up onto the Hummer.

"Well, hell," she muttered, and then carefully climbed down. She walked around to Maguire. "Earthquake."

"You're talking in shorthand again." Maguire tipped the gas can forward.

"El Paso is within the radius of the fault line that runs along the base of the Franklin Mountains."

"Ah. That would explain this bloody mess."

"I checked the map. We need to stay close to 62/180. Fort Bliss is southwest-ish from here."

"Southwest-ish? Is that a real direction?"

"New world, new language, Maguire," Baumer said without missing a beat.

"Ooooh…can I make up words, too?"

Baumer smirked. "I'm sure any of the words you would come up with would not be fit for tender ears or mixed company."

"Hey, I'm a lifer. In basic training, the mess hall, they served alphabet soup with just four letters. I'm a product of my environment," Maguire countered.

"Frightening thought, that." Baumer returned her focus to the horizon. "Okay. If we trend northwest from here, we'll hopefully run into the post boundaries. I did desert training here about a lifetime ago. I think I can get us there."

"Overland, I'm guessing." Maguire let the last of the fuel in the can fill the tank, then set the can on the ground.

"Of course. The roads are crap, but then again, out in the desert we might drive right into a crevasse," Baumer mused.

"Six of one, half dozen of the other," Maguire agreed. "We've got eight cans left, so we're good on go juice. When we get to a town and take a look-see, we can restock."

"Sounds good." She handed over the binoculars. "Keep a lookout for drop offs and bad guys."

Maguire chuckled. "I live to serve." She stowed the fuel can quickly, then with a sigh of regret, tossed her brownie out of the Hummer and clambered her way to the top hatch.

Baumer shook her head as she moved back into the driver's seat. She was not looking forward to the next forty or so miles before they got to what she hoped would be El Paso.

＊＊＊

Baumer's neck and shoulders ached with tension. The last hour and a half had been an exercise in operating on hyper-alert. Three times they came across drop offs too deep to traverse, and had to drive along the edges until they found a crossing point. The last crossing had been executed with a prayer on her lips. She could actually hear ground falling away from her tires and hitting bottom way, way down.

Maguire ducked down into the Hummer. "You are not going to believe this, but there's something up ahead."

"Care to be more specific?"

"It's kind of hard to describe." Maguire's forehead scrunched with her non-explanation. "Just keep rolling forward, half a klick up. You should see it soon." Maguire popped back up to her scout position.

Ten minutes later, Baumer had stopped the Hummer a hundred meters from what could best be described as a large shack. The sides were weathered boards, and the tin roof was rusted away in several spots. She leaned on the horn to alert anyone inside that company was arriving.

"What are you doing?" Maguire asked in a harsh whisper, head quickly swiveling left and right.

"Why are you whispering? I'm announcing our presence. Let's put it this way, if you lived here who would you trust more, the people who say 'hi, I'm here,' or those who just walk up to your door without a hello?"

Maguire opened her mouth to reply, closed it with a click of her jaw, and shook her head. "You get me killed, and I'm going to haunt you. I'm Irish, so I can do that."

"I'll keep that in mind." Baumer became silent, sure that she'd heard something. She turned her head. There was absolutely nothing moving except a hot, sluggish wind.

She twisted her body to look at Maguire, who shrugged as she continued to scan the area. Baumer slowly rolled the Hummer forward, but kept her hand near the gearshift just in case she had to pop into reverse. She kept rolling until she reached what she guessed had once been a driveway. With a twist of the key, the engine stilled.

Baumer exited the vehicle and picked up her M4. She kept the weapon pointed down, not wanting to appear too aggressive but not wanting to look like a potential victim either. Maguire clambered down from her spot and took up a similar stance.

Back to back, they slowly turned 180 degrees. Not too far in the distance, the Franklin Mountains stared back at them.

"Even amidst all of this insanity, it's beautiful," Baumer murmured as she moved to stand next to Maguire.

"Very beautiful, if you can get past the harsh conditions," a young female voice said from behind them. "I'd appreciate it if you'd keep your weapons pointed at the ground."

"Okay," Baumer readily agreed. "Mind if we turn around?"

"That's fine. Just so you know, I've got a shotgun on you."

Baumer and Maguire turned slowly, both keeping the barrels of their weapons pointing to the ground. The sight that greeted them was a slim young woman with impossibly straight hair, so black it was almost blue. Her shotgun definitely commanded their attention.

"I'm Lieutenant Baumer, this is Staff Sergeant Maguire, US Army. I'd shake your hand, but…"

The young woman chuckled but did not lower her own weapon. "Victoria Lejos. You're coming from the wrong direction to be soldiers from the base."

"Yeah. We're rolling in from Hood towards Arizona."

The woman seemed to digest the information as her gaze pinned them in place. "It's just the two of you? No one else dropped off a mile back and is tracking behind you?"

Baumer didn't hesitate. "Just us. We didn't find anyone else…alive when we came up from our hole. It's a long story."

Victoria nodded. "Keep 'em safed and come in out of this heat. Hope you won't be too offended if I warn you that I will shoot you if I have to."

Maguire looked at Baumer. "I like her."

"You like girls with guns? What a shock," Baumer said dryly.

Victoria led them into the shack, which was burning hot inside. She halted at a half open wood plank door. "My granddad built this place, and yes, he meant it to look like this." She pulled the door open and waved them through.

Baumer and Maguire hesitated before they stepped in. When Victoria closed the door, the room began to move down, and the two soldiers shared a look of surprise.

Victoria laughed. "Everyone called my granddad a kook and a lunatic. Turns out, he was right."

"I'm guessing there's a story there," Baumer hazarded.

"Yeah, sort of a long one, but we have time. Feel like some lemonade? With ice." Her grin was sly.

"Ice? Real ice," Maguire repeated with disbelief.

Victoria grinned. "Solar power."

"A suspicious mind might wonder why you're showing two strangers your inner sanctum," Baumer said casually.

Victoria nodded. "Yeah, but then that suspicious mind doesn't know how to get the elevator back up to the top," she countered. "And an honest person knows enough to voice the thought you just did. College aside, I've lived in the area my whole life. For the most part, soldiers are honest and trustworthy."

The elevator halted with a small jolt. Victoria pushed a button that opened the double steel, sealed door that faced them, and she led the way into a very comfortable looking room.

"Feel free to take a seat." She slung the shotgun over her shoulder, barrel down. "I'll get the lemonade, then we can talk."

Baumer and Maguire looked at one another, then Baumer shrugged and Maguire proceeded to look around. The contents of the room were comfortably worn, and the family photos were about what one would expect. What was not expected were the framed degrees from three different universities, including one from MIT.

"Wow, someone is hugely smart," Maguire muttered.

"No kidding." Baumer looked at the framed photos. "Same man with some serious dignitaries. Here's one of him and General Brannon."

"General of the Army Brannon?"

"I only know of the one," Baumer confirmed.

"His younger brother's a one-star. He was my CO in Alaska. I guess I should say he *was* a one-star," Maguire corrected. "Damn, this is hard to get used to."

"That's my granddad," Victoria said quietly as she placed the glasses of lemonade on the coffee table. "He's brilliant to the point of making you feel really dumb. Never play Jeopardy or Trivial Pursuit with him."

Baumer and Maguire nodded acknowledgement as they joined Victoria on the couch.

"Sorry. Natural curiosity." Maguire picked up an offered glass. Sure enough, there were ice cubes floating in it.

"It's quite all right. Granddad does the same thing. Sorry about the reception. We've had some less than welcome visitors." She took a long sip of her drink. "I know you've got questions."

Baumer placed the cool glass against her forehead. "Only about a million." She frowned. "Earthquake?"

"Yeah, a big one, but Granddad planned well when he built all of this. It took us a couple of weeks to clean up after that one. I'm sure glad he's as brilliant as he is quirky. He installed a vertical/horizontal spring system, just in case."

Baumer was stunned. "Like they do in Japan?"

"Yeah. He worked in Japan for years on similar systems. I'm guessing whatever hit California was huge. We have a HAM radio, and sometimes we can raise northern Oregon but not much in California anymore. We had contact with a station agent in the old Fort Ord area about a week ago, but Cramer, the soldier we talked with, hasn't been active lately. Last time we talked, he sounded…sick." She rolled her glass in her hands. "Before that, he said there had been multiple nuke detonations, just above surface."

"Standard Soviet doctrine, adopted by jihadists," Baumer said quietly.

"Whatever it was, it worked. We haven't had a lot of contact since then. We get some transmissions from Idaho and Montana, and made a few contacts in Illinois, but most of the time it's dead quiet."

"How did you survive?" Maguire asked as delicately as possible.

Victoria almost laughed. "Pure damn dumb luck. There are two levels below this one. Granddad spent a lot of time working for the government, decades really, and just got it into his head that the world was going to come to an end at some point. They paid him a beggar's fortune for his brains, and he invested a lot of it, made a bigger fortune by guessing right, I suppose. Apple computers, ground floor. Internet Explorer, ground floor." Her laugh came in a short bellow. "Tetris, he invested a hundred grand in that game company. Who knew? Ten million dollar return. Anything with a different sounding name, he went for. The longer he worked for the government, the more 'paranoid' he became."

"And that's why he built this place." Baumer sipped her lemonade and nearly swooned. "This is very good."

Victoria smiled. "Thanks." She took a deep breath. "Yeah, he spent a mint on this installation. Air filtration system, solar batteries hidden around all the crap outside, rehydration water system, titanium piping system, EMP shielding times three layers—you name it, it's here."

"Where is he?"

Victoria contemplated her answer for a long moment. "Headed to Canada. There's someone there. She's important to him."

"So, you are station keeping, so to speak," Maguire clarified.

"Yeah." She took a sip and set the glass down. "He was having problems with figuring out what he should have entertainment wise." She shook her head. "So I came with four boxes of books about everything, even stuff that would aggravate the hell out of him. We were down on the lowest level when his DEFCON alarm went off." She fell silent. "He sealed the doors before I could even think of reacting."

"Noble would love your granddad," Baumer mused aloud.

"Rachel Noble?" The pitch of Victoria's voice rose, as her interest was piqued.

"Yeah, you've heard of her?"

"Are you kidding? Granddad says she was one of his most brilliant students. I met her once. She and Granddad spent the whole night talking about something they called the final quantum. It was very intense and way over my head at the time. She survived? Of course she survived." Victoria answered her own question. "Jesus, I'll have to let him know."

"What did they mean by the final quantum?" Maguire asked.

Victoria's head gave a half shake. "I was fourteen, I didn't catch all of it, but it had to do with multiple weapon strikes and the mathematical probabilities of successful survival. Like I said, over my head at the time."

"At the time?" Baumer repeated.

"Well, yes. Once I hit MIT, I almost figured it out in theory, but I didn't know all the variables. Still don't. If I did, I could do an analysis and work out a statistical theory of mutually assured destruction, with and without sustainment of any living matter. What was once a fail-safe doctrine of the threat of nuclear deterrence because of mutual annihilation became obsolete when coercive credibility was no longer a valid ultimatum."

Baumer and Maguire looked at each other, then back at Victoria with a visually observable lack of understanding.

Victoria smiled at their blank looks, but soldiered on. "The calculations have a lot to do with the relationship of photon wavelengths to nuclear energy changes and understanding hydrogen atom energy, and color, light, and emissions once calibrated through a spectrometer and the effect on different life forms, animal, vegetable, mineral, et cetera."

Maguire smiled and leaned back. "Apple, tree; apple, ground."

Victoria looked over at Maguire. "Huh?"

"She's being annoying, ignore her. But she's saying that you and your granddad might be a great deal alike," Baumer translated.

"I'll take that as a compliment." Victoria smiled. "As I was saying, more simply put, if I had the variables, I could figure out what the hell happened and who started this shit."

"Does it matter at this point?" Maguire took another sip of her lemonade, still clearly marveling at having real ice cubes.

Baumer nodded. "I think it matters a whole lot. What if the perpetrators managed to take out most of the world without killing themselves? Are they going to pack their bags and move here once everything clears out?"

Victoria cleared her throat. "Who says it was an outside threat?"

Baumer and Maguire both stared at her.

"Someone is responsible for genocide on an unprecedented scale, ladies. The last three decades there's been a growing mistrust of our own government. Granddad got out for a reason." She took a long breath. "I'm not a conspiracy nut, but something came undone and I'm not naïve enough to think our politicians didn't have something to do with it. By action or inaction, I couldn't say. We have to consider the government's past."

Baumer thought that over for a minute. "I hate to admit this, but she's got a point." She anticipated Maguire's expression of disbelief. "According to Prescott, Noble got out because the government was ignoring what she was telling them. It's not like she was pulling this stuff out of her backside. She had solid evidence that human intelligence agents were given or heard for themselves, and it came from the bad guys themselves. You have to ask yourself why that evidence was ignored. Let's face some hard truths like adults: politics became big money. A lot of those public servants left politics to become millionaires, billionaires even, by supporting and pushing the agenda of false flag-waving interest groups. And then there are those who became millionaires while they were in office by the same methods. They loved the money and power a lot more than they loved this country."

"And let's not forget the rabid jingoists who were being elected at lightning speed," Victoria added. "They would do anything to get their wars, regardless of whether or not the ends justified the means."

Maguire didn't look pleased with the supposition. "I never

really understood two-faced patriotism. Either you love your country and all it stands for, or you don't. It's a basic thought process that seems simple, for all its complexity. The mere idea that Americans could have caused this cataclysm makes my brain itch."

"Having listened to my granddad's observations most of my life, nothing would shock me," Victoria said.

"And you can figure this out?" Maguire didn't sound convinced.

Victoria nodded. "Between me and Granddad? Oh yeah. He's got a computer system you would not believe, as well as back doors embedded into whatever system is left in DC." She shrugged. "He's not real trusting, not now and not when he was younger."

"I'm just a soldier. I have no desire—"

"If it *was* our government, Mags, then for some reason they were trying to kill you, me, and everyone else that they should have been protecting. I'd like to know why the hell I'm running around like a refugee in a third world country," Baumer said.

For a moment there was a tense silence between the two soldiers. Maguire blinked first. "I'll grant you that."

"And honestly, now there are no 'just anyones,'" Victoria said quietly. "Every surviving person has a skill, no matter what it may be. You're both soldiers. Regardless of rank, you're now the standing army, and by default, its leaders. I'm a statistical analyst. Granddad and Noble might be the last intelligence analysts left. Survivalists are now our hunters and militia. See what I mean? We don't know who or what is left, but we need every remaining material asset and the services of every single person."

"Sounds like you've thought about this a lot," Baumer observed.

"I've had a lot of free time. I've read most of the books I brought Granddad. If I had known I was going to be here indefinitely, I would have brought my own favorites along." Victoria managed a smile. "I propose you two crash here for the night."

Baumer didn't hide her relief. "Under the circumstances, I hope you don't fault me for being happy to hear that."

"No problem. It'll be nice to talk to someone other than myself for a change. We will have to pull your Hummer into that thing that looks like a falling down barn."

"So what is it really?" Maguire asked.

"A falling down barn." Victoria laughed. "But I know your vehicle will fit inside. We'll just have to fight with the doors a little bit."

"I'll drive it in. Mags, you've got cover duty. Victoria, lead the way." Baumer stood and reached into her pocket for the key.

They rode the elevator up to ground level and began the garaging exercise. Maguire scanned the immediate perimeter with her M4, the scope never lingering too long in any one place, while the other two struggled to open the barn door. Then Baumer drove the Hummer into the cavernous space. She and Victoria wrestled the door closed, and then tried to brush out the tracks as much as possible.

"How often do you get people coming through?" Maguire asked as she kept scanning the perimeter.

"Every once in a while." Victoria chewed her lip in thought. "You say you're going to Arizona, right?"

Baumer trusted Victoria enough by that point to concede that little bit of information. "Yeah. We have some other refugees to pick up."

"Watch your back at Las Cruces. I'm not sure what's going on, but some of our visitors don't have much good to say about it. One group said they lost four of their party there. Everyone's been tight lipped about it, mostly the terrified variety of tight lipped."

Chapter Five

Watch your back at Las Cruces.

The sentence circled around in Maguire's mind as they moved closer to where Baumer had calculated Fort Bliss was located. Because of Victoria's warning, they had decided that once they executed a re-supply, they would go overland instead of using the road.

"You know," Baumer began as they took a break from making their own road, "I think Victoria was interested in you. Just staying there with her might not have been so bad. I mean, who knows if we'll ever find any place safer."

Maguire responded with a lopsided grin. "I thought that cognac knocked you out last night, right after you finished scribbling in your little notebook."

"It did to some extent, and no knocking my notebook. It's got a lot of important information I should remember, so it might come in handy in the future. But—" Baumer stopped chewing on cold fried chicken and studied her companion's expression. "Wait a second... Was I knocked out on purpose? Did you and Victoria—?"

"Come on, L. T., you know me: mission first."

"Really?" Baumer smirked. "And since we were securely several stories underground, just exactly what was your mission last night?"

Maguire knew she was blushing, but tried to just ignore Baumer. "Mags?" the lieutenant persisted.

"Finish your chicken while it's still fresh enough for you to enjoy. It's probably the last home-cooked meal you'll get for a while."

"You're changing the subject."

Maguire shook her head and smiled, and they continued their meal in companionable silence.

When she'd finished, Baumer said, "I know it's not your style to kiss and tell. I've always respected that about you. If you and Victoria got together last night, well, I think that's great. You just, well, you told me you never do one-night stands."

"I don't. We...didn't, Jess. We talked, compared scars."

"That's all?"

"She kissed me."

"Smart woman. If she'd waited for you to make the first move, she'd be waiting until she was covered in cobwebs."

"Funny. Not."

"But true." Baumer smirked. "Would you have stayed if she'd asked?"

"She did ask. If it is meant to be, we will meet again. Until that time, we have a mission that must be completed."

"And you always complete your mission." Baumer smiled as she secured her trash, wiped her hands, and turned the engine over.

In a move Maguire knew must have been ingrained, Baumer looked to her left to make sure there was no looming traffic. Within moments she was up to cruising speed.

"No task too tough, Ma'am," Maguire finally responded, staring out the passenger window without taking particular note of anything. When she spoke again, she said, "I was married once. She was the love of my life."

Maguire tugged a cigarette from a pack and placed it between her lips. The Zippo followed and flared. "I've had lovers since Moira left me, but 'none so fair as can compare.' Before all this began, I still had hope that we'd get back together someday, be a family again."

"And now?"

"With a ninety percent mortality rate, Ma'am, now I have only my mission." Maguire sighed. "And a good friend I must get to safety."

"Just for the record, the friend is happy that you're here with her." Baumer yelped as they hit a nasty dip in the desert. "Sorry."

Maguire smiled. "It's an awful road that you've chosen." She spotted something off in the distance and pulled out her binoculars. "Well now, I think we've found your fort." She scanned the terrain and let out a low whistle. "Slow down."

"What ya got?" Baumer asked loudly enough to be heard over the engine.

"Downed fence, trashed vehicles. Looks like it was all exodus here."

"How can you tell?"

Maguire's smile was more of a grimace. "It's all pointing in our direction." She lowered her binoculars. "This truly sucks, Ma'am."

"Again with the understatement," Baumer commented dryly as she drove toward the chaos.

Five minutes later they arrived at the downed fence, and both women exited the vehicle, weapons at the ready. They automatically fell into tactical positioning—Maguire in the lead, with Baumer back and slightly to her right, ready to cover both flanks. They walked slowly, taking time to scan what was left of each body they came to. The vehicles that were not completely destroyed were inspected for anything they could re-purpose for their own use. It turned out not to be worth the effort.

After an hour or so, they rested with their backs against the last destroyed vehicle and Baumer took a sip from her canteen. "I counted twelve with obvious bullet holes."

"Front and back," Maguire confirmed as she accepted the offered canteen. She took a long sip. "I'm guessing those are the ones that were trying to keep the others from leaving."

"Agreed. Not sure we have much choice but to go in."

"We pretty much have to. Eight cans of gas won't get us to Huachuca, so we need to scrounge." Maguire field stripped her cigarette and discarded the remains.

"Running low on smokes?" Baumer teased with a genuine smile.

"Smokes, chew. We'll hit the Class Six store, maybe the commissary. Hopefully they haven't been stripped bare. If we can't get to your friends, we will need to resupply food, gas…anything we can find."

"Gotta love human vices," Baumer quipped.

"You'd better hope there are some stores left." Maguire smiled. "If I get hungry enough, I'll be selling you as a dancing girl to any survivor we come across who has a steak."

Baumer laughed. "You've never seen me dance. You wouldn't even get an appetizer for me." She looked back toward the Hummer. "Okay, let's get into the post proper. Scrounge first, or find someplace to bed down first?"

Maguire shrugged. "You're the L.T. You decide."

"Yeah, but with just us two, it's almost a democracy. If we hook up or pull others in, then tag, I'm it."

Maguire saluted. "Roger that, Ma'am."

"You know, you could call me Jessica or Jess." She slid her canteen back into its holder.

"I tried that, but it felt out of place," Maguire said with a shake of her head. "You're my L.T."

"Your choice. We're wasting daylight. Let's move. We'll scrounge for two or three hours, then find shelter. I want to move fast, but no taking chances. We do not separate."

"Roger that, Ma'am. I'll take each point. You are low, I am high. If doors gotta be kicked in—"

"We pass them by. No chances, Mags. We have an opportunity to get to Huachuca and then sanctuary. We get there alive, we die of old age, got it?"

"I got it. Mind if I don't like it all that much?" Maguire groused. "There might be Unfriendlies here who could be lying in wait to take us out."

"They'd more than likely outnumber us, so they'd be out here already. I'm sure we tripped all kinds of sensors. We have to be smart about this. We're just trespassing and then moving through. We get in, crash, then leave. We don't have to live here."

Maguire grunted. "Got it."

"Look at the bright side—I might let you shoot something at some point."

Maguire blinked and then laughed. "That's fine then."

"Well then, soldier, let's move." Baumer strode away towards their vehicle.

***

It was daunting to see that an area as huge as Bliss could

have become a veritable ghost town. Maguire and Baumer had no doubt there were other survivors like them, but it was possible they were still below ground. They might also have moved on to find others…or perhaps they were watching them at that very moment.

They found several signs that displayed insignias other than the common FORSCOM red, white, and blue circle. The crest revealed no more than that Bliss had been assigned as a Forces Command post. It was the other signs, or the remaining pieces of them, that told a more interesting story about the largest military installation in the USA. The further they traveled inside the post boundaries, the more unit insignias they located: one armored division and brigade, a cavalry logistics command, an air defense artillery brigade, a joint task force, and a unit that had Maguire shaking her head in bewilderment.

"Wow. Unfeckinbelievable," Maguire said as she knelt by a dented and curled metal emblem.

"What?"

"This makes even less sense." Maguire tapped the sign. "The 32nd Army and Air Missile Defense Command was here."

"So was the German Air Force Air Defense Center." Baumer pointed to the sign that held an Iron Cross with the word 'Luftstreitkräfte' under it. "I forgot they did their tactical training here and at Holloman. Looks like they all got caught with their pants down."

"That's just another missing piece of this massive puzzle." Maguire stood and looked at the death and destruction surrounding them. "The 32nd AAMDC should never have been caught unawares. They are always on alert, ready to deploy, to defend at any minute. I did some training with someone who was assigned here. They employ in-country analysts to constantly filter intel to them, and then continuously train based on that intel."

"Then that makes this whole thing even more curious," Baumer said. "Why wouldn't they have been alerted to, at the very least, grumblings of some sort of smaller scale strike, much less…" she looked around, "this?"

"Good question. Their post mission is to perform critical theater-level air and missile defense planning. There is no way they would not have had *something* in place to fight this. They never, ever should have been ambushed like…like Pearl Harbor."

Baumer studied her sergeant. It was clear that Maguire was upset, as she was nearly vibrating.

"Mags, we don't know that they didn't have a defensive strategy in place. This attack was on an unprecedented scale, and you are thinking rationally and with logic, as though these forces actually had time to act."

The look of shock on Maguire's face did not fade.

"Look, we can't even be sure that our own government, or some part of it, wasn't behind whatever happened. If political forces beyond the military were playing both ends against the middle, it isn't difficult to see how we got wiped out. We need to find out who, and why."

Maguire stood stock still.

"Let's move, Mags. We're not going to learn anything more if we don't move out. Scrounge time."

Maguire looked around at the destruction surrounding her. After a few moments, Baumer's command apparently sank in, as she drew herself erect and responded, "Right, scrounge," but her voice shook.

"You good, troop?" Baumer asked.

Maguire ran a slow hand over her face as she steadied herself. "I'm good, L.T. Just taking a hard knock to my brainpan. I'm good."

"Okay, let's move smartly," she ordered, then murmured, "I wish that the platoon of butterflies in my stomach was not also moving smartly."

"Roger that, Ma'am." Maguire gripped her rifle in preparation for moving out. "Moving smartly, butterflies and all."

***

Baumer rolled the mattress out on the lower berth, and it bounced on the tight springs of the double rack bunk. With darkness falling, the only reasonable place to crash for the night was what looked like it had been a Vietnam-era barracks.

According to the fading sign by the front gate, it had been the brig. Crashing there for the night made sense to her. No one in their right mind would think to look there, if anyone was looking. She heard Maguire rolling out her own mattress six feet away.

"Nice digs, L.T."

Baumer couldn't tell whether or not her companion was being a smart ass. "Would *you* look here?"

Maguire stood up and stretched her back. "Actually, no."

"Score one for the officer corps," Baumer quipped.

"I wish we'd found more things we could use, though."

The scrounging mission had been a bust. The PX, commissary, and Class Six stores were nearly cleaned out. The only thing they'd managed to gather were six five-gallon cans of fuel and two cartons of smokes that fortunately were Maguire's brand. Regardless, if she had not found them in a sealed container, she would have had to leave them behind rather than risking them being contaminated.

"We can't win 'em all, Sergeant. At least we've got the fuel."

"True that." Maguire lay down on her bunk. "How long to Huachuca?"

"Eight, maybe ten hours, or maybe a day or two, depending on what we run into. With the extra fuel, I think we can afford to hammer down. I just wish I knew what the roads were like ahead of us. The effects of the earthquake have really been slowing us down." Baumer flopped down to rest. "Regardless of what challenges the trip presents, I'm not looking forward to Las Cruces."

"I'll be up top, weapons hot, entering and leaving," Maguire promised in a deadly tone.

"I trust you, Mags."

"Thanks." Maguire lit a cigarette.

Baumer was quiet for a time, then turned over and rested her head on her hand as she looked at Maguire. "What was your Moira like?"

Maguire blinked and turned her head on the pillow. "Why?"

"Curiosity. You don't seem like the type to be tamed, so

I'm curious about what this woman was like."

Maguire snorted. "Oh, she was lovely. Tall, willowy, red hair, all Irish. Green eyes clear as cut emeralds when she was happy. Same green eyes turned dark as jade when she was angry. Usually at me. I was on leave visiting my mother in Ireland, and there was Moira."

A smile flitted across her face. "I was lost from the first glance. She took a look at me in my uniform and asked what I was doing in an American uniform instead of an Irish one." She glanced at Baumer. "Terrible snob, that woman."

"But I'm assuming she finally went out with you, since she married you," Baumer prodded.

"It took most of my leave time to convince her I wasn't a complete hooligan. One night I cooked dinner for her, and then we went out to one of the fish houses, since what I'd made wasn't fit for consumption. She liked the effort, though."

Maguire took another drag and let the smoke out slowly. "Every spare moment I could get off duty, I was flying to Ireland or flying Moira to see me. I had to beg her to come see me the first time, and even then she insisted on paying for half the fare. That was just her way."

"She made you work for it." Baumer laughed. "Why did you love her?"

Maguire leaned back and thought for a moment. "I think because she made me work for it. I couldn't rely on being charming, I had to be me. There was just something about her that called to my heart. I've never had that reaction to a woman before or since."

"Why'd she leave?"

"She'd had enough of being a soldier's wife. We were married for seven years and lived together a total of three. I was always off somewhere on deployment. My mother died, and Moira was at the funeral alone. I couldn't be spared from a mission. That did her in. When she went back home to Ireland, she took my life with her. She begged me to sign the divorce papers. She said that she did love me, but she knew that I wouldn't ever leave the Army.

"I saw her after the boondoggle in Korea, when I was training for Fianoglagh. She told me she was proud of me, and then she walked away." Maguire flicked some ash on the floor. "Don't feel sorry for me, L.T. I'm lucky. I had my heart's desire for seven years, and I know what it feels like to have walked with love by my side. I've been looked at as if I'm the only person in the world that matters. I know people who've never had that from their first breath to their last."

Baumer took a long couple of seconds to respond. "I don't feel sorry for you, Mags." She sighed. "I'm jealous, I think."

"You'll find love when you least expect it, L.T." Maguire took a last drag and then snuffed out the smoke.

"I actually had it once. I guess, like you, the Army and the wars won out without us meaning it to. I'd be happy to have something like that again once the world makes sense again."

"If the world ever makes sense again." Maguire closed her eyes.

Chapter Six

Las Cruces. The City of the Crosses. Mindful of Victoria's warning, they entered the outer limits of Doña Ana County with caution. Their early morning drive had been occupied with finding ways around the devastated airfields at Bliss and White Sands. What the earthquake hadn't destroyed, the attack had. Foraging for supplies at White Sands did not result in much success. Whatever hadn't been looted or destroyed was almost certainly contaminated. They scored a single small container of sealed, boxed MREs that they stocked in their vehicle.

Up to this point, they had been fortunate to travel without running into any hostiles. The little hairs on the back on Maguire's neck advised her that they had run out of luck. She ducked down from her turret.

"L.T., we're being watched," Maguire called in a low voice.

"I feel it too, Mags." She drove slowly, so as to not seem aggressive. It was possible that the bad element they had been warned about had somehow been neutralized, and they didn't want to engage with any friendlies.

"Hold up. I see a hand-painted sign up ahead." Maguire focused her field glasses on the printing. "Oh, shit!"

"What? Anytime you are less than unflappable, Maguire, I know I need to take particular notice."

She let the binoculars drop. "It says 'Welcome to Fort Mescalero.'"

Baumer slowed the Hummer. "So?"

"So…the Mescalero is a band of the Apache nation."

"So? It's not like they're going to surround the wagons, right? What's the problem?"

"You know that I'm three-quarters Irish, right?"

"Right."

"Well, the other quarter is Comanche."

"And?" Baumer prodded impatiently.

"The Apache and the Comanche are natural enemies."

"Yeah, *a couple generations* ago. And I won't tell them if you don't."

"If they don't turn out to be friendly, I'll be disrespecting one-quarter of my heritage by trying to make peace."

Baumer shot her an incredulous glance, then returned her attention to the terrain. "I understand that tradition and legacy are important to you, but I will kick *all* quarters of your ass if your pride picks a fight. Are we clear on that, Staff Sergeant?"

Maguire chuckled at Baumer's reprimand. "Yes, Ma'am. Loud and clear."

"What's so funny?"

"Shades of the Old West." Maguire nodded toward the sign.

Baumer glanced over and saw a long line of well-armed Native Americans with weapons pointed directly at them. "Jesus! Where'd they come from?"

"They can be very stealthy. Looks like, somehow, there may have been an uprising. I hope we don't die today, because theirs is a story I'd love to hear."

"Don't you Native American types say 'today is a good day to die'?"

"That's Klingons, Ma'am." Maguire sounded completely serious. "Comanche don't like dying, Ma'am. We prefer to live to harass and kill another day."

"Uh huh. Now you tell me."

"You didn't ask before, Ma'am."

Baumer snorted. "Technicalities. We really have to clear up these technicalities, you know." She killed the engine but left the keys in the ignition. "Leave the heavy weapons inside, but we take our sidearms."

Maguire stood up by her gun and made a show of placing the weapon on safe and adjusting the barrel into the up position, then she ducked back down into the body of the Hummer. She exchanged her helmet and goggles for her black beret.

"Ready, Ma'am."

Baumer took a deep breath and released it slowly, then

nodded. "Let's go," she ordered.

They exited the vehicle together and slowly walked forward, their hands well away from their sidearms but not raised in surrender. They stopped fifty meters in front of the vehicle and waited for someone to step forward.

"If one person twitches, we haul butt back to the wheels and get out of Dodge," Baumer ordered in a low voice.

"Roger, Ma'am. I'll be cover. You have the keys, so don't wait for me. I'll be there, trust me."

After a tense few moments, two men broke away from the main group and started forward.

Neither soldier moved. Maguire counted at least twenty high-powered weapons pointed at them. If they had to run, it was going to be a short-lived sprint.

Finally the two men were in front of them. Each wore his hair long, in the old way, tied in double braids. The taller of the two handed his M4 carbine to his compatriot.

"You are dangerously close to trespassing. This is Apache land now. The first person to say 'How' dies." His tone was deceptively calm.

Maguire studied him for a moment, and then said softly, "Would marúawe or ya'ateh be more acceptable?"

His head snapped around to look at her. "At least you didn't say 'How.'"

"Maybe I should say 'death from above.'" Her eyes flicked toward his arm. "Your tattoo. Is that for show, or did you earn it?"

He glanced at his forearm. "I earned it."

"Airborne or Air Assault?" she shot back.

"Airborne."

Maguire nodded. "Good, then we can talk. I don't speak dope on a rope. I do speak Airborne."

"You also speak Comanche," he accused.

"A few words, thanks to my grandmother, who learned it from her mother," Maguire admitted. "I'm third generation 101st Airborne Screaming Eagle, if that satisfies you."

"Still a few generations behind me. Where are you going?"

"I don't trust you *that* much." Maguire smiled to take the sting out of her refusal. "After all, we just met."

"And I'm not asking to hear myself speak," he snapped back.

"Your manners are what I would expect from an Apache," Maguire said evenly, ignoring Baumer's low groan. "We are not enemies in this. My friend and I are just passing through. We've seen your sign, and I know better than to attack my traditional enemy on what is my weak ground. But if you really piss me off, then you and I will face off and you will die. Do you really want to die today?"

"Do you?" His smile wasn't pleasant.

Maguire smiled back, just as ugly. "That depends. Blades."

He blinked. "Blades?"

"If you wish to die today, then you will do it on my blade. No firearms, no one else in the middle to save you, just you and me and sharp blades." Maguire stared at him and let him see what was in her eyes, in her soul. "Just you and me."

"What makes you think I might not like blades?"

Maguire shook her head. "Because you blinked."

For a long moment there was silence, then the leader laughed. "I hate blades."

"So do I, but I can fight with them," Maguire answered seriously.

"Then we will put aside stupid things and speak soldier to soldier."

His words held promise, and Maguire nodded. "Staff Sergeant Maguire. To my side is Lieutenant Baumer. We're out of Hood, and our destination is to the west. That is all I can tell you of our plans. I hope that will satisfy you."

"For now it will." He nodded at Baumer. "Captain Red Horse, at your service."

Baumer and Maguire snapped to attention and rendered salutes. Red Horse stared at them a moment, and then slowly returned the gesture of respect and acknowledgement of authority.

"Sir, please excuse our trespassing, but Triple A didn't have you on the map." Baumer smiled.

Red Horse didn't laugh, but he did manage a thin smile. "I'm sure. Until we came together here, Fort Mescalero didn't exist. It's been a long couple of months."

"Would it be impolite to ask how Fort Mescalero came to be?" Baumer said.

Red Horse thought about it for a moment, then sighed. "Most of us had already begun to gather before the attacks. I can't tell you why—an unsettling in the air, maybe. After all hell broke loose? It just seemed like a natural progression to organize. We had a ceremony, and no, I'm not going to reveal what the ceremony was. The earth shook for a long time and everything electronic died. Those of us who'd done time in uniform figured it out. We lost a number of our people to the earthquake, some to radiation, and some to fear."

Baumer shook her head. "It wasn't radiation. The winds were all wrong for that. California got nuked along the coast according to what we could glean from the few contacts we were able to make, but the winds would have taken the radiation over the Rockies, not here. What you are getting hit with is most likely residual upheaval, fissures belching up whatever the earth hides under her crust."

"Do you have anything that might help? We have a couple of serious cases."

Maguire wondered if Baumer realized how difficult it had been for him to swallow his pride and ask for help. To her, it was abundantly clear how much dignity that had cost him.

"Sergeant, in the back of the Hummer I have a medic bag. Take out half of the z packs and bring them here," Baumer ordered.

Maguire double-timed it back to the Hummer. As she reached the rear tires, she could still faintly hear the conversation.

"I think those meds will do some good. Now it's my turn to ask for help. We have to get west. How bad is Las Cruces?" Baumer asked.

***

Baumer, Maguire, and the Apache leader walked toward a dune that, closer up, looked man-made. Red Horse led them around a ledge and downward into what looked like a cave beneath the mound of white sand. Two guards stepped aside to

45

let their captain pass, and Baumer and Maguire followed Red Horse into a small network of tunnels. Eventually he stopped at the door to a room and gestured them inside. He spoke softly to a man in a desert camo military uniform, and the man nodded and hurried away.

"One of our practitioners will be up to get your medical bag." He nodded to the chairs and Baumer took a seat while Maguire looked around.

"Where are we exactly? I mean, what do you call this place, other than Fort Mescalero?" Maguire asked.

"These are the outer dunes, where the local adrenaline junkies used to have ATV, dune buggy, and off-road cycle competitions. One of my uncles bought this land years ago and decided that instead of living above ground and dealing with the heat and sand storms, he'd construct this building. He was really a visionary. This place is quite functional even without electricity."

"Did he build this just for his family? Because it looks huge," Baumer commented.

"His family includes about three hundred members," Red Horse said.

"Fertile little bugger, wasn't he?" Baumer cracked.

"Um...L.T., in most Native American nations, the entire tribe is family," Maguire said quietly.

"Actually, you are both right." Red Horse nodded. "He had nineteen children." At the look on Baumer's face, he added, "Three wives, and not at the same time."

Baumer waved off the additional information. "I wasn't going to ask."

"How did you know we were coming?" Maguire asked. "Scouts?"

"Yes, but that's the third tier of our perimeter alarm," he told them. "It's really quite clever. My uncle set up mini seismographs. The sand is a great absorber, but it's also an effective channel for movement. By the readings we can tell force and duration, which alerts us as to whether our impending company is a large, medium or small group. The other ingenious thing he did was to install periscopes at intervals."

"Periscopes?" Baumer repeated, intrigued.

"You mean, instead of electronic surveillance which can be detected, defective, or gunked up by the weather, he employed the use of tubes, mirrors, and prisms," Maguire said in clear admiration.

"Exactly. The way the system is set up is that initially the seismographs alert us to motion. We monitor the area the activity is coming from, and we can tell from the recording of the vibrations whether or not it's Mother Nature. We can quickly isolate which quadrant is impacted and raise the periscopes in that area."

Baumer considered that for a moment. "Aren't you concerned someone will see them?"

"Did you?" Red Horse asked with a wry grin.

"Good point," Baumer said.

"If we need more information, we send out the scouts."

A woman dressed in buff-colored scrubs trotted into the room. "Naiche said you might have some medicines we could put to use." Her eyes swept the room and focused on Baumer and Maguire. "Hi." She shook hands with each woman in turn. "Katy Brusuelas Dark Moon."

Red Horse introduced the two visitors as he passed the bag to Dark Moon. "Bring back what you don't or can't use."

She looked through the bag and teared up at the sight of the z packs. She glanced at Baumer and Maguire. "You will save many lives with this gift."

"I hope so," Baumer answered fervently. "I hope they outlive all of this. And keep what you don't use now. You might need it later."

Dark Moon clutched the bag to her chest, an instinctive gesture of protection. "They will sing songs of the generosity of two uniformed strangers. Your names will live for every generation to come."

Maguire scratched her head. "Could you make sure they leave my name out?"

"Afraid to be singled out, Comanche?" Red Horse teased.

"More like afraid my ancestors might hear of it and not be so understanding," Maguire answered honestly.

"We'll just think of a complimentary name to call you by in the songs then," Dark Moon promised, hugging the bag to her body. "I hate to meet and run, but I have patients. Thank you seems so…inadequate."

After she had gone, Red Horse turned to Baumer. "I will make sure you are somehow compensated for whatever we use. Since paper money and coin are now useless, you shall have something for your trip. Or you may stay here with us, if you wish."

Baumer smiled. "Offer appreciated, but we have committed to being elsewhere. Anyway, you owe us nothing. We still abide by the Army ethos. We still have half, so we're good."

"Are you sure the people you've committed to meet out west are still there?"

"They were as recently as a couple of days ago," Maguire said.

Red Horse nodded. "If that falls through, you are welcome to come back here, Creator willing."

"We'll keep that in mind, and thank you. So," Baumer said, "you were going to tell us about Las Cruces."

"How did you hear about the unrest there?"

"We heard it from a reliable source at another location."

"I respect that you are keeping your sources and contacts confidential. I expect you will be no less honorable about your stay here."

"You have our word, Captain Red Horse," Maguire said.

Red Horse arched an eyebrow. "The word of a Comanche?"

"The word of a soldier," Maguire said seriously.

Red Horse nodded in acceptance. "Our reservation is about a hundred miles north of here, near Ruidoso," he provided. "When Reckoning happened, we spread out to see what was affected, who was left. We found that many stray tribal members, Apache and others from related nations, had survived in numbers…seemingly more than other groups."

"Is that what people are calling what happened? Reckoning?" Baumer inserted.

"Until we know what really happened, yes," Red Horse said. "What are you calling it?"

"We don't really have a name for it. We've been referring to it as Day Zero."

"I guess that's what happens when there is no media to name a catastrophic event for the rest of us. We're still trying to figure out what that was. Nobody seems to have any intel. We thought maybe the closer we got to the military installations, the better the likelihood that we would get information and reinforcements. But..." Red Horse sighed. "Cannon, Kirtland, and Holloman were not only destroyed, but uninhabitable. Of course, habitation may be okay now, but I doubt it. Like White Sands, most military bases were attacked with chemicals. If you weren't underground, and I mean deep underground, you died."

"We saw some of the same outcome. Pretty ugly stuff," Maguire said.

"We had to cremate what casualties we found. It was the only way to stop the spread of bacteria from the decay."

"Weren't you concerned that the fires would alert others to your presence?" Maguire asked.

"It couldn't be helped. We have to give the land back to Mother to nurture and mend as quickly as she can."

Baumer looked at Maguire. "Mother?"

"Mother Earth," Maguire supplied.

Baumer nodded as Red Horse continued.

"On our way here, we ran into small groups of survivors, who mostly wanted to know if we knew what had happened. We could only tell them the basics. They weren't violent, as most were sick from radiation or chemical poisoning. My guess is they are gone now. We have a vanguard patrolling the areas so the bodies will be disposed of. We're trying to recon and repair as we go."

"And Las Cruces wasn't so friendly?" Baumer guessed.

"We found that the university had been taken over by mercenaries and refugees. I don't expect their stronghold to last, though," Red Horse said. "A majority of them were also exposed—came out of their shelters too soon, drank unfiltered water, or ate contaminated food. They're dying off at a pretty steady rate. In the meantime, they're desperate, and that makes them an unreasonably nasty element to deal with. Now that the air is breathable and the land is recovering, the survivalists are starting to show up to claim territory. The fighting has been brutal at times. They want to colonize, and my people aren't going to fall for that again."

"Can't blame you there," Maguire mumbled.

"As it stands right now, we're maintaining our boundaries and keeping their group restricted to the university. They're showing no signs of wanting to work together to assess remaining resources or organize a workable society."

"Well…the new world status is still very young. Everybody is understandably a little freaked," Baumer said. "Nobody is even sure who they can trust and who they can't."

"You and I decided we could trust each other with just a few words," Red Horse said. "It's not that difficult. We offered them an opportunity, but they don't want to share. They want it all. We can't have that. Not again."

They were interrupted by a rumbling, and a shaking of the ground. Maguire and Baumer looked anxiously at Red Horse.

He smiled when the ground stilled. "Aftershock," he assured them.

A man dressed in jeans, hiking boots, denim shirt, and bandana stuck his head into the room. "Joseph, there's movement in the northwest quadrant that's not quake-related."

"Let me know when you have more," Red Horse said to him.

Maguire quirked an eyebrow. "Joseph?"

"My first name. My full name is Joseph Cochise Red Horse."

"Cochise? Like…?"

"Grandson, a few times removed."

"That would be about six generations, wouldn't it?" Maguire calculated.

"Yes. Cochise was Chiricahua. Four generations ago, my great, great grandmother married into the Mescalero. When the Chiricahua were released after being prisoners of war at Fort Sill, they were given the choice of staying at Sill or relocating to where our tribes were, here in New Mexico. Some stayed, some migrated. My great, great grandmother came to Ruidoso and fell in love with my great, great grandfather." He moved toward the door. "I would prepare a grand feast in your honor, but all we have to eat is pretty much the same thing you have probably been eating—MREs and stored canned goods."

Baumer nodded. "Thanks, but we're actually fine. We had a freeze-dried breakfast before we left Bliss."

"I must go check on the activity in the quadrant. Please relax until I get back." Red Horse nodded at them and then left the room.

Baumer turned to Maguire. "Wow. What an interesting development. Good thing they found us before the people from the university did."

"Red Horse is an honorable man from a sovereign bloodline."

"How much do you know about your Comanche ancestors?" Baumer asked.

"Enough to have selective amnesia while we're accepting the hospitality of the Apache."

Baumer arched an eyebrow. "I require an actual answer, Sergeant." The tone of her voice brooked no argument.

Maguire shook her head in resignation. "My Comanche ancestor ran with Quanah Parker's band of Quahadi Comanche. His name was Chogan. All we really know is that he left a wife and three daughters when he died at the hands of the white man's cavalry in the plains of what's now the panhandle of Texas. Before him, his father fought the Apache wherever the Apache were."

Baumer absorbed the information. "It could have been worse. You could have my family history. Try explaining to your recruiter that your great grandfather died at the Battle of the Bulge, serving on the *other* side."

Chapter Seven

The movement in the northwest quadrant turned out to be their own scouts returning from a mission to assess the situation to the western side of the university. Red Horse spent some time presenting possible strategy options to get Baumer and Maguire safely past Las Cruces, and then offered them a billet for the night.

Despite Red Horse's apology for having nothing to provide his guests with a feast, the people under his command fed Baumer and Maguire well. As they dined on canned beets, spinach, potatoes, tuna fish and soup, they were told of the history of the Western Apache. Despite the fact that the word "apache" meant "enemy" in several native languages, including Comanche, Maguire found herself fascinated by the saga. Because her Irish heritage was more the focus in her family, she knew only minimal bits and pieces about her Native American background.

Listening to Dark Moon speak of her past with such pride made Maguire regret that she didn't know more about her Comanche heritage. She wanted to ask if anyone knew whether any Comanche bands had survived, but Dark Moon's last story had been of how the Apache had been violently displaced from the southern plains and central Texas by tribes of Comanche in the early eighteenth century, so Maguire stayed silent. She did promise herself that she would do some research of her own, if she ever got the opportunity. If Red Horse had mentioned to anyone that she had Comanche blood running through her veins, they had yet to react to it. Perhaps given the magnitude of what had happened in the world, even a long standing blood enmity had been forgotten in the need for all the survivors to work together. Maguire suddenly wondered if maybe their warring ancestral tribes had grown to have anything in common other than Native blood. Perhaps linguistics might be a communal basic.

"What dialect of Apache do you speak?" Maguire asked.

"English," Red Horse answered. "The younger generations don't show an interest in learning or perpetuating our languages, so our native tongues are dying out. Athapaskan is the most popular Apache dialect, and Chiricahua-Mescalero is variously considered to be bastardized Athapaskan or a separate language altogether."

Dark Moon picked up the thread. "Athapaskan is what was used in the storytelling. Apache told animal stories with the wolf as the main character. For example, the wolf brought fire to people, the wolf was very smart. Storytelling has always been a way we communicate our history."

"Given the current circumstances, will you make an effort to join with other nations and tribes?" Baumer asked.

"Uh…that's not as easy as it sounds, L.T.," Maguire said.

"She is correct," Red Horse said. "There are not just tribes, but individual bands, each band led by its own chief. The chief is chosen by a tribal council, and all decisions are made by councilmembers who have to agree before any action is taken."

"So…a chief is more like a…a mediator than the leader of the band," Baumer summarized.

"Yes. And each council has customs that differ slightly, or sometimes a great deal, from those of other councils. What is not offensive to one may be highly insulting to another, which makes it difficult for the nations to come together," Red Horse explained.

"Even now? Even after all that's happened?" Baumer asked incredulously.

"We'll have to see," Red Horse said. "It is possible that all the plains nations could come together, at least initially."

Maguire frowned. "The last time that happened was at Little Big Horn."

"Exactly my point," Red Horse said. "So, we'll have to see."

After a moment, Maguire chuckled. "Sorry, but it sounds a lot like the Irish. Clans fought each other over the most stupid of offenses, while the Brits just sat back and waited for those most pissed off to come to them for whatever 'help' they might need. When that happened, they pounced, and took my land for their own."

"Your land? Isn't America your land?" Red Horse challenged.

Maguire took in a slow breath. "My father was an American soldier, but my mother was Irish and I was born in Ireland. I've spent half my life in Ireland and half in the U.S. Recounting it all would take a generation." She thought for a moment. "It's like growing up on a rez but having to go into the white man's world to make your way."

Red Horse nodded. "When you put it like that, you make sense." He took a cup of coffee offered by one of the runners. "I hope our red nations can join together, but there's no guarantee. We have to find out what's going on in our new world before we can build a nation."

Baumer took a sip of her water. "I agree. There is no way anyone can really move forward until there is intel about who might be in charge of the government."

"I'd love to meet up with whoever's in charge of this FUBAR," Red Horse muttered in a flare of anger. "I'd like to know why so many of our people have died. I can't figure out how it happened, but it shouldn't have happened at all."

"Do you have communication capability?" Baumer risked the question.

Red Horse answered cautiously. "You will accept a yes or no for an answer?"

Baumer nodded. "If you do, if we get that answer before you do, I'd be happy to share that information."

"Why?" Red Horse asked. "It's not that I don't believe you, I'm just curious."

"We need to find people we can trust and form alliances with them, possibly even generate a skeletal frame for new governance. Whether the perpetrators were our enemies or, God forbid, our own government, we will all need each other to fight them. If it was any element within our government and they allowed this to happen, I certainly don't want them in charge of my life, or yours."

Red Horse took a long time to smile, then he looked at Maguire. "Are you sure she's not Apache?"

Maguire chuckled. "I'm actually thinking she's adopted Irish."

Whatever Red Horse was going to say was forestalled as one of the scouts dashed into the room and whispered in his ear. Red Horse nodded and put down his cup. "You really want to see what's going on in Las Cruces?"

Baumer glanced at Maguire, then said, "Yes."

"Then saddle up. They're busy tonight. We'll have to go two klicks underground, but I think it might be an eye opener for you."

Baumer and Maguire gathered up what they would need for the trip, and within moments they were following Red Horse and the scout. Maguire gave silent thanks that she'd had the time to work out during the interval between doomsday and now. Baumer was starting to suck wind a little over halfway there. Finally the ground sloped upward and they ducked out through another man-made dune. In the distance they could make out the glow of a huge bonfire.

"They do this from time to time. They catch an outsider, or someone tries to defect. Fair warning, it's not pretty." Red Horse's voice was grim.

Baumer grabbed Maguire's binoculars and focused them on the scene, then nearly dropped them. "Oh my God," she croaked, but she brought them up again.

Framed in her sights were three men and two women who were being crucified. She watched as nails were pounded into feet. She couldn't hear the noise itself, but it seemed as if the crowd cheered as each nail was pounded home. About to lose her lunch, she dropped the glasses.

Maguire grabbed them before they could hit the ground. She put them to her eyes just in time to see blades piercing the left side of each of the five victims. "Jesus, Mary, and Joseph, this is fecking medieval!"

"You'll have to pass through their perimeter. They have everything else cut off for fifteen, twenty miles. Beyond that, there is earthquake damage," Red Horse said grimly. "We've scouted as far as we dare, and we haven't yet found a clear way around."

"This is going to suck as bad as Korea," Maguire muttered

as she watched the carnage.

Red Horse regarded her closely. "You were in Korea?"

"Yeah. It was a huge vat of suckage," she answered matter-of-factly.

"I have to agree." He did not look away when Maguire's gaze found his.

She nodded once and returned to her binoculars.

"If we go in guns hot as a diversion, can you release those who want out?" Maguire asked.

"There won't be that many, and I'm not sure it's worth it to my troops," he admitted.

Baumer nodded agreement. "We can't save everyone, Mags."

Maguire sighed. "I know."

"It was a good thought, though." Red Horse tucked away his own binoculars. "Come on, we should go. I don't really want to watch those poor souls get finished off. I'm guessing you'll see them up close enough tomorrow."

***

Baumer's back rested against a cool wall as she watched the fire in the pit. The options that were available to them ran on a loop through her mind. None of them were appealing. Any attempt to pass through the Las Cruces perimeter was going to be unpleasant at best. For the first time in the last few hours, there was a quiet that seemed comforting, even if her thoughts were not. A plate slid into her peripheral view.

"One of the ladies decided you needed some fried apples." Red Horse sat down by the wall, native style. "She even put on some of her cinnamon." He handed her the plate. "*I* don't even get cinnamon." His gentle smile morphed into a feigned pout.

Baumer's return smile was conspiratorial. "I'll sneak you some, if it won't get you in trouble with her."

Red Horse laughed. "Deal." He gazed at her for a long moment. "You're worried."

"You think?" Baumer's tone was wry. "I've got the driving skills to get us through the terrain, I hope. I just don't know what else they have to throw at us."

He shook his head. "It won't matter. Ignore what you think you should look for, *do* what you know." His voice was both sympathetic and confident.

She chuckled. "Infantry psychology?"

His expression darkened. "Infantry?" He shook his head vigorously. "Air...borne," he said slowly, as if to a slow child. "Airborne. We drop from the sky."

"I was always told only two things drop from the sky— birdshit and idiots." Baumer waited for his reaction.

Red Horse grinned. "That saying was made up by someone who couldn't make it through Ranger school. Sounds like we had some of the same instructors at OCS."

"I wouldn't doubt it." Baumer noticed that his eyes kept coming back to her plate, and she laughed quietly. "I can hear you salivating from here." Baumer extended her dish towards him. "Go on, take one." She smiled as he speared an apple slice with his knife. "I'll tell you a secret, Joseph Red Horse. I'm scared out of my mind."

"You should be. But are you going to let that stop you?" He savored a bite of the treat.

She watched his face softened in his enjoyment, and for just a second she could imagine him as a five-year-old boy.

"I don't want to," she said finally.

"But?" he asked around his chewing.

"It will be more than just me out there. That's what concerns me," she admitted.

"Don't worry about your Sergeant, Jessica. She can handle herself. Let her take the heat off of you," he advised. "Just drive. That's all you have to do."

Baumer knew that he was making incredibly simple sense. "I'm building a mountain, aren't I?"

"You are an officer. It's what you were taught to do. But don't forget to trust those around you. Your Irish Comanche is very capable, and she views you as a friend." He took a breath. "Don't tell her but, I know her name, I know her reputation. You couldn't do Korea and *not* know. She'll keep the heat off of you," he assured her. "Just do whatever you have to do."

"Thank you." Baumer exhaled slowly. "How do you do this? Bring so many together after such devastation?"

He shrugged. "I don't know. I was here when it all happened. After Korea, I just wanted to come home and not do anything. And I did. I came home, worked the land, worked at doing not a lot more. Then this happened and we did not have anyone to step up. My sister shamed me into it."

Baumer grinned. "I should thank her."

"I wish you could." His eyes filled with sadness. "You are three weeks too late," he whispered. "Your z packs would have saved her."

She angrily slapped the wall beside her. "I am so sorry."

He shook his head. "Don't." He took her hand and brushed it with a gentle touch. "You are not responsible for everything that's gone on. You can't do that, or the guilt will eat you alive."

"Too late." She took a deep breath and let it out slowly. "I have these moments where I just want to stick my head in the sand."

"When you have those moments, look to the sky instead," he advised.

"Why?"

"Sticking your head in the sand only keeps you in the dark. And also, sand can scrape. Look up at the starlight instead. It's a much nicer view."

Chapter Eight

Maguire tugged on the chinstrap of her helmet to make sure it was snug before she opened the door of the Hummer. An unfamiliar quiver of fear rumbled through her, and she hated it. Nothing was natural about deliberately going into a possible free-fire zone, and she had to fight the fear. And the fear was justified. An early morning recon from one of the man-made dunes showed a hell storm potential.

Baumer joined Maguire at the Hummer. "This is going to suck in a big way."

"Now look who's understating." At Baumer's feigned glare, Maguire grinned. "Six miles, Ma'am. It ain't nothing but a thing," the sergeant said with more bravado than she felt.

"Bull, Sergeant. It is a big thing. Don't think I didn't note all the roadblocks and barriers the scavengers have set up. Good thing my dad taught me to drive."

"NASCAR driver, was he?"

Baumer laughed. "Heck no. Demolition derby." She smiled innocently.

Maguire blinked slowly as she tugged her chinstrap tighter. "Feck me. Just don't drive through it backwards."

Red Horse joined them at the Humvee. "Good luck. If you happen back this way, I hope we're here."

"Thank you, Captain. I hope you're here, too. You are a valued ally." Baumer's voice held hope that could not be disguised. She snapped to attention and saluted. Maguire was a millisecond behind.

"I'm not a Captain anymore." His voice was husky with emotion.

"In my book, you are, Sir," Baumer answered. "And if you disagree with that, then I guess you are a head of state. These people are your people, and you are their leader. Either way, you rate the salute."

Red Horse returned the salute, then dropped his hand. "I hope you make it."

"If we find any answers as to the genesis of this catastrophe, we'll send them. Thank you for trusting me with your com capability, Sir," Baumer said sincerely.

"It's Joseph." He turned to Maguire. "Shoot as well as your ancestors, Comanche. Death from above."

"Currahee, Sir. Hooah. You are a man of honor." After a short pause, she added with a grin, "For an Apache."

He looked at Baumer. "I do believe, despite her smart ass ways, that you are in good hands. We'll be watching. If it looks like it's going to shit, we'll lend a hand."

Baumer touched his shoulder. "Don't. We either get through or we die, but do not risk your people for us. You must make sure that your people survive."

It was a long moment before he stepped away, and then watched as they got into the vehicle. Baumer took the wheel with confidence, while Maguire squirreled her way into the exposed gun turret. As Maguire drew down her dark lens goggles, she flashed him a grin, then pulled back on the cocking handle, loading her machine gun.

Maguire leaned down and flashed the same grin at Baumer. "If this is it, Ma'am, I'm happy it's with you."

"Forget that, Maguire. I am not dying today," Baumer shouted over the noise of the engine.

"Roger that." Maguire tugged her chinstrap tight. "Drive fast, lady, and don't hit anything that's gonna hurt."

Baumer flashed a decidedly un-officer-like finger gesture and hit the gas.

"Oh, this might hurt," Maguire said aloud as she hung on to the Hybrid.

Baumer maintained speed while keeping an eye on the distance to the first barricade. In her peripheral vision, she could see a gathering of the university people.

Maguire ducked down slightly to shout, "Weapons."

"Wait 'til we take fire!" Baumer shouted back.

"What?"

"Let them shoot first, then give 'em hell."

"Hell I can do," she agreed, then added in a mutter, "Not so crazy about the rest, though." Maguire straightened up and tracked the gathering with the barrel of her Hybrid. She had to shift her body every now and then, but she was mostly comfortable with her position.

Baumer twisted around the first barricade then straightened out, her wheels cutting hard in the dirt covered road. She eyeballed the three barricades she could see and groaned but did not falter.

Maguire ducked the two shots that struck her limited turret shelter. The pinging sound told her that someone had possession of an M16 and was making halfway good use of it. She swiveled to her right to face the flak, and then fired about three feet away from her intended target as a warning.

Return rounds were fired, and Maguire gritted her teeth and looked down to check that her rigged ammo belt was still in good condition and not going to fail her.

"Hang on!" Baumer shouted.

"Sure, like I'm going anywhere," Maguire muttered behind her Hybrid, knowing full well that her L.T. could not hear her. Another ping sounded entirely too close to her, and a sliver of metal from a ricochet cut her left cheek, splattering her turret with blood and pissing her off.

"That's fecking it!" She ducked down for half a second. "Taking sustained fire. Hell being unleashed, Ma'am. I will send them to their God."

Maguire stood up and let loose a hailstorm directly into the middle of the gathering crowd. Mists of blood spouted up from direct hits, while those who were not hit dove in all directions.

"Five miles!" Baumer shouted as she dodged around another barrier.

Maguire had to take her hand off the gun grip to keep her balance and then was right back in position. Her Hybrid barked out three-round bursts to conserve ammo, but her rounds were hitting what she aimed at; she could tell by the people falling like ten pins. She sucked in a breath and kept firing at a steady rate.

She heard Baumer's loud gasp, and a quick glance told her that the next barrier would send them airborne.

"High top, hang on!" Baumer shouted, and then their wheels left the ground.

Maguire's teeth rattled and she tasted blood from where she bit her cheek just after the wheels touched ground again. "Feck!" She opened up with her gun and kept up a steady stream of firing both left and right.

"Three miles," Baumer announced.

Maguire's brains tried to unscramble themselves as she shook her head and kept looking forward. *"I bet your daddy didn't teach you how to deal with this,"* ran through her head as she peripherally watched Baumer fight wheels that wanted to go left when they needed to go right. Baumer strong-armed the vehicle to the right and was rewarded with two hundred feet of straight ahead driving.

Focusing on the enemy, Maguire took advantage of the even line. Her bullets tore into the leading rank of weapons firing at her; more heads and necks exploded in mists of blood. She felt nothing as she watched them fall. They were just so many targets hitting the ground. And she was still taking fire. Like a swarm of insistent mosquitoes, metal kept ticking off her turret. She scanned the area until her gaze settled on the only high point. The bell tower still in range of her was the only logical source of the continued barrage. She aimed as best she could at sixty miles an hour. Fifty seconds of sustained fire of 7.62mm ammunition reduced the enemy sniper nest to Swiss cheese. There was no further return fire.

"Hooah!" Maguire pumped a victorious fist, even as she became aware of the blood trailing down her cheek.

"One mile," Baumer called up.

Maguire divided her attention between the insurgent blitz and her lieutenant, as Baumer tried to maneuver through a trap of deep, soft sand. She fought it hard, cutting her wheels left and right, slowing her speed to twenty miles an hour.

The streak of a rocket propelled grenade cut dangerously close to the nose of the Hummer, and Maguire was about to yell to Baumer not to slow down any more if she could help it when Baumer gunned the engine hard. The Hummer lurched forward and avoided the RPG explosion by about ten feet.

Maguire's head snapped side to side, but her finger was

still on the trigger, firing, defying all the rules of good fire control. Several more of the enemy fell, even if by accident or luck.

"We're clear!" Baumer shouted as incoming fire stopped and the road evened out under their wheels.

"Thank God." Maguire sagged down from her position, blood staining her face. Reflexively, she turned and looked at her ammo—two hundred rounds left, if her count was right. She sighed. "We cut it close."

Baumer glanced at her. "You're hit," she worried, as she kept her hands on the wheel.

"Ricochet. Ain't nothing but a thing, Ma'am," Maguire cracked. "Nice driving."

"Thank my daddy," Baumer quipped as she looked in the rear-view mirror.

***

Baumer eased the vehicle to a slow stop under the cover of a deserted gas station two hours outside of Las Cruces. She reached back and tapped Maguire's leg. When a goggled face peered at her, she said, "Dismount, Sergeant. I need a break, and we need to check on your face."

"My face is fine, L.T.," Maguire objected, but when Baumer scowled at her, Maguire finished with, "Dismounting as ordered, Ma'am." She proceeded to do just that as Baumer exited the Hummer, opened the back hatch, and rummaged through the medic bag with shaking hands.

Baumer's hands stilled, and she let her head fall forward as she took a deep breath and released it slowly. The adrenaline was bottoming out, and now she was deathly tired. She closed her eyes, and then arms wrapped around her and squeezed her tight, and she felt the warmth of Maguire's body against her back.

"You all right?" Maguire whispered.

Baumer almost laughed. "I have no idea." For just a moment, she let herself sag into Maguire. "We've just begun this and I'm tired of it already. I'm not sure I can do this."

"You've already done this *and* bought the kilt. One month

and a half on your own on that long hike back to civilization," Maguire reminded her.

Baumer arched an eyebrow. "Aren't you tired?"

"Exhausted."

"You could have the decency to show it." There was a hint of annoyance in Baumer's tone.

Maguire grinned despite the obvious pain it caused. "What? And destroy my goddess of war image?" She hesitated a moment, then said, "My unit in Korea was supposed to conduct a brief delaying action, a day at most." She swallowed. "It wasn't until eight days later that we were relieved. You've already done more than that. Alone, I would not have survived in Afghanistan or Korea. You survived alone. And you're not alone this time, L.T." She tightened her embrace.

For a moment, Baumer did not feel like a lieutenant in the United States Army; she felt like Jessica Baumer, whoever that might be. She sucked in a breath. "Thank you."

"For as long as this mission takes, I'll walk beside you," Maguire promised.

Baumer gathered herself and patted Maguire's hand. "I'm okay now. Thanks." She stepped out of the embrace and turned to face her friend and comrade in arms. "Now, your wound."

Maguire tried not to squirm as Baumer liberally poured peroxide on her cheek, used tweezers to withdraw a small sliver of metal, and then applied two Steri strips.

ChapterNine

"L.T., just so that I'm in the loop, who are these friends of yours?"

"Took you long enough to ask. Curious, are you?"

"Call me the proverbial cat. I know of them, but not about them, if that make sense."

Baumer smiled. "Devon Prescott and I were stationed at Taji together for six months in 2004. She was a PFC at the time. She got out as a staff sergeant."

"Why?" Maguire asked.

"She intended to be a career soldier, but she could no longer outrun the Don't Ask, Don't Tell witch hunt that always seemed to be nipping at her heels."

"Glad that's over. Not that I guess it matters now," Maguire said.

"She got out after her third tour, before she could get caught and crucified. The next year, it was repealed."

"Bet that frustrated the hell out of her," Maguire said.

"Not really. Immediately after her separation from the service, several private military contractors courted her for her IP skills. The company she finally chose, Sansleau, was the civilian contractor for arid operations on American soil. The company provided training and technical support for paramilitary venues in dry, desert areas, and they paid Prescott an obscene amount of money for her skills."

"I've read up on them. Something like a hundred k for six months work?"

"Only if you're stateside. That doubles, even triples if you are assigned outside the USA. Plus, a majority of the higher ups had no issue with her sexual orientation. She was at Fort Huachuca as the liaison for the tracking and improvement of desert training."

"Hands on?"

"No. She implemented and filed the paperwork. I'm sure she thought she had died and gone to heaven, well, until all this."

"And what about the woman who is there with her—Szabo?"

Baumer's smile radiated warmth. "Szab is…delightful. She's a jack-of-all-trades, mistress of none. You two should get along just fine."

Baumer rumbled the Hummer to a halt and killed the engine. She was not looking forward to stepping out into the Arizona heat. She spared a moment to think of Maguire, who had spent half of the trip inside the vehicle and the other half exposed to the sun, heat, and wind. Even though Maguire claimed that it didn't bother her, Baumer felt somewhat guilty. Maguire had gone from moderately pale to an interesting shade of tan and pink. The ricochet wound on her cheek was still oozing blood, but didn't appear to be infected.

Maguire dropped down from the turret, pulled off her helmet, and wiped some sweat from her forehead. She set her helmet down. "You're sure you want us to go out there with just our sidearms?"

"I know Prescott," Baumer insisted. "If she were under duress, she would have coded that information and passed it along. So yes, just sidearms, even if yours isn't exactly regulation," she teased.

"I don't like the Beretta, I like the Sig." Maguire would not budge. "I guess the Army could just bring me up on charges for breaking the regs."

"When I find someone with more rank than me, remind me to suggest it." Baumer almost sounded serious. With that she pushed the door open and the heat sucked her breath from her. "Jesus! I thought Texas was hot."

Maguire snagged her black beret from the seat and positioned it on her head. "How many times were you in Iraq?"

"More than was safe, and the temperature never felt like this."

"Bullshit. It was just the same." Maguire stifled a smile as she adjusted the tactical holster that held her Sig.

"No, this is a dry heat," Baumer bantered.

"So is an oven, but I wouldn't want to live in one." She slammed the door closed and joined Baumer.

The buildings were what Baumer expected—squat, white or beige, with brass plaques displaying building names that mostly belonged to fallen soldiers of distinction.

The creak of a door opening caused them to swivel their heads, looking for the source. Baumer smiled widely as she recognized Prescott. It had not been all that long ago that she was sure she'd never again see one of her favorite soldiers.

"Jess! How the fuck are you?" Prescott pulled Baumer into a hug. The ever-changing color of her hazel eyes twinkled at the sight of her good friend and former commanding officer. "I was hoping to hell you had survived the attacks, but I'm glad Szabo was the one who picked you up on the computer, because I think I would have fallen over dead from shock at hearing your voice."

Baumer returned her hug and then pulled back a bit to look at her friend. Prescott's dark hair was longer than she'd ever seen it, and her perpetual tan was gone, replaced by the sallow shade of someone who had spent too much time indoors. Other than that, she looked good. "I never had a doubt about you surviving. You're too mean to die of anything but old age."

"Now that's the truth." Prescott laughed, then suddenly turned serious. "Honestly, it was a fluke that Szabo and I were in the dungeon when the shit hit the fan. I was in trouble again. I got caught doing a better job than my homophobic, misogynistic military supervisor."

"Nice to know some things never change." Baumer grinned then relinquished her grip on her former troop. "Pres, I'd like you to meet Staff Sergeant Branna Maguire. She was my fellow lab rat. Maguire, this is Devon Prescott."

Baumer watched with amusement as Maguire suffered through the age-old army ritual of being sized up as the newbie. If it bothered her, she did not show it, she merely gazed back at the appraising eyes. The slight widening of Prescott's eyes at seeing Maguire's shoulder tab did not go unnoticed, and Baumer knew there would be questions later.

Prescott returned her attention to her friend. "Did you run

into any trouble on your way here?"

"Only on the northwest side of Las Cruces. Before we made the attempt to get through, we encountered a tribe of Apache on the southeast road. It was encouraging to see how they are surviving and even thriving. They have reverted to their ancestral skills at living off the land and fighting for what's theirs. They escorted us to the edge of the city and offered to come get us if we couldn't get through. They will be worthy allies if we get to Noble's sanctuary." Baumer took a breath. "I'm not sure I can describe Las Cruces. It was barbaric. People are so desperate to survive, they are slaughtering one another rather than working together.

"You also might want to make note of Deming, New Mexico," Baumer continued. "We encountered a large gang, mostly male, that was determined to get our Hummer away from us and take our supplies. I'm not sure that it was as bad as Las Cruces, but if it hadn't been for Maguire's dead eye and my determined driving skills, they would have killed us."

"I think dying—at least right away—wouldn't have been your worst immediate worry," Prescott said solemnly.

"I would have eaten my gun before giving in to that," Maguire said.

Prescott eyeballed Maguire again. "I hope you would have had the decency to take Jessica with you."

Maguire's expression matched Prescott's in intensity. "I always take care of my own."

"Good to know." Prescott nodded approvingly.

Baumer chose to ignore the verbal cockfight that appeared to be brewing between the two women. "We're going to have to make sure we stay off all the main roads when we leave. And we're going to have to stockpile food and water. It seems that anything roadside that wasn't destroyed in the initial attack has already been cleaned out. Also, almost everywhere we've been, the roads that lead to what's left of the cities and towns are barricaded and guarded by survivors who don't want to share."

"I figured it might be like that. What kind of population are we talking about in these groups you've passed?"

"It varies," Maguire said. "The group that ambushed us was large, maybe a hundred in total, and that was only the ones we could see. Only about fifteen came after us with vehicles and weapons, the rest stayed behind the barricades. We don't have any idea how many others were entrenched in what's left of Las Cruces. Other groups we passed were small. They didn't seem any less dangerous, but there were less than twenty in view."

Prescott nodded as she absorbed this information. "Come on, Szab's cooking chow. Might as well enjoy normal food while we can." She turned to lead the way to the mess hall.

Baumer saw a hint of a scowl on Maguire's face, so she fell in step beside the perceptive troop. "What's up, Mags?"

Maguire kept her voice low. "I recognize your friend's command walk. Was she ever a drill sergeant?"

"She did a year and a half as a drill sergeant. Why?"

"Great." Maguire rolled her eyes. "Almost all the former drill sergeants I've known stubbornly believe that they are always absolutely right. If your buddy is the same, it could be a long trip to wherever it is we are going."

"She's more civilian than military now, so I wouldn't worry about it," Baumer reassured her. "Is that the only reason you two are prickly around each other? It wouldn't be because she defected to the civilian contractor side, would it?"

"No, Ma'am. I am actually fine with that. Sansleau has the best reputation for trying to stay within the parameters of the law of any of the contractors."

"Then what's the problem?"

Maguire sighed. "I don't know yet. Maybe it's nothing but a personality clash."

Baumer nodded. "I know you will soldier through whatever it is." She quickened her pace and waved Maguire forward until she could hear Maguire's footsteps crunching on the gravel behind her.

Baumer's eyes tracked around in a tactical grid. She could tell where there had been bodies. Those areas were now clear, but there were tire marks around them. Prescott and Szabo had been busy between computer conversations.

The smell of cooking meat reached them, and Maguire and Baumer both started to drool. Their own kitchenette in the lab had had the basics, but the meat had been consumed first out of fear that they would lose power and the perishables would spoil.

They had eaten the last hamburger weeks earlier. Other than the time Victoria had served them fried chicken, it had been MREs and trail mix.

"We ain't much in the way of culinary talent, but anyone can grill a steak on the right equipment." Prescott pulled back the bar lock in the front door. "We haven't had any company, but I don't like to take chances." She turned on her heel and looked at the two new arrivals. "Speaking of which, did you secure the Hybrid?"

Maguire answered by reaching into her right breast pocket and pulling out the firing pin. "Three tours in Afghanistan and one especially memorable one in Korea. Give me just a touch of credit." Her smile was anything but sincere as she carefully placed the firing pin back into her pocket.

"If you two are finished peeing around each other..." Baumer said. A pointed look finished her sentence for her. She turned toward the person moving around the kitchen. "Szab!"

"Hey there, L.T.," Specialist 4th Class Natalia Szabo called from behind the serving line where the stoves and ovens were located. Her dark Slavic features lit up at seeing Baumer. "Long time, no see." There was clear admiration on her face.

Baumer knew that Szabo held her and her service experience in high regard. "Szabo, priyatno videt tebya, moi drug," Baumer responded with affection.

"Your Russian's getting better. And it's good to see you, too."

"Nope, it's all I remember. What'd you make?"

"Steaks, fried potatoes, and corn—basic stuff that even I can't mess up." The ingenuous grin on her face spoke to her honesty. She passed loaded plates over, and then pulled off her apron. "I even set the table."

Baumer turned her head to look at the table. Szabo had used the good table linens normally reserved for VIPs. Her eyes misted. "Thank you, my friends. I can't believe you still have meat. Or power," she added, almost to herself. "You cooked." She gestured to Szabo. "You get first seat." There was an order in her soft voice. Flushing slightly, Szabo took a chair. The others took a seat, and they all tucked into dinner.

***

For a long time, the only sounds were those of silverware clinking on plates, chewing, and appreciative murmuring. After the initial edge of hunger was taken off, there were requests for salt, pepper, and bread.

Maguire finished first and pushed her plate away. She sat back in contentment and watched the other three as only one new to their company could. Part of her felt slighted by Prescott's condescension because she did not share their bond, but another part of her understood. Prescott did not know her or her abilities, so Maguire was willing to give her a little latitude.

Baumer was the last to finish. Maguire liked the fact that the officer was enjoying her food, lingering over it. Knowing what the lieutenant had endured during her month long trek back to US lines, Maguire understood.

Maguire waited until she was sure everyone had finished eating before she began gathering up the plates and silverware. When Baumer and Szabo tried to help, she waved them off. She noticed that Prescott did not offer to lift a finger. She mentally ticked off another point against the woman.

With so few dishes, it didn't take long to load the dishwasher racks and start the cycle. She then took a grill brush and cleaned the grill. When she finished, she checked her watch. It was almost time. From her spot at the grill, she looked back over her shoulder at the others.

"Recall still at 1800 on this base?"

There was a long silence until Szabo spoke. "Actually, here it is 1815. The post CO was a late leaver."

"Which direction is the flag from the front door?"

"Southwest." Szabo ignored Prescott's glare and continued to roll up the tablecloth.

"Thank you...Szabo. What is your rank?"

"I am Spec 4 promotable, although I don't think I'll ever see sergeant again now."

Maguire smiled. "For that dinner alone, I would recommend you."

"There is no more Army, Maguire," Prescott broke in. Her voice and manner were weary. "There's no more reveille, recall,

PT, or anything else."

Maguire straightened. "Until I am officially notified that the Army is dissolved, I will render *all* courtesies and honors as dictated by regulations. If you have an issue with that, Prescott, that is your problem. Now, will the doors open when I push on them, or do I have to shoot them out?"

Prescott sat erect in her seat and stared at Maguire. Maguire shook her head, turned toward the doors, and drew her Sig.

"All right! The doors will open when you push on them."

"Wow," Szabo said in clear surprise. "I've never known you to back down so readily, Pres."

"I didn't back down," Prescott said defensively, still eyeballing Maguire warily. "I just don't want to sweep up the glass." She watched as Maguire replaced her sidearm and strode out the doors.

Baumer stood and tugged on her uniform, straightening it. "I know tensions are really high right now, but Maguire is not the enemy. Maybe you should look up the little boondoggle in Korea, Pres. You might learn a thing or two. As far as I'm concerned, the Army still stands, and courtesies are still observed." With that, she followed after Maguire, then turned and looked back at the others. "I fully expect these doors to open when we return. Szabo, you coming? I will understand if you don't."

Szabo deliberated for a moment, then grabbed her beret and headed towards the door without a glance at Prescott. "I am coming. I'm still in. I can only hope that eventually we find some payroll geek to issue my back pay." She grinned and jogged up to Baumer, and together they walked out of view.

***

Prescott stewed in frustrated anger for a few moments, then pushed away from her chair, moved to the door, and watched as the three women snapped to attention and rendered crisp salutes.

"What the hell did she mean? Look into Korea and learn something?" Prescott muttered. She would research that later, after everyone was asleep. They might have lost connectivity to the World Wide Web, but up until a month ago, she could still access internal military records and archived events. She mentally thanked whatever deity might be out there that they could still find gas for their generators.

She waited until honors were rendered, even though in her mind, the Army, the country were gone. In their place was something else, something that could only be imagined in nightmares.

Baumer, Szabo, and Maguire completed their salutes and executed a sharp about-face. Together they marched back to the door of the mess hall. Maguire pulled the door open, then waited until the other two entered the mess hall before she stepped over the threshold.

ChapterTen

Maguire and Baumer were shown to their sleeping quarters. Maguire expected they would be equipped with racks, like they had been back at their Bliss set-up, but this private area was more like a four-person dorm room. The beds were actual single beds as opposed to cots or bunks. On Prescott and Szabo's side of the room were two sections with a "lived-in" look. The side Maguire and Baumer were to occupy had two areas with bedding rolled up on mattresses, and the desks and walls were clear of any personalization. The questioning looks on their faces prompted an explanation from Szabo.

"Collins and Nazarian." She pointed to the beds. "They were our relief. They were caught outside. Pres and I were on duty when everything went down. The post had been on a 72-hour lockdown while several battalions were participating in a drill. We were doing twelve shifts of six hours on, six hours off, as everyone in this building except the four of us were needed for the exercise. When we got word the drill was over, we had just relieved them. Nazarian suggested that she and Collins get some fresh air and some edible food. They showered and left to go to town. An hour later, the drill went live and everybody outside was, well, gone."

"What about everybody inside?" Maguire asked.

"In the beginning, it seemed as though there were quite a few of us left, because we have a few below-ground buildings. Once we realized what had happened, we did a roll call. Of course, because of the electromagnetic pulse, everything above ground that required a plug was fried. That truncated our computer communications for about twenty-four hours. During that time, we still had our portables and we were able to count at least forty-three survivors before our batteries died. Then satellite signals started to come back. A little jury-rigging on my part, and we were able to reach out farther than the post."

"So where are the others?" Baumer asked

Szabo shrugged. "I don't know. I think a majority of them went outside too soon, in search of family or loved ones or signs of other life. A couple of the grease monkeys were down under with us for a while. They had been working on some secret project and got stuck in the motor pool."

"What happened to them?" Baumer asked.

"We don't know. We assume they took a Hummer and left. One day they were there, the next day they weren't. Pres and I have checked every inch of this place since the air cleared. Whoever else was here is either dead or vanished. We're the only two left. Pres is suspicious that the original exercise was never a drill."

Maguire asked, "Why is that?"

"Think about it. We have a fully equipped Intelligence Center here, and they had no clue we were about to be nuked? One aspect of the exercise was to improve our time evac'ing troops and equipment from Libby Airfield and Sierra Vista to NORAD. We don't have airfield surveillance, so we don't know who and what went or who and what, if anything, was brought back."

"It wouldn't surprise me if the top brass knew and left us peons to vaporize or die by whatever means," Baumer said, readily acknowledging Szabo's scenario.

"Are you two sure Noble is still out there?" Maguire asked.

The door opened behind them, and Prescott walked in. She was carrying a small cooler, which she set on a table. "Noble is there. I spoke with her yesterday." She opened the cooler and pulled out four bottles of beer. "I thought we could use some refreshment while we discuss our next move."

Maguire accepted a bottle. "And it's ice cold." She twisted the cap off and waited for the others to do the same, then lifted her bottle toward the other women. When they clinked the bottles together, Maguire said, "Sláinte!" She and the others took a long, satisfying swallow.

"Wow. This is a treat. How'd you get this?" Baumer asked.

Prescott and Szabo smiled. "The motor pool boys had it. We didn't dare touch anything above-ground, but we scavenged all the underground food and beverage sources. It amounted to a five-day supply at every sublevel, which is what has kept us going. We save the beer and the steak for a special occasion," Prescott said.

"Well," Maguire looked over the sweating bottle of brew, "it ain't Irish, but it's beer, and after a month of being deprived of a good malt, it tastes feckin' great to me."

Szabo grinned and raised her beer in a toast. "Here's to feckin' great!"

"So, when do we get moving again?" Baumer asked.

"In a hurry to leave our safe haven, Jess?" Prescott sipped her beer.

"What's really safe anymore, Pres?" Baumer asked before Maguire could. "Even though this isn't a big post, comparatively speaking, you don't know who might be holing up here or what their intentions might be, whether they are military, contractor, or civilian. You don't know who may have wandered on post or crawled out of some hidey hole after you did your initial sweep.

"We don't really know much of anything anymore beyond what's right in front of us. We say it is luck that the communication satellites are still orbiting in perfect working condition, but is it? Or is it by design? I would venture a guess that most of those who survived, outside the loop of whoever started this, don't have the technical skills of Szabo or the intel background that you do, or the trained survival skills that each of us has. People wanting to survive will do just about anything to live another day.

"Believe me, dinner and this beer have been unbelievably great, but if we stay here, we're sitting ducks for whatever the next phase may be, whether it's by plan or a result of desperation. Just my humble opinion, but a military installation is no longer one of the most protected places to be. I want to get where we're going, take a breath, and make any future decisions from there."

Szabo frowned. "If we make it."

"We'll make it."

Prescott's assurance was met by skepticism from the lieutenant. "How can you be so sure?"

"Because failure isn't an option," Maguire interjected.

"Hooah, Sergeant." Prescott took another drink. "Besides, our awesome mode of transportation gives us an edge."

"Yeah, who would have thought my tinkering and tweaking over the last couple years would be paying off," Szabo said proudly.

"No shit." Prescott grinned, then sobered. "I still think we should have developed a 4 x 4 version."

Szabo shrugged. "If this had happened next year..." She shook her head. "At least we have her now."

***

Baumer and Maguire followed as Prescott led the way into a dark, cavernous room, their footsteps echoing off the high walls. There was an oddly self-satisfied grin on her face. Szabo's face showed only unbridled enthusiasm. Baumer looked around with a professional eye. There was an impressive array of computer equipment—sensors that she assumed were diagnostic tools, and a rack of some gear that reminded her of cell phone batteries only economy sized.

"It's neat, isn't it?" Prescott smiled with pride. "Szabo has done a huge amount of work on this project. She might not look it, but she has a programming brain like you would not believe." She pushed a button on the wall, and lights began blazing in sequence. In the middle of the cavern, a tarp covered shape came into view.

"You won't believe this thing." Pride was clear in Szabo's voice. "She is like nothing you have seen. Three years of my life, devoted to her."

"Well, the L.T. can marry you two, if you want," Maguire joked.

Szabo walked over to the main worktable, where she picked up a bulky wired control and grinned as she pushed a button. A faint metallic whirring sound fired up, and the tarp began moving up and away.

Once the tarp had cleared away, Maguire said, "It's an RV."

Prescott grinned. "For everyone else, it's the RV from

hell." She began walking its perimeter and pointing out its features. "Up top, imbedded with the running lights are cameras—one for each corner and overlapping coverage fifteen degrees at edges. No blind spots. All cameras have FLIR, that way we are not blind in the dark."

Baumer was impressed. "FLIR? Forward Looking Infrared?"

"Yep. The headlights can operate in standard mode, or if we need to blind an enemy…" She thought a moment and then shrugged. "Basically, just think of this as the space shuttle driving down the freeway.

"The outer body is a double shell of Kevlar. Between those two shells, pure lead. Just to give you an idea of her impermeability, she could take a bazooka round from World War Two with no problem. All glass is bullet resistant, but it makes opening the windows kinda hard. We have a one-hundred-gallon water reservoir on a filtration system, but the filters have a fifty-run cycle life. Bad news is that we only have one spare set of filters, so we only cycle when we get to half usage, by that I mean after we use fifty gallons of water. So we have to conserve. Drinking water will have to be bottled, and that's going to add weight."

"We can work something out, maybe top off some camel backpacks, for drinking only," Baumer mused. "That leaves water for cooking and showers on maybe a two or three-day rotation, depending on what kind of work we're doing. If we can find a clean water source, could we drain the used and restock the tanks?"

Szabo nodded. "We've thought about it, but that would mean hauling test kits, and that would take up space and add weight."

"You won't need them," Maguire said. "Just test the old fashioned way."

"Which would be what?" Prescott arched an eyebrow.

"Animals. Watch a water source in the morning or at night. If an animal drinks from it and doesn't die, it's safe. You don't hunt much, do you?" Maguire responded in a neutral tone.

"Not game, no. Besides, we're not sure how many animals survived," Prescott said dismissively. After a moment, she added, "You know, Maguire, I feel like you started challenging me the moment you arrived here and I don't like it. Just because I'm no longer an official grunt doesn't mean I've lost all my military instincts regarding my survival training."

Maguire let Prescott's words roll right off her but out of the corner of her eye, she saw Baumer cross her arms. "Not challenging you, Prescott, I'm just direct. I don't have time to coddle anyone."

"Not asking for coddling, Sergeant, I'm—"

"Oh, good lord, enough!" Baumer snapped. She looked at Prescott. "Continue, please."

Maguire hid a grin while Prescott audibly sighed. "Inside is a very small kitchenette, and the sleeping accommodations are minimal."

"How minimal?" Baumer walked around the vehicle, running her hands over the body.

"Pull down racks." Szabo's regretful tone indicated what she thought of the racks. "But it was the only way to do it. I myself will be sleeping under the computer station."

"Computer station?" Baumer tore her gaze away from the RV to stare at Szabo.

"Best the military could build with NASA, NSA, and every other capital letter agency in the field. As long as the satellites keep flying, I can access whatever information we might need."

Maguire let out a low whistle. "That might come in very handy indeed."

"Down side is that it's an energy hog. Two car batteries run the damn thing. Which means we will most likely be scrounging batteries wherever we can," Prescott explained. "She's an energy-consuming beast, but she'll get us where we're going. The batteries that run the engine and just about everything else are solar charged. Best case, we stop in bright sunlight for four hours with the engine off, and we are in back in business."

"What about inclement weather?"

"We're fucked," Szabo said bluntly. "Any time we're below sixty-five percent, we have to stay put and wait while we recharge. Try to operate with energy output that low, and we could fry the whole system. She's a showpiece, but untested in a real world situation."

Baumer finished her walk-around. "I have got to say that you did beautiful work from what I can see. We'll just have to monitor systems and adjust them accordingly."

"That was the order for the first test run." Szabo laughed. "Isn't that how the instruction books are written?"

Prescott managed a real grin for a change. "I would guess that's a roger. Everything else is living space and, just for you, Maguire, hatches up top to allow gun access if we need it. Do me a favor though, measure each hatch to front and back, I'd hate to have to explain to the government why you put holes in this toy."

"I thought you said there was no government," Maguire challenged.

"Mags…" Baumer cautioned with a sigh.

"Right, no non-essential holes in the vehicle or they can bill me," Maguire agreed. "I'll check the angles, find the blind spots with each weapon system, and put up range cards for each. That way, if I'm dead, the rest of you will know what you're doing."

Prescott was not amused. "You say shit like that on purpose, don't you?"

Perplexed by Prescott's objection, Maguire shook her head. "I always give voice to the truth. The honest truth is that I have combat experience and training. You three are not trained the same. If anything should happen to me, I would have failed all of you if I hadn't done and said 'shit like that.' Whether or not you like it does not come into play. I'd rather piss you off than get you killed."

Prescott stepped forward. "Well, you're there."

"At the fuck ease, soldiers," Baumer snapped. "Pres, drop the boulder on your shoulder, and Maguire, find a different way of saying shit like that. Let's just agree to disagree." Her voice volume rose substantially as she added, "And I'm going to shoot the next person who drives me to cussing."

"Yes, Ma'am," Maguire answered automatically.

Prescott had the grace to look ashamed. "Sorry, Jess."

Szabo nearly fell over. "Damn, L.T.! I've never, ever heard you curse. Substitute some very interesting words for curses, maybe, but never out and out curse."

"Well, that's what these two are doing to me. Now," Baumer took a breath, "if we're all acting like human beings again, what else do we need for this little adventure?"

For a moment there was silence, then Maguire raised her hand. "How much weight has been allowed for ammo?"

Szabo grinned. "Since we don't have a lot of luggage, I can spare you five hundred pounds for ammo."

Maguire did the math in her head. "Crap. That means light on the Hybrid and heavy on the M4s, plus nine mil for the sidearms. My kingdom for a fifty sniper rifle," she grumbled.

"Sorry, no can do on that one, Irish." Szabo shrugged. "The weight limits are strict."

"What if we dumped the ammo cans and just went with loose ammo?" Prescott asked with a flash of creativity.

"We'd have to make sure not to tangle it up—maybe bungee the Hybrid ammo, use cubbies to hold preloaded mags for the other calibers separately, but that could work. And it would save us three pounds for each ammo can," Baumer calculated. Every eye was on her. "What? I got stuck in supply for nine months after my last tour. I did learn something."

Maguire laughed until she was doubled over. "Oh, you did, L.T. You did. It's perfect. Keep this up, and I'll make you an honorary Irish Ranger."

"In that same vein, we could cut open all the MRE bags and cardboard boxes. That will save us a little as well," Szabo offered.

"We could each choose four sets of clothes and dump the rest. It's what we worked with in the field." Prescott got into the swing of the weight saving. "We come across a clean water supply, then we can wash stuff without depleting our own water supply. We might have to stock up on deodorant, but it ain't like the PX is overrun right now."

"Or we could bring along containers of moist towelettes. That would at least save us from using our limited water supply to bathe if we can't find a natural source for a day or two," Baumer suggested.

"Good idea, L.T.," Szabo said. "And we're stocked up on tampons, just FYI." She couldn't seem to help the small smile that appeared at the mention of *delicate* matters.

Chapter Eleven

They moved out at the traditional zero-dark-thirty, with Szabo at the wheel of the RV. It was no longer what anyone would consider a "recreational" vehicle. There was nothing leisurely or enjoyable about what was now essentially an armored personnel carrier, or anything fun or relaxing about the journey on which they were embarking. As Szabo drove, she called out other "R" words that could replace "recreational" in the vehicle's designation. "Reconnaissance!" she shouted out to anyone who was listening.

Prescott was seated at the console, observing a number of monitors. One terminal displayed video of whatever was being captured by the 360-degree panning camera mounted on the roof. Another screen kept track at all times of the infrared perimeter that surrounded the vehicle. Anything warm-blooded that entered the hundred-foot circumference set off an alarm to warn the RV's occupants. The program was designed for threat assessment, devised by Prescott to work similarly to the radar transmission that advised them of the current weather in the immediate vicinity of the RV.

"Reassembled, maybe," Prescott countered with a chuckle.

Baumer slid into the swivel seat next to Prescott. "Everything working the way it should?"

"Just because this is all put together with spit and a curse? Have you no faith?" Prescott's tone was pure sarcasm.

Baumer swatted her shoulder. "I guess I've become a chronic skeptic. I don't know why. It's not as if we've recently had an apocalypse or anything."

"Maguire asleep?" Szabo glanced at Baumer in the rear-view mirror.

"She was until you shouted out something a moment ago," Baumer said, not unkindly. "I want her to be rested for her watch tonight."

"Oops. Sorry. With all the noise this contraption is making, I thought she wouldn't hear me."

"It's more Maguire's training than it was your mistake, Szab," Baumer said. "A mouse farting two counties over would wake her from a sound sleep. She's on heightened alert, and I certainly can't fault her for that."

"Redeemed," Szabo said, more quietly this time.

"Reincarnated," Prescott offered.

Szabo nodded her approval. "Oooh…Szab likey."

Baumer studied one of the monitors and watched the topography change with every mile they slowly covered. One of the screens was showing changing numbers that she immediately recognized as longitude and latitude. The small window in the corner of that screen displayed readings that were unfamiliar. Pointing to the area in question, she asked Prescott, "What are those other numbers?"

"That's the AQI, Air Quality Index. It reads and interprets the five major pollutants—ground ozone, particle, carbon, sulfur, and nitrogen dioxides. This gauge here," Prescott tapped the screen, "measures and calculates levels of nuclear, biologic, and chemical presence. If the AQI of any the five pollutants goes over 300, it will flash red. The unhealthy air level used to be anything over 100, but since the big burst, I guess they figured if we were still alive, 100 must be for wimps."

Baumer leaned forward and squinted at the numbers. "They're all somewhere in the two hundreds."

"Yeah. What we're breathing now used to be maroon on the AQI color chart and classified as 'very unhealthy.' The further north we go and the higher the altitude, the more often we will be breathing decent quality air. Good thing Noble is where she is." Prescott gestured to the screen. "Anyway, if all the lights flash red, we just hunker down inside here and wait it out. If there is any kind of a nuclear, biologic, or chemical presence in the atmosphere, we'll hear an audible alarm."

"And how do we deal with that?"

"We pray, Jess. This contraption is everything but airtight."

They stared at each other, absorbing the hopelessness of that fact.

"Revolutionary," Szabo said.

Prescott raised an eyebrow. "Re-armament."

"How does this work?" Baumer pointed to the screen that displayed the perimeter stats.

"Pretty much the same way the weather program does. A microwave signal beams toward a target and listens for its reflection, then analyzes how the frequency of the returned signal has been altered by the object's motion."

Baumer stared at her for a moment. "Do you come with subtitles?"

"Didn't you and Maguire have to interpret numbers and graphs in your Army rathole?" Prescott asked pointedly.

"Actually, no. Our programs did all that for us. And we had a reference screen for everything. Come on, Pres, you remember how it was. They only fed us what they wanted us to know. Our terminals were restricted."

"It's like Doppler radar, actually. It's all about motion detection. Except these programs are a bit more advanced. Not top of the line, of course, but the best we could do with what we had."

"Rigmarole." Szabo said. "Hey, I like that! Get it? RIGmarole."

Prescott glared at her. "If you weren't driving, I'd throw something at you."

"Impressive, though." Baumer tapped the screen.

Prescott leaned back in her chair. "Doesn't it just kill you that the military spent obscene amounts of money on state-of-the-art technical equipment and data, and yet bought their physical defense weapons from the lowest bidder?"

"Guys, I'm seeing some smoke off to the far left." Szabo's tone was serious.

Baumer swung out of her chair and took up a position behind the driver's seat. "That's an affirmative," she confirmed. "Pres, can you zoom in with the camera on your one o'clock?"

"Got it." Prescott made the necessary adjustments. "Oh man! This isn't good."

Szabo stopped the vehicle while Baumer returned to the monitor and discovered what Prescott was referring to.

The door to the sleeping compartment slid open, and

Maguire poked her head out. "Fee Fi Fo Fun, I smell a reason to get my gun."

***

The young woman stared blankly at the sky beyond the shoulder of the stinking hulk of a man who was sweating and grunting above her. She had no more tears to cry; dehydration had seen to that. She had no screams left in her; she had screamed herself hoarse days ago. She felt as if she had been deserted by her faith, that her fealty to any supreme being had been a travesty of her innocence. Everyone she loved had died, so why was she forced to live? She felt she had been too good of a person to survive just to become a war whore and worse, an incubator for the children of these monsters.

She wanted to kill herself, but they never gave her an opportunity. She was the only woman they had, and they used her to take of their physical needs and to be the first of many to propagate their new world order. They called her their Eve, told her she would be the first mother of the new civilization.

While they traveled, she did not see another living female. She longed for the day they would find a replacement for her. She hoped that they would trade her for new flesh, and that would leave her free to exit this terrible new world that she had not asked for. Despite her anguish, she was torn about wishing that same torture to be borne by another. The cycle of terror and torture would begin for another victim. The Lord had abandoned her in her time of need, and so she was loath to pray that she be spared this abomination at the expense of another woman's violation.

Finished slamming his disgusting body into her, her attacker pulled out, stood up, and then stepped aside for the next man to take his turn. After him, there would be a third and then a fourth...

Just as their body parts were about to couple, a shot rang out. The sound of it seemed close, but did not originate within the small group of five men surrounding her. The gunshot distracted her rapists, which mercifully stopped the assault against her.

TheEnd

***

"Afternoon, boys," Maguire said in as polite a tone as she could muster. She looked at the half-naked young woman on the ground, and nodded acknowledgement. "Ma'am."

The victim stared at the three women who stood in a wide half-circle. She looked at once terrified and grateful as she reached for one of the men's shirts to cover herself.

Maguire, Baumer, and Prescott stood confidently before the four men and their captive. The trio was armed to the teeth with every weapon that would be both effective and convenient to carry. Baumer and Prescott held their Colt M4 Tactical Assault Rifles in a loose port arms, while Maguire's TAS was in a ready position that could turn them all into dead men in a heartbeat.

One man, apparently the leader, took a step toward the trio. "Where the hell did you bitches come from?"

"Now that's not very nice," Baumer said. "For all you know, we could be your saviors, come to alleviate your suffering and transport you to a place where you can get proper shelter, food, and water."

Confused optimism appeared on the faces of the four men, while the woman looked terrified.

"Damn, Lieutenant, now you went and got their hopes up." A dark smile split Maguire's face. The look let the men know the last thing these women would be was good Samaritans who were on their side.

The man who was next in line to take his turn with the woman said belligerently, "What the hell do you want, then?"

"Well first, we'll take the woman," Maguire said.

The man who acted as if he was in charge glanced contemptuously at the captive, then shifted his eyes to his men and nodded at the woman. One of them grabbed her by the hair, yanked her to her feet, and held her in front of him with a knife at her throat. The leader glared at his uninvited guests. "You can have her in exchange for some of your weapons…and fuel. I'm betting you didn't hike here."

"Oh goodie. A betting man," Baumer said. "How about this? We'll bet you that you'll turn this woman over to us with absolutely no fuss, and then you'll all walk away."

"Or?"

"Or you won't walk away at all." Baumer's voice was flat, matter-of-fact, as if holding out death as their only option was an everyday occurrence for her.

"Your offer sucks," the leader said. "I don't like it, so I'll say no."

"Pretty cocky for a piece of shit rapist who, in case you haven't noticed, is way outgunned," Prescott observed drily.

"Rapist? Me? Like if you dykes get hold of this fine piece of ass, you won't use her for the same purpose. She ain't good for much else."

Maguire noticed the question now in the woman's eyes, and her expression of terror.

"Dykes, huh? That's a pretty big assumption on your part," Baumer said.

"But we'll take it as a compliment," Prescott added.

"Yeah, wear it proudly, you dyke bitches." Maguire's eyes never left the woman, or the raider who had her at knifepoint. The captive female's face and bare shoulder were badly bruised, and Maguire was certain there were also bruises, both physical and psychological, that were not visible.

"You're taking a big chance here with your demands," another man spat.

This one might almost have been considered handsome, if it hadn't been for the recent scar running from his forehead to his right cheek. It was healing, but still raw and angry.

"There are many of us, you know," he continued. "You could be surrounded right now."

"Many of you? Meaning many scumbag assholes? Yeah, we know. We've already taken out most of those in this immediate area. But you guys? We know there are just four of you. And of course the woman," Baumer said.

Maguire was getting tired of the foreplay; she was ready to fuck them up. There would be no redeeming this bunch. Besides, if there were others in the outlying area that they hadn't seen, the sound of repeated gunfire would certainly draw them closer.

"It's pretty evident you don't have much respect for

women, so you probably couldn't imagine that we'd have brains enough to scout the area first," Baumer said. "We spotted your group before you even laid her down. While you were all getting off, we made sure you were alone in this sector."

The woman's look of fear suddenly turned to outrage. "You saw they were about to rape me and did nothing to stop them?" And then she seemed surprised that she had a voice with which to speak.

The leader sneered. "I told you. It's not your virtue or safety they're interested in."

Maguire stepped forward aggressively, right eye still on her sights. "Shut up!" It was not a suggestion. Her voice softened as she addressed the woman. "What's your name?"

"Anna," the young woman croaked, her voice hoarse. She cleared her throat.

"How long have you been traveling with these men?" Maguire asked.

"Four days." The voice was a little stronger.

"So I gather today was not the first time you were…attacked…by them?"

"No."

"We really should get moving," Prescott urged. "Let's get the girl and get out of here."

"I second that," Baumer said.

"It's unanimous." Maguire adjusted her aim so that her sights were fixed on the man with the knife. "Don't you love democracy?"

Baumer almost smiled. "Maguire, you got him?"

"I've got him," she confirmed.

"Fire."

Within seconds, all five men were dead and Anna was crouched with her face toward the ground, hands laced together on the back of her head.

While Prescott made sure the men were dead and Maguire searched the camp for any usable supplies, Baumer tapped Anna's shoulder. "Are you okay?"

Anna lifted her head and saw the blood spatter on her. "I…I think I'm shot."

"Do you hurt anywhere?" Then, realizing how that could be

construed, Baumer's eyes softened in sympathy. "Anywhere new?"

Anna weakly stood, still clutching the shirt against her lower body. "N-no." She looked around at the corpses of her attackers. "They're all dead?"

"Yes. Trust me, they would have tracked us down and killed us all if we hadn't taken them out." Baumer reached over and picked up Anna's torn and filthy denim skirt. "Put this back on for now. We have some spare BDUs you can put on when we get back to the RV. You can also take a quick shower and--"

Anna ignored the skirt being held out to her. "Will I be any better off with you?"

"What?" The voice belonged to Prescott, who had been checking out the meager pickings from the men's SUV. She stomped right up to Anna. "Are you crazy? You think you would have been safer with them?"

"Is what they said true? Are you lesbians?" Anna's question came across more as offensive than frightened.

"What the fuck difference does that make?" Prescott's demeanor was almost menacing.

"Pres, come on." Baumer grabbed her friend by the arm. "Calm down. You're scaring her."

Prescott's eyes seemed to burn a hole right through Anna. "Better scared than dead, isn't it, little girl?"

"I'm not a little girl!" Anna choked out.

Prescott stood nose to nose with Anna. "Then don't act like one!" She stepped back. "I don't know what you've been brought up to believe, and I don't care, but we're not predators. All we are trying to do is survive, got it? Didn't we all endure enough judgment before the apocalypse? We don't have time to deal with any of that shit now! If you want to live, come with us. If you want to die, stay here." Prescott turned to walk away.

"Pres!" Baumer's voice held a note of warning.

Prescott turned around to face Baumer. "No! I am not going to have this fight the rest of the way to Noble's. I'm not putting my life on the line for some ingrate who drinks our water, accepts our hospitality, uses up a portion of our limited rations, and still thinks she would have been better off with the men who brutalized her!"

Maguire had heard enough. "What's going on?" She noted the stubborn glares passing between Prescott and Anna.

"Prescott wants to leave Anna here because Anna seems to be a bit of a homophobe," Baumer explained tersely.

"I'm not a homophobe!" Anna yelled, her voice cracking with dryness and emotion. "I don't want to be left here. All I wanted to know was if I was any safer with you. You just gunned down these unarmed men—"

"Who had been raping you for four days!" Prescott countered in exasperation. "There is a war going on all around you, or haven't you noticed?"

"I noticed!" Tears glistened in Anna's eyes. "I just didn't think you would be as ruthless as they were. You saw that I was going to be raped, and you just let it happen!"

"Anna, as much as we would have liked to save you from this most recent humiliation at their hands, we had to make sure we could save you and save ourselves as well. First thing you need to remember from this point on, never bring a victim to a crime." Baumer's tone was gentle but resonated with conviction.

"Are you accusing me of being responsible for what happened to me?" Anna asked, her expression angry.

"No," Baumer replied. "I'm telling you that we need to assess any potentially dangerous situation with our own safety being the first priority. If we had just busted into your little campfire without any kind of recon, we might have all been victims. There might have been others who weren't immediately present, and they could have come back and surrounded us. We had to act to evaluate that possible threat before we stepped up to save you. I wasn't accusing you of anything, Anna."

"It's a new world, kiddo," Maguire said. "Kill or be killed. It's all about the 'gots' now. Who gots and who doesn't gots. The doesn't gots want to be the gots, and will do anything to attain that status. The difference between them and us? We won't use you for our pleasure. We will use whatever skills you have, and as long as you can pull your own weight, you'll be an equal member of the team. If you don't, and if at any point you betray us or out us in a situation that might get us killed? Yes, we will kill you. But force you to have sex? No. We don't do that."

Anna paled but nodded. "That's fair."

"What skills do you have?" Baumer asked, holding out the skirt again.

Anna took the tattered garment and quickly put it on. "Um...I can sew. And I can keep everything clean, and...um...I can cook."

Maguire looked at Baumer with a delighted expression, then back to Anna. "Excellent. Welcome aboard."

"Hey! What the hell is wrong with my cooking?" Prescott asked in annoyance.

"Other than that we can't eat it? Not a damned thing," Maguire teased.

"Fine," Prescott spat. "I'm going back to the RV to tell Szabo to pull around so we can load up and get out of here. It'll be dark soon."

"I'm sorry." Anna sounded as though she meant it. "I really didn't mean to sound ungrateful. I—"

"Forget it," Maguire told her. "Like I said, as long as you pitch in and pull your weight, what's in your head is in your head, as long as it doesn't become a danger to me or my friends."

Anna pointed to Prescott's retreating back. "What about her?"

"Trust me, she'll deal. She always does." Baumer gestured around the small camping area. "So, what have we got?"

"They didn't have much fuel left, a little in the tank and an empty five-gallon gas can, but their battery is practically new, so that'll help. They had three canteens of water, an armload of MREs, some first aid supplies, their weapons and some ammo, a few blankets, and five sleeping bags. Then there was a camp shovel, a nasty-looking hibachi, a dead HAM radio, a dead Coleman lantern, and this crappy tent. We should at least be able use the material for something. There was a cooler, devoid of any ice, of course, but...best of all? Seven bottles of Budweiser."

"They had five cases the night they picked me up," Anna volunteered.

"I'm so glad they had their priorities in order," Baumer said drily. "Now I wish I'd made that bet years ago, back in the dayroom. One of the guys said the only thing that would survive would be cockroaches. And I said, 'No, it'll be cockroaches and Bud.' He said 'Wanna bet?' and darned if I shouldn't have. Although I doubt he's around to pay up."

They all turned at the sound of the RV and saw it driving slowly around the bend, Prescott walking beside it.

"Ready to get out of here?" Baumer said to Anna.

"More than ready." She gingerly took two steps forward.

"Stop," Baumer ordered, and Anna immediately stilled, cringing in fear. "Sit," came the second command, and Anna dropped.

Weapon up, Maguire quickly executed a visual 360. "L.T.?"

"Sorry, Mags. No danger. Anna, what's wrong with your feet?"

Fresh tears rolled down the young face. "They took my shoes."

"On it," Maguire said without having to be ordered. She adjusted her sling and dropped her rifle so that it hung in front of her as she walked over to Anna. After inspecting both feet, she sighed. "You are going to stand up and I'm going to piggyback you to the RV. No arguments, unless you really want to walk that far."

Anna nodded, then stood painfully as Maguire turned away from her. With little difficulty, she was hoisted onto Maguire's back.

Chapter Twelve

Szabo parked the RV and got out. "Cool, more supplies. Let me get them inventoried and stowed, and—" She stopped in mid-step at the sight of Anna being piggybacked by Maguire. "Whoa! Who have we here?"

"This is Anna," Maguire said. "She was a captive of the bunch we just took out. She needs to get cleaned up a little and find a change of clothes. Think you can help her with that?"

Szabo looked at Anna again and promptly blushed, suddenly struck mute.

Prescott noticed the awkward silence, saw Szabo's dumbstruck expression, and then looked over and saw Anna's deer-in-headlights look. "Trust me, Szab, she doesn't need you to help her bathe. Just grab her some clean clothes from our pile."

"Oh, yeah, sure. I knew that. I was just..." Szabo looked at Anna again, turned pink and ducked back inside the RV. "I'll get you some clothes," she called from within the vehicle.

Prescott shook her head and mumbled, "Oh yeah, the little princess won't be at all distracting."

Baumer turned to Anna and gestured toward the RV. "Don't pay any attention to her, Anna. She came out of the womb crabby. As soon as Szabo comes out with your clothes, we'll get Mags to set you down. After that, you can go in the back where the shower is and wash yourself off. It will have to be brief. As I'm sure you know, water is a precious commodity. We also have sanitized wet wipes, which will help. Then you can change into something cleaner. Anything you might need in the way of feminine products, I'm sure we have it. If you can't find it, ask."

A set of clean desert BDUs identical to what the others were wearing was shoved forward at Anna from the doorway of the RV. "Um…here…" Szabo said. She avoided making eye contact with the young woman.

"Thanks." Anna took the clothes.

Szabo stepped out of the vehicle so that Anna could enter. Before Anna disappeared inside, Szabo cleared her throat and said, "They're a set of mine. We're about the same size, so they should fit."

Anna nodded and then shuffled slowly toward the back.

Szabo shoved her hands in her pockets and spun around, only to be greeted by the stares of her three compadres. "What?"

"I have never in my life seen you tongue-tied," Baumer said.

Prescott nodded. "Me neither."

"I haven't known you that long, but it seems as if you are acting a little peculiar," Maguire added.

Szabo tilted her head in the direction of the RV. "Is she…uh…who…" Szabo scratched an invisible itch on her head. "What is her story?"

"Oooh, down, girl," Prescott said. "Get that thought right out of your head."

"What? No, I…shit, Pres, you know I wouldn't have the nerve, anyway. I mean, yeah, she's beautiful, even though she's filthy, but I know we don't have time for that stuff." Szabo looked at the ground and scuffed at the dirt with the toe of her boot.

"Szab, she's…she's been gang raped by those bastards we just killed, and it's been going on for days. She's traumatized and she's frightened of everybody, including us."

Szabo's eyes softened and her expression completely re-formed into a look of sincere compassion.

Baumer looked directly at Prescott. "We need to take it easy on her. She's a civilian, and this is her worst nightmare."

"Hell, Jess, it's the worst nightmare for all of us," Prescott said.

"But we're better trained for—"

Prescott put up her hand. "Please don't say it. None of us were trained for…for whatever the fuck this is. We were trained for short-term survival in the most unimaginable circumstances, but never for something like this."

"The lieutenant's right," Maguire said, as she finished adding their latest acquisitions to the inventory list.

"Of course, you'd agree with her. I think you were born with a damned rifle in your hand," Prescott spat as she helped stack the new supplies.

"The L.T. is right. This is war, and we were trained for war. We are trained to adjust to the circumstances that surround us, no matter what situation we are in. That young woman in there knows nothing of that kind of life. Her only chance of survival is if we help her."

"Look, we can't pick up every straggler we come across or rescue every fair maiden in distress. We can't do it and survive this thing ourselves. We're limited by the resources we have and how we use them." Prescott's voice was even, reasonable.

"Point taken," Baumer said. "But we won't turn our back on this one. The decision has been made."

"What? No voting? No democracy? You make the decision and it is so?" Prescott challenged. She stopped stacking and leaned against the side of the RV.

"Fine. Let's vote. All for helping Anna, raise your hand." Baumer's hand went up, as did Maguire's and Szabo's.

"There's your democracy, Pres." Baumer put her hand down. "Now stop playing the grumpy naysayer. We've got much bigger things to concern ourselves with."

Maguire peered at Prescott, who stood stewing in anger. "Don't you love a democracy?"

Baumer groaned.

"Maguire, you're an asshole," Prescott muttered.

"Now that's an established truth." Her Irish brogue bled through hard.

***

Szabo rolled out from under her computer station. "It's too hot." They had made it a good twenty miles from where they had picked up Anna before the RV showed signs of overheating. Szabo drove the huge vehicle into a flank of trees and shut the engine off. After a brief discussion, they decided to camp there for the night, let the beast cool down, and start fresh in the morning.

Maguire sat up in her sleeping rack. "Hey, Szab, would it hurt anything if I open a hatch?"

"No, it should be fine, and I'll give you my firstborn if you do."

Maguire stood up on her rack and lifted the hatch, setting it into position. A breath of air instantly flowed into the RV. She also took the opportunity to scan three hundred and sixty degrees. There was nothing moving in the immediate area. She dropped back down. Even though they had concealed the RV as well as they could under the circumstances, Maguire felt a measure of vulnerability at not having been able to get further away from the men's camp. She watched as Szabo tinkered with the cooling system.

"How much longer?" Prescott asked from her own position on the floor near the small stove.

"Five minutes less than the last time you asked," Baumer barked. "Take a nap or something."

"Too damned warm and too wound up," Prescott protested. "I told you we should have picked up some crossword puzzle books at the PX."

"And what would you do once you've cheated your way through them? Besides, you wouldn't let me bring the chess set." Szabo sounded as though she was pouting.

"I was tired of you kicking my ass," Prescott defended.

"Jesus, are you two really adults?" Baumer asked in exasperation. "I was hoping that sort of thing would be a thing of the past."

"This grousing is nothing like the stuff back in the barracks," Szabo said.

"Well, how about you both knock it off. We're here for the night, so deal with it. Mags, you take first watch. I'll take second watch, and Pres, I'll wake you up for the last one."

"What about me?" Anna asked.

"For now, I think you should try and get as much rest as you can. We can't guarantee when you'll get any more. But if you want to get up with me when it's my turn, I'll start training you to know what to look and listen for." Baumer turned to

Szabo. "Since we need you to pilot this monster, you need to sleep as well."

"Sleep," Szabo said with a dreamy expression. "Another soon to be precious commodity. One of the things I know I'll miss. And strangely, I'll miss traffic jams," Szabo admitted with a wry smile. "And my e-mail. I'd give almost anything for a Big Mac."

Prescott shifted on the floor. "I'll miss baseball. This would happen the year my team was finally winning for a change."

"I already miss the smell of home baked biscuits." Anna's response caused drool factor ten in everyone. "Not store bought. We used to make double batches on the farm."

"Good one, princess." Prescott actually sounded sincere.

"Fudgesicles." Baumer nearly groaned. "I'll really miss those."

"Good Irish whiskey," Maguire tossed in. "Not the crap most American's drink, but the good stuff."

"And ice cold beer," Anna added. The others stared at her. "What? I'm old enough to drink. I started drinking beer long before I reached the legal age."

"What, that 3-2 stuff that's mostly beer-flavored water?" Prescott asked.

Anna made a disgusted face. "No, Killian's."

Maguire gave Anna's arm a squeeze. "Feckin' A! I like you better and better every minute. A lass after my own heart!"

Anna blushed at Maguire's display of emotion, and Prescott chuckled and shook her head.

"You do come out with some surprises." Prescott sighed. "I'll miss freshly picked raspberries. And watermelon."

"And a twice-baked potato," Szabo joined in. "Loaded."

"Pizza," Anna added. "Definitely pizza."

"Okay, we need to stop this," Baumer said. "You're making me hungry and thirsty for things we can't have. I have a great imagination, but not even I can pretend an MRE is any of the foods I'll really miss."

It was quiet for a long minute until Szabo broke the silence. "I'll miss sex." She looked around at the others. "I know I didn't have it very often, but I wonder if I'll live to find that kind of intimacy again at least once before I die."

Anna looked away. "Sex isn't always about intimacy."

Szabo and Baumer exchanged glances, and Szabo reached over and patted Anna's knee. "You're right. I'm sorry. I apologize for reawakening that nightmare for you."

"That nightmare had not gone away." Anna's voice was barely audible.

"And it won't any time soon," Baumer acknowledged. "But we're with you now, and we will do our best to make sure you never have to worry about that again." She stretched. "Tomorrow's going to be another long day. Let's hit our racks and rest while we can."

* * *

A drive that should have taken a hair over twelve hours took nearly fifty. They needed to stay parallel to Interstates 89 and 70, without traveling too close to the highways. Fortunately, the further north they got, the less damaged the topography appeared to be, which made it easier to stay out of sight and out of mind of insurgent groups of survivalists. Whenever they found an abandoned vehicle, either on the "road" or near an isolated house, they would check it for fuel. They had scavenged enough to get them as far as Flagstaff, which was intact but deserted, and then around the Grand Canyon, whose majesty and calm were deceiving.

Regardless of where they went, they could not escape the reminders of death, even when they barely brushed by the outlying districts. Decaying human bodies and animal carcasses littered what were once populated areas. When they left Arizona and crossed the state line, the once beautiful landscape became increasingly rugged and fragmented, causing the travelers to sometimes slow to mere miles per hour in order to reach their next projected location with the RV undamaged.

They stopped on the outskirts of what was once Emery County, Utah, where Prescott, Baumer, and Maguire exited the vehicle for reconnaissance. Szabo and Anna stayed behind. Szabo monitored the surveillance, and Anna manned the radio. Anna wasn't really sure what she was doing yet, but it comforted her to know that she had Szabo right next to her if she messed up. Szabo could easily have handled all of the communications devices, but letting Anna help was a way of making her feel involved and included. And it kept her out of harm's way, insofar as that was possible under the circumstances. Radio traffic had been minimal when the trio returned an hour later.

"So, what's the scoop?" Szabo asked.

"We're fucked if we try to circumvent Castle Dale," Prescott said, shrugging off her backpack and utility harness.

Szabo looked at Baumer, then back at Prescott "Why is that?"

"Too much destruction from quake and aftershocks, and clearly there's been a lot of fighting as well," Prescott answered. "I have a lot of faith in your baby here," she patted the dashboard, "but all of the access roads and infrastructure have been destroyed, and to go around would take us at least a week out of our way."

"Um…wouldn't an extra week be better than risking our lives going directly into town?" Anna asked timidly.

Prescott rolled her eyes as she shook her head. "It's a risk either way, Princess. If we go around, we run the risk of trashing the Rigmarole on the terrain and running out of fuel. Without our transportation, we won't make it to the other side anyway. It's too hazardous."

"Oh." Anna swiveled the chair around to face away from Prescott.

Baumer removed her helmet and rested her hand on Anna's shoulder as she gave Prescott a reprimanding glare. "It was a legitimate question."

"It's also legitimate that we could wait to be saved by the Utes," Prescott said.

"Do you mean the Native American tribe, or are you channeling *My Cousin Vinny* and telling us we need to wait to be saved by the lord of the flies?" Szabo teased.

Prescott burst out laughing. "Thanks, Szab. I needed that. No, we were advised that the…the…"

"Unitah and Ouray Band of Northern Ute," Maguire supplied.

"Yeah, them. Their reservation is huge. It sprawls out over

seven counties, but mostly this one, so they are a force to be reckoned with, for the good, is what we were told."

Szabo looked suitably impressed. "Who told you that?"

Maguire answers. "We ran across what was left of a group of refugees. They had just been in a firefight with a band of mercenaries. The refugees had been holed up at the last standing steam electric generating plant on the eastern slope of the plateau. They had to go into Castle Dale for supplies, but the mercs outgunned and outmanned them, and those refugees who lived had to retreat. So now the town is falling. They said it was a matter of time before whatever businesses that were still standing would be looted and burned."

"Do you think there are any medical supply stores in that town, or drugstores? I don't care if we get anything else, but we need medicines and medical supplies." Szabo's eyes cut towards Anna. "I'm worried about your feet. My oversized boots are not helping them heal. And soap and water aren't enough, but some peroxide or alcohol—"

"We are not risking getting killed because of my feet," Anna protested.

Prescott looked up. "It's a risk either way, Princess. At least this way I might also find a crossword book, which," she glared at Szabo, "I'm bringing out with me."

Without missing a beat, Szabo retorted, "Look in the kid's section. You'll know those words. And perhaps they'll have a travel size chess set." She grinned at the stream of curses from Prescott's mouth.

"Looks like we're going to find out."

***

Anna watched the street from her lookout spot behind the dark main entrance of the abandoned Walgreens. Since her feet were still quite tender from walking barefoot when she'd been a captive with the raiders, she had been set on watch. She looked down at the soft pair of soled slippers that Prescott had discovered and then tossed in her direction. They helped a little. She was trying to decide if Prescott had deliberately searched them out to ease her discomfort or for some other reason. She could not figure out what made the infuriating woman tick.

Thinking she heard something, Anna cocked her head toward the street and tried to filter out the sounds of her new friends rummaging through the store. There it was again, but very faint. She peered out along the street but could not see anything, so she limped over to Baumer's position to report it.

"I heard something outside, like breaking glass," she whispered.

"Which direction?"

"To the right from the front doors. I looked but I couldn't see anyone." She turned her head back toward the street.

"Stay here. I'll get the others." Baumer made quick work of rounding up Maguire, Szabo, and Prescott. The four came back to Anna's position without their rucksacks and carrying their M4s, ready for their orders to confront the potential danger.

"Szab, you got a look at the map. What's to the right of our position?" Baumer questioned.

Szabo closed her eyes and visualized the map. "For the three blocks to the right—a bank, two bars, a medical clinic, a hardware store, an elementary school, and an ice cream shop. Beyond that, open land and apartment buildings." She opened her eyes. "Money is useless now, so the bank would of no use to anyone. Most of the places around here have no electric, so there's probably no ice cream."

"Bar or doctor's office?" Maguire asked.

"Gotta be the doctor's," Baumer reasoned. "They might have medications there, right?"

"But what kind, and would they be worth getting our asses in dutch for?" Prescott asked just above a whisper. Everyone looked at her. "Hey, someone's gotta ask the hard questions."

"Well, if it was me, I'd be hitting the bar." Maguire chuckled, and it broke the tension.

Baumer considered for a moment. "Doctor's office, it is. Maguire, you got point. Everyone else cover. If you see a threat, make sure it's a threat before you light it up. Hand signals only, and tap your head if we have to beat feet. If we run into something, we rally, discuss, and then move."

She was greeted with three whispered, "Roger."

"Szab, access that brain of yours again and tell me where

the doctor's office is," Maguire requested as she slid magazines for the M4 into several pockets.

Szabo was quiet for a moment. "Across the street, four buildings down." There was an impish grin on her face as she added, "Would it be helpful to know about the back alley?"

"Szab, one of these days you are going to have to tell me how you do that," Baumer muttered.

"It's easy. You just stare at the map 'til your eyes bleed," Szabo stated with a hint of sarcasm.

Baumer, Szabo, and Maguire moved into the shadows in front of the main door.

"Princess, you stay here until we come back. Anybody comes in and finds you here, you blow this for all you're worth." Prescott handed Anna a metal whistle she had found in one of the aisles." Anna nodded and Prescott grunted and then went to catch up to the others at the front door.

"I fucking hate urban warfare," Maguire muttered.

"You're Irish. I thought that was inbred in you all," Prescott jibed.

"Wrong part of Ireland. You really need to look these things up," Maguire shot back.

"Fight about it later," Baumer whispered. "Maguire, you're up."

Maguire slid her night vision goggles down, took a quick peek out the door to the right, and then drew her head back inside. She mouthed "clear" and pointed to herself, then across the street. At Baumer's nod, she bolted across the road to the corner of a building. Without turning, she held up her hand and made a fist.

***

Maguire disappeared into the alley, leaving the others to each watch a different section of the street. When she returned, she signaled the others to cross the street quickly. They dashed across the road, weapons pointing down the street.

They followed Maguire at a combat run as she led them up the alley to another alley and cut to the right along the rear of the buildings. As they advanced, they could hear the sounds of destruction growing louder. They slowed as Maguire slowed.

The doctor's office was a square red brick building with a lot of windows. Maguire halted and turned to her teammates. She pointed to herself and Prescott, then her eyes, and then to the building. Baumer and Prescott nodded.

Prescott and Maguire used the darkening sky and the sparse cover to their advantage, losing sight of Baumer when they turned the far corner of the building. Five minutes later Maguire reappeared behind Baumer and Szabo. Noticing her L.T.'s breathing was ragged, she tapped Baumer on the shoulder and saw Baumer make an effort to slow her breaths. When Maguire had Baumer's and Szabo's full attention, she backed away. She held up four fingers, then one of their few flash bang grenades. Given Baumer's expression, Maguire knew she must be sporting a seriously scary grin. The lieutenant shouldn't have been surprised; she knew how much Maguire loved wargames.

Baumer nodded and glanced at Szabo, then they both caught up to Maguire.

Maguire leaned in close to her ear. "Three bogeys, one friendly. They're bunched up. We can go in through the broken windows. As much noise as they're making, we have a good shot at not being detected before we are ready to be seen."

Chapter Thirteen

Struck by yet another backhand, the doctor slammed to the ground. He had instantly recognized the leader of the men who had broken into his office. Now he was pulled back up to his feet and then thrown into what was left of his bookshelf. His head banged against several thick medical books. He barely had time to cry out in pain before a knee jabbed into his stomach. Instantly he lost what little he'd had to eat for dinner.

"I told you I was gonna kill you if I ever caught you in this office again," his attacker snarled. "You ain't got no cops to save your ass this time, you fucker."

"I told you what happened," the doctor gasped, receiving another knee to the belly in response.

"You killed my kid!" the man shouted into his ear as he was yanked upright.

The others were trashing his office, dumping out medications and contaminating them. He watched as one of the men drew a deadly looking hunting knife and waved it around.

The doctor gathered his courage and glared at his assailant. "*You* are the one who kicked your daughter in the stomach," he rasped.

"Kill him and get it over with!" one of the attackers shouted.

"I wanna make him hurt before I kill 'im. Hear that, Mister 'I'm a Doctor'? I'm gonna take my time killing you."

A large young man grinned as he pointed a nickel-plated .44 revolver at the doctor. "I can put six holes in him for you, no vital organs, just a lot of pain."

The one with the knife quickly stepped forward. "Fuck that! I'll kill him for you right now."

As the blade settled against his throat, the doctor closed his eyes and thought a quick prayer. He and the man with the knife were both knocked over by the sudden percussive explosion, and he suddenly had ringing in his ears. When the doctor opened his eyes, for a long moment he thought he was dreaming, then he became acutely aware of the pressure on his chest.

Four camouflaged figures entered quickly, one of them firing off a single shot that put down the man with the gun, who lurched forward and fell on the doctor.

One of them pulled the body off him. He shook his head to relieve the ringing in his ears as the two surviving attackers were hogtied. One of the rescuers knelt in front of him. He could see the woman's lips moving, but could not hear her. She patted him on the shoulder, which for some reason caused him to relax just a little.

***

"Szab, on lookout," Baumer shouted as she checked on the victim.

"Like no one heard the flash bang?" Prescott laughed as she kicked the now knifeless, zip tied idiot in the head. She checked to be sure that her kick had rendered him completely out of it. "Goal."

Maguire shook her head. "You're sick."

"So says Quick Draw Maguire," Prescott snapped back.

She smiled. "He had a gun"

"He was too busy drooling on himself to fire it."

"Children, later, huh?" Baumer chided. Those two were giving her a headache. "Pres, Maguire, check out the rest of the office. See if the good doctor here has any supplies left that we can use." When they immediately began checking the cabinets, she turned her attention to the man bleeding on the floor. "So, what do we do with you?"

He blinked at her but did not respond, obviously having no idea what she had said.

***

Anna was busying herself with going through what was left

of the Walgreens pharmacy, looking for anything they might be able to use, when she heard the loud bang and then a single shot. She waited in silence for a few moments, and then went back to rummaging. The pharmacy had not exactly been looted. Some shelves were bare, but others held some remnants, and at this point, every little bit helped. She allowed herself a smile when she found several pouches of tuna fish that were still within the expiration date. It would definitely be a welcome addition to their menu.

She kept an eye on the front of the building as much as possible while she foraged. A shadow in front of the window caught her attention, and she froze. Two quick flicks of light, and she let out her breath. Maguire stalked in with her M4 at the ready.

Anna snapped her fingers twice, as she'd been taught, and Maguire lowered her weapon. Her hand signal brought the rest of the team inside, along with one extra person.

"You've been busy," Maguire murmured as she went over to a small pile of items near where they'd left their rucksacks.

Anna shrugged. "I didn't know what else to do."

"Good job," Maguire said without turning her head.

"Szab, feel like seeing what we can use to make some chow?" Baumer asked as she guided the newcomer to take a seat on the floor.

"Sure. I saw some canned stuff earlier."

"I found some tuna packs," Anna offered hesitantly.

"I think I love you." The Russian immigrant grinned. "I'll check to see if there is anything else left."

"Anna, meet Doctor Porras. Doc, this is Anna, our other civilian," Baumer said with a small smile. "Pres, you're with me. I want to make sure we don't have any additional unwelcome company outside. I'll walk the store perimeter. You take two blocks out."

"I could do that alone," Prescott grumbled.

Baumer raised an eyebrow. "And I could have shot you six years ago. Your point?"

Prescott didn't even blink. "Following you, oh mighty leader."

"What would you like me to do?" Porras asked.

Baumer looked at his battered face. "Rest, and see if there's anything here that you can use to take care of those cuts on your face." She turned and gave Prescott the signal to move out.

***

Porras watched in amazement as they disappeared into the shadows, then he turned to Anna. "Hello."

"Hi. Welcome to the strangest group of people you're ever going to meet."

"They must be particularly strange if they're worse than what I've been meeting lately," Porras said.

Her smile was empathetic. "I've got some peroxide and gauze if you want it." She pointed to a backpack.

He felt as though he had fallen into an episode of *The Twilight Zone*, but he managed a nod. "That's very kind of you. Thanks."

He nearly had a heart attack when Maguire dropped the rucksacks near him and then settled her body down next to Anna.

"There's an employee latrine in the back. Darker than the rest of this place," she dug a compact flashlight out of one of her cargo pockets, "but you can use my flashlight. Careful though, it's one of those brings-the-sun kind of lights."

Porras' expression showed his confusion, and Anna stifled a rare giggle. "It's an LED. Just don't look directly into the light."

"Speak from experience, do you?" Porras asked with a hint of wry amusement.

"Way big experience," Anna corrected.

He took the flashlight and backpack. "I'll be back shortly."

"Hey, Doc?" Maguire called. "When you're patched up, would you mind taking a look at Anna's feet? She's been having some trouble with 'em."

"I'll do what I can," he promised.

"Maguire," Anna groaned.

"Hush, kiddo. Your feet are trashed. You need someone to look at them, and let's face it, us four are not doctors," Maguire said gently. "Where's the L.T. and Prescott?"

"Out making sure that there's no one else around."

Maguire nodded. "We call that checking an extended perimeter."

Anna filed that tidbit of information in her brain. "Can I ask you something?"

"Sure."

"Sometimes you sound American and sometimes you sound Irish. How come?" Anna asked hesitantly.

Maguire chuckled. "My mother was full Irish, my father was an American soldier of Irish descent, with some Comanche Indian tossed in just for fun and grins. They met when he was stationed in Germany and she was working for an Irish travel agency." She leaned back against the shelving. "When he wasn't deployed, we lived where ever he was stationed; when he was deployed, we lived in Ireland with my mother's family." She smiled at the memory. "I've even got dual citizenship."

"That is so cool. Until now, I hadn't even left my state." Her voice was filled with both wonder and disappointment.

"Well, now you can say that you have traveled," Maguire offered.

"You should keep a journal," Szabo whispered to Anna as she stopped in front of them. "I will see if I can find you something to write in. Don't tell Pres." She was carrying several cans in a store tote bag. She sat down next to her friends and placed the bag on the floor. "Now hand over the tuna fish, or the mick gets it."

Anna laughed. "You sound like an old gangster movie."

Szabo winked and shot Maguire in the arm with a water gun. A wet splotch ran down Maguire's arm. "You thought I was kidding? It's just a flesh wound. Next one won't be. Gimme the fish."

"I give, I give." Anna handed over the tuna packs. "Just don't hurt her anymore." She played along, and that made her smile. She hadn't felt like playing in a long time.

"I knew you'd see it my way, doll face." Szabo grinned, then broke out laughing.

"Szab." Maguire's voice had an edgy tone to it. "That better be water."

"Only the best for you, Mags. Right out of the employee

toilet." Szabo grinned, then took off running, Maguire in hot pursuit.

Baumer re-entered at that moment, and sent a questioning glance at Anna, who shrugged her shoulders with an innocent expression that was not very convincing.

***

Doctor Kyle Porras was walking back to something they called the Rigmarole with the women who had saved him. He was still dazed by the beating he had taken earlier, but the persistent ringing in his ears was finally diminishing. As unobtrusively as possible, he studied his companions, wondering what their stories were. The young one who was introduced as Anna said they were the strangest group of people he was ever going to meet. She didn't elaborate and he didn't persist, mostly because he would not have been able to clearly hear the story at that time.

Even though Anna was wearing military clothing and looked fit enough, she didn't have the military bearing of the other four women. Plus she wasn't armed to the teeth like they were. Her manner seemed sweet and cautious, while the others seemed absolutely fine with kicking ass and taking names afterwards. They seemed to be confident in their mission and skilled at defending themselves as well as others in need of protection.

It was clear that Baumer was the leader of this band. The others might not always agree with her, but there was no doubt that she was in charge, at least for now. Prescott reminded him of the rebellious older sister who had to question just to question. Szabo was the youngest sister, fast to smile and surprisingly quick witted, but he could tell that under all the humor, she was serious. Maguire quite frankly scared the hell out of him. He shook his head. Prescott and Maguire reminded him of children vying for the attention of a favorite schoolteacher. Baumer was the schoolteacher.

Just when he was sure that he could walk no further, they reached their destination. His mouth fell open at the sight of an RV.

"Say hello to Rigmarole." Szab grinned. "Rigmarole, this is Dr. Porras."

"Um...hello, Rigmarole." For some reason, Porras did not feel like a fool for saying it. It felt more like relief.

Szab looked at her friends. "He can stay." She grinned and pulled the door open.

ChapterFourteen

Anna jerked awake, then automatically checked around to make sure she was safe and that she had not roused the others. She often had nightmares, but she was getting better about reacting to them. Oddly, talking to Szabo seemed to help. She checked her watch. Judging by the glowing hands, she knew that Szabo would be the one on duty.

She stole from her rack and tiptoed to the door of the RV, which was open to let in some air. Anna stepped down from the RV and walked as quietly as she could to Szabo's position. She snapped her fingers twice.

Szabo turned her head and motioned for Anna to join her. She kept her eyes on the perimeter as she softly said, "Nightmare?"

"Again."

"This might sound trite, but they do go away after time."

"It's never going to go away." Anna felt like crying again. "You must be getting tired of the 'princess' falling apart night after night."

Szabo was quiet for several minutes. "I will never be tired of you, Anna. You have become *moi drug*, my friend." She took another moment. "I remember this one night in Iraq when the L.T. was still a sergeant. I was just a private, so new I was shiny. I had worked a very long day in Supply and was late getting off duty. Almost everyone else was asleep, but I really wanted a shower.

"There had been reports of women being attacked, but I thought 'I am a soldier, I am trained.' There were two of them." She shifted her gaze to Anna. "Jess found me after. Took me to the clinic. She called the MPs. When the men were found, Jess and I both discovered the ends to which the Army would go to protect combat experienced soldiers. They were released back to duty pending the investigation, and Jessica was labeled a troublemaker."

Anna did not know what to say, so she said nothing for a while. Finally she asked, "How…how did you get over it?"

Szabo shook her head. "You do not 'get over' it, you get through it. You get beyond it in order to live your life, in order to reclaim what someone else believed they could take from you."

"How?" she rasped, her throat tight.

"It is both simple and frustratingly difficult. Accept what happened and believe what you know to be true—it was not your fault, you did nothing to bring that on yourself. You cannot change what is in other people's hearts." Szabo sighed. "I know I sound like a public service announcement, but that's four years of therapy condensed into a few sentences."

"I'm sorry." Anna drew in a deep breath. "All these nights I've sat with you, crying on your shoulder... It must have been hard listening to me making you relive—"

"Anna, truly, I don't relive it. I have sealed it in its own little box within my past. I only told you so that you will know that you are not alone, that I do understand how you are feeling. Four men or two, three hours of abuse or four days," she shook her head, "the end result is the same. I will listen as many nights as it takes to help you move forward."

Anna rested her head on Szabo's shoulder. "Thank you."

"You're welcome. Now, tell me more about your home. What you have told me is very different from what I knew."

"It was nice. We had a four-bedroom house. My folks had one room and us kids each had a room of our own. When I needed 'me' time, I could go to my room to get away from my brothers and sister. We had a big kitchen. I think there was room in there for three people to have lined up side-by-side with arms stretched out. The kitchen was my favorite place after the barn. I loved our horses and dogs."

"It sounds very nice. Very different from what we had, but just as nice."

Anna was curious. "What do you mean?"

"I was born in Russia. I remember being little and my mother crying because I said I was hungry. I don't think we had much. I recall always being cold. When we moved to the United States—I was seven or maybe nine, I do not recall exactly—we had food and blankets and my parents had a real bed. I thought we were rich. It was like being a princess. Now I know how little we had compared to others, but we were better off here than in Russia."

Without taking her eyes off the horizon, she said, "After a time, we were able to bring my aunt to America, also her three children. Eight of us in our tiny space. My whole life we lived in apartments, never a house. But it was still different from Russia. It was cramped, but free. I don't know how else to say it." She glanced at Anna. "But I think it would be nice to try living in a house, at least for a time."

"When we get to where we're going, we can find a house for you," Anna promised.

"You sound so sure," Szabo teased. "You will be my house finder?"

"You're my friend, so yes, I'll find you a house."

Szabo rested a hand on Anna's shoulder. "I am honored to be your friend."

"I don't have many. It's nice to have a new one."

For a long while they said nothing. Finally Anna gathered up the courage to give voice to her curiosity. "Talia? How come you're only a specialist? I mean, I've been listening to you guys talk, and you've been in the Army a while and…"

"I got into trouble twice. Given my history, I should have been given a dishonorable discharge, but due to the fact that I have a very smart brain that they needed, I was not kicked out. They did reduce me in rank and dock my pay each time though," Szabo answered.

"What did you do?"

Szabo grinned. "Each time one of my fellow soldiers was molested by other soldiers… How would Pres put it? Oh, yeah—I kicked their balls into their lungs." Her grin blossomed. "I was punished, and they went to the hospital. I feel like it was an even trade."

Anna was astonished. "And they didn't kick you out of the military?"

"Have you *seen* my gray matter?" Szabo asked with a

heavy Russian accent.

***

The next morning, after a breakfast of canned hominy, rolled oats, and the contents of five small jars of cocktail wieners raided from the drugstore, the group policed their mess and then discussed their strategy for the day.

Maguire looked around the gathered group. "We've been pretty lucky the last couple of days, and I don't want to take that luck for granted. Before we move out, we should scout ahead."

"I agree," Baumer said. "Szabo needs to recalibrate some of the RV equipment and then make the appropriate adjustments. Taking time for advance recon would give her the time to do that."

"I'll move out in a direction that is 90 degrees from Maguire's zone, beyond the scope of what Szab's cameras can see," Prescott offered. "That way, we'll have a thorough idea of whatever is ahead."

"Okay. Anna and I will look for springs and other water sources," Baumer said. "Doc, you can stay with Szabo and give her a hand if she needs it."

"Nah, Doc. No offense, but you'd just be in the way," Szabo said without animosity.

"She's right," Porras agreed. "I've never been any good at the mechanical or technical stuff. Why don't I take one of those poles and tag along with Anna and Jessica. If they find water, I can try to catch us some fish while they filter and replenish our drinking supply. I can always help carry everything back."

"Wouldn't trust that the fish are safe to eat," Prescott cautioned.

"True. And really, shouldn't someone stay here with Szab?" Maguire asked.

"I'll be fine." Szabo waved her off. "I have the perimeter sensors and all my other alarm gadgets, as well as that adorable little MAC10 we got from town. You guys will be gone two to four hours at the most. We're pretty well camouflaged in this nice little area off the road. Trust me, it's all good."

Maguire shook her head. "I don't know. I don't like it."

"Jeez, Maguire, you're not the only one with skills." There was a hint of hurt in Szabo's tone. "I can take care of myself. And I certainly know enough to hold 'em off until you all can come to my rescue."

"I wasn't insulting you, Szab, I just care, that's all," Maguire said. "We'll be ranging pretty far away this time."

"I appreciate that, but I do need to get this stuff done, preferably before we move this big, bad girl again."

"Fine, but if those perimeter alarms go off, I don't care what you're doing, you get the hell out of this thing and get yourself deep into the brush, you got it?"

Szabo flashed a smile and saluted Baumer. "Yes, Ma'am, I got it."

***

Three hours had passed, and Szabo had just finished taking parts out of one damaged system to patch up a sister system. She was halfway through her list of repairs when she decided to take a break and crawl underneath the RV to ensure all was okay with the underbelly of the beast. She had finished tightening up the 6-point valve when she saw a pair of boots. The size of the footwear made her think that Doc must have come back for something he had forgotten. She was about to call out when she remembered that Doc didn't have such footwear.

The first pair of boots was joined by another, then another. Szabo held her breath when she heard a deep, male voice say, "What the fuck do we got ourselves here, boys?"

"Dunno. Looks like someone's home," another male voice answered.

"I don't think so," the first voice said. "It's too...I don't know...military looking. Let's see what's inside."

Oh God, oh God, please don't let them find me here! Why didn't the flippin' perimeter alarm go off? Where did they come from? Jesus, I hope they didn't find any of the others. Szabo watched as the RV shifted with the weight of a body as it climbed the few steps to the interior.

"Holy fucking shit! You guys gotta see this in here! It's a

damned gold mine of weapons and supplies and a shitload of technological stuff!"

Another man joined the first. His voice was clear and commanding. Szabo decided it was likely he was the leader.

"Damn! Somethin' ain't right here. No one would leave this gem unattended." He walked to the door. "You two, check over there in the brush, and you three, spread out and go track that road back there!"

Szabo had counted at least seven men. If she could get to a semiautomatic weapon, she might have a chance of getting all of them, or at least most of them. Please, God, don't let them look under here.

"What do you think?" the first guy asked. "Take what we can, fuck up what we can't?"

"What's this? Damn! Surveillance cameras. I wonder what their range is. Hey, you can pan and zoom with these, too. Let's use them to look around and see if we have company, and where they are."

Shit! Please don't find the others. Please, God, don't let them see any of the others!

"Nope, don't see anyone."

Szabo let out a quiet sigh of relief.

"Wait—what was that?"

She held her breath again.

"Looks like it could be tracks but it's hard to tell, even zooming in. Could be animal tracks."

She exhaled again.

"I still say no one would leave this vehicle unattended like this: fully stocked, cameras running, computers on," the leader said. "Someone's gotta be around here."

"Hey...maybe it's whoever slaughtered our guys near Winslow."

"That would be too much justice," the leader said. He stepped to the door, then down to the ground. "Hey!" he called to the men he had sent out to scout. "Get all your asses back here! We need to start stripping this motherfucker."

Szabo wondered why it was that when she wasn't required to stay completely still, she could do it, but as soon as she *had* to, some part of her would always twitch. She heard the thudding of several feet jogging toward the RV from different directions, then she heard someone call from a short distance away, "Hey, there's someone under the rig!"

Chapter Fifteen

Maguire crawled through the brush to the edge of the road, where she halted. Taking in shallow breaths, her eyes scanned the area. Seeing no enemy, she moved forward, the stock of her M4 pressed against her cheek. She quick-stepped to the RV and ducked her head inside the door. She was able to see just enough to tell her that no one was inside, and that the interior had been completely trashed. She ducked back out and scanned the road to the back side of the RV. It took a moment for her eyes to adjust to the changes in shadows from the trees. When they did, she swallowed hard to keep the bile from erupting past her lips. "No, no, no, no, no…" She cross-slung her weapon and ran as fast as she could.

Suspended by ropes around her wrists, Szabo dangled from one of the satellite bases atop the RV. Her naked, bleeding body twitched with muscle spasms that protested the life oozing out of the numerous wounds.

Maguire was sure that Szabo was dead, until she heard a desperate, gurgled "Mags," from Szabo's bloodied lips.

Maguire drew her knife as she skidded to a stop. She quickly cut the main rope and slid underneath Szabo, catching the Russian on her shoulder and easing her to the ground. Maguire pulled her canteen from its case and twisted off the cap.

"It is my fault," Szabo wheezed. "You told me…" she took a deep breath that made her moan in pain, "…told me to pay attention, but the satellite was not—"

"Shhh. It's okay. Try to drink some water." Maguire eased a measure of liquid into Szabo's mouth. "How many, Talia? What did they look like?"

"Ten men. Said we killed some comrades. Must've been…Anna's guys. … They were tracking us. …

Didn't…say…" She tried to breathe in, but groaned when she took in too much air. "I told them…nothing." Her body convulsed. "They…took…destroyed everything."

Maguire set the canteen down and brushed Szabo's hair away from her sweaty, bloody face. "Which way did they leave, my girl?"

"West," the tortured woman managed. "I told them…you'd gone… west."

"The rest of the team will be here soon. You'll be fine." Maguire forced herself to sound calm as she gauged the many deep knife cuts on Szabo's torso and the semen dried on her bruised thighs.

"I am the child of … Russian immigrants … but I am not stupid, my angry … Irish friend. I will soon die." She took in a rattling breath. "They drove ice pick into … both lungs … Only alive this long … because I am stubborn." She smiled, showing broken teeth.

Maguire smiled softly. "But you grill a mean cow."

"Not so mean … if it ends up in my pan." She tried to smile, but only managed a grimace. "There is a dead … man. Bury him. … He tried to stop … them. They shot … him."

Maguire tried to make her more comfortable by raising her up a little, but Szabo shook her head. It was not the time to show emotion; it was the time to be strong for her friend. Maguire tried to keep her voice from breaking, when she said, "Tell me what to do."

Szabo at Maguire. There was peace in her eyes. "End it. Please."

Emotional strength be damned, tears sprang to Maguire's eyes, blurring her vision. "I can't."

"You can. I would ask only you … this thing. You are the only … one strong enough." She coughed up some blood, then rested for a moment. "Tell Jess … I know she … tried for me. Please."

Maguire looked skyward, as though she might find strength there, and then back at Szabo. "I will ease your pain, my friend." She locked her gaze on Szabo. "I promise you something, *duit an mionn fola*. These men will not live a long life. I promise you that on my blood."

"A blood oath? The ... *klyatvu sem'i krovi.* ... I am your ... family?" Her breathing was coming in shorter puffs now.

Maguire wrapped her arms around Szabo as tightly as she dared without causing more pain. "You are my family. We can just say it took you a long time to get to Ireland."

"I went there ... once. It was ... very green." She smiled around her pain again. "You come from ... a country very ... beautiful. Please ... end it, moi drug," she pleaded.

Maguire held her closer. "What *does* moi drug mean?"

"My friend," Szabo whispered.

As the words left her mouth, Maguire twisted Szabo's neck. "Be at peace, moi drug. I swear to you that I will cut their beating hearts from their bodies." She kissed Szabo's gory brow and gently laid her on the ground. Maguire used every ounce of willpower she possessed to hold back a guttural scream of anger and grief that would have echoed off the mesas and alerted their enemies that they had returned to the RV.

***

The Irish woman leaned toward the ground and dragged a measure of dirt away, then another, then over and over again until the dirt gave way to firmer earth. When she could not make a dent in the ground with her fingers, she drew her knife and continued to work on Szabo's grave.

She worked with a single-minded determination, so she barely heard the ATV, barely registered Baumer, Anna, Prescott, and Doc returning. She heard the women gasp and saw young Anna turn her body against Doc Porras, away from the grisly scene.

"Son-of-a-fucking-bitch!" Prescott slid to her knees beside Szabo's body and pounded her fists against the ground in uncontrolled rage.

"Szab!" Baumer cried in an anguished whisper. "No!"

"Maguire, what happened?" Prescott's eyes never left the body of her friend.

Ignoring questions and comments alike, Maguire worked single-mindedly on digging the grave.

"Maguire! Damn it!" Prescott swiped at angry tears.

Baumer was crying openly. "How did this happen?" She accepted the blanket Anna had retrieved from the RV and used it to cover Szabo's body. "Maguire, answer me!" Baumer ordered.

When Maguire just continued to dig, Prescott jumped to her feet and took a threatening step in her direction, and Baumer grabbed a handful of Prescott's pants. "No, Pres," Baumer said. "Leave her alone. She has her own system of coping, and trying to force her to answer will just delay her compartmentalizing the situation. She'll tell us when she can put it all into words."

After several deep breaths, Prescott calmed down. She found the head of a broken claw hammer to use as a tool, then she knelt and quietly began to work beside Maguire. No words were spoken, nor was there even any acknowledgement between the two diggers.

Only after Maguire had searched for and found the man Szabo had spoken about, and dragged him to the grave, did she become somewhat aware of her surroundings. When Prescott argued against laying him to rest in the same grave as Szabo, the sharpened point of Maguire's blade invited Prescott to back off.

"What is wrong with you?" Prescott demanded. She didn't like being threatened, but she knew better than to mess with Maguire's unpredictable temper. "How can you bury that scumbag with her? You're disgracing her sacrifice!"

"It's what she wanted," Maguire said finally.

"How the fuck would you know anything about what she wanted?" Prescott's tone was bitter.

"She told me." Maguire wiped sweat off her face with the back of her sleeve. "Before she died."

"She was alive when you got to her?" Baumer asked in surprise.

"Barely...but enough to tell me that this guy tried to stop the rest from doing what they did to her."

"Did she say anything about who they were?"

"She thought they might be connected to the group we took Anna from."

"Why would she think that?" Prescott eyeballed Anna, who looked steadily back at her.

"They told her we killed some of their comrades, and they were wearing the same armbands as the guys we took out when we rescued Anna."

"There were more?" Prescott charged toward Anna. "You never said anything about there being more men in that band!"

Anna cowered behind Doc. "I didn't know there were more. They talked about others, but I never saw any of them. I thought they were all dead."

Prescott looked skyward. "Great! Just fucking great!"

"So, what do you think? They went to join up with their group and found them all dead, so they followed our tracks?" Baumer surmised.

"That would make the most sense. We certainly left enough visual signs behind us along the way," Maguire said.

***

Baumer could see that Maguire was preoccupied, and was frankly surprised that she was talking to them at all. Baumer, Prescott, and Doc moved forward and helped Maguire slide both bodies into the hole.

Maguire stood to the side of the grave as Prescott and Baumer each said her words of sorrow and good-bye to the good-humored Russian immigrant soldier who cooked better than anyone admitted, programmed a mean RV, and made everyone laugh.

"We should really cremate them, you know." Doc's voice startled the others out of their haze. "Less chance of disease if we don't leave anything behind but ashes."

"I know, but she wanted to be buried," Maguire said flatly. She turned away from him and looked down at her friend. *"Beidh mé a choinneáil ar mo gealltanas mo chara."*

"What the hell was that?" Prescott asked.

"A promise," Maguire whispered.

She, Prescott, and Doc began shoving handfuls of dirt into the hole until it was full and the moon was starting to shine in the night sky. Anna and Baumer prepared a meal from the two MREs they found in Szabo's backpack, but no one really felt like eating. When the meager ration of food was set in front of them, they picked at it, but eventually cleaned their mess kits.

"I wonder why they didn't leave anyone lying in wait for us." Anna's face was puffy from crying.

"Why bother? By stripping the Rig, they probably think they sentenced us to die," Baumer said.

"Big mistake on their part," Maguire muttered.

"I say we take two hours to rest, and then we continue north," Prescott offered quietly. "If they're heading west, hopefully we won't run into them again. Unless they're lying in wait somewhere up ahead."

"If they tortured our alleged direction out of Szabo, I'm pretty sure that's the direction they'll head," Baumer said. "Their kind wouldn't think a slip of a girl like Szab would be able to lie to them under such duress." Baumer buried her head in her hands and sniffed back tears. "That poor woman. It's not human what they did to her."

"They're not human," Anna said quietly. "Nobody can afford to have human emotions anymore, not if they want to stay alive." She pulled her knees up close to her chest and rested her chin on them, looking straight ahead.

The other three regarded her soberly. "Out of the mouths of babes," Baumer said finally.

"Is there anything left to salvage in the RV?" Doc asked.

"They cleaned it all out. What they didn't take, they destroyed. The Hybrid is gone and so is all the extra ammo. What we're carrying is what we've got," Baumer said grimly. "All we have is what's left in our individual rucksacks."

"Son-of-a-bitch!" Prescott shook her head. "That'll barely get us to Noble's compound." She looked over at Maguire. "Just how good are your hunting skills?"

"If there are any surviving, uncontaminated animals out there, I will find them and we will eat." Maguire dumped the contents of her waterproof ruck and began to reorganize, creating two piles.

"What're you doing?" Baumer asked. "I thought we were going to rest,"

"You go ahead. I'm going west. I'll give you what I don't need out of my ruck." Maguire started to refill her sack with the bare essentials.

Prescott exploded. "Excuse me? You're what? Maguire, don't be a fool. I understand the need for vengeance, hell, we all do, but we need you with us more than we need you dead."

"What do you think you're doing, Mags?" There was dismay in Baumer's voice.

"I'm going west," she repeated, her voice calm, level. "You all rest up, pack up what's needed and then head north. I'll catch up to you. Don't shoot me when I come back in."

"I don't think you've thought this through, my friend." Prescott sounded as if she was vexed.

"Prescott, let's not kid each other," Maguire said softly. "You and I are far from being friends. We're a team and we will continue to work as a team, because it's what we need to do to survive. I can count my friends on one hand, and you aren't one of them."

"Fine. Agreed. We aren't friends. But you're certainly not working as a part of our team right now. You're behaving like a merc. You won't help the team any if you don't come back."

"Don't doubt me, Prescott," Maguire said jauntily.

"You're not fucking superwoman, Maguire! Baumer says you're good at what you do, so I believe her, but no way in hell are you going to be able to ambush a bunch of homicidal men, kill them all, and then walk away without a scratch!"

Maguire dropped the armband that she had taken off the dead man. "Those who wear this killed Szab. I made a promise, and I'm keeping it. Come with me if you want."

"Then both of us would be dead, and I'm the only one who can get us to Noble's." She studied the set of Maguire's jaw and knew she was wasting her breath. "You've lost your mind," Prescott muttered, shaking her head.

"And yet, I'm still going. If you try to stop me, you'll end up dead." She sighed out loud. "I have no real desire to kill any of you, so just agree to let me go."

Prescott shrugged. "If you're bound and determined to go on this suicide mission, I'm not going to stop you."

Baumer tilted her head in reflection. "Can you really get them all, Mags? Without getting yourself killed?"

"Yeah, I can." She tapped the tab on her shoulder. "Irish Army Ranger Wing. I passed the course. I'm going to cut the head off that snake, for Szabo and for us."

"What the hell is an Irish Army Ranger Wing?" Prescott jibed. "And I don't care if you passed the course. Passing a course is not the same—"

"Irish commando school, originally trained by US Army Rangers. You really should look these things up." Maguire's voice was flat as she stared at Prescott. "Korea was *not* a school, and what I learned there could be called inhuman. How I killed men there was beyond barbaric."

"It's still a suicide mission," Prescott argued.

Baumer made her decision without taking the usual vote. "Go get 'em, Maguire. We'll be heading north by the compass. Catch up with us when you can." She stood up and pulled Maguire into a hug. "Don't you go getting yourself killed. I can't have two of you on my conscience. You promise me if you can't get them all, you'll forget it and get your pig-headed Irish ass back to us. If you leave any alive, they'll be after us again."

"How can you justify wasting ammunition on targets that may never be a threat to us again?" Prescott asked.

Maguire pulled herself away from Baumer. "I made a promise."

"How upright and decent of you." Prescott rubbed her weary eyes. "Szabo is dead. She won't know you didn't fulfill your promise."

"I'll know," Maguire said solemnly. "And don't worry, if I do this right, I won't need any ammunition."

Baumer clapped her sergeant's shoulder. "Godspeed, Maguire."

Maguire nodded, hoisted her rucksack over her shoulder and slung her rifle, and turned to walk away.

"Maguire."

Maguire stopped, and everyone looked in Anna's direction. "Yes?"

"Kill them twice for me, 'kay?" Anna's voice sounded small but determined.

"You got it, kiddo. For you and for Szab." And Maguire disappeared into the darkness.

Chapter Sixteen

Maguire silently shifted in her hiding spot, the clear area at the base of a waist-high shrub with heavy, leafy limbs. It reminded her of playing elves and hobbits under the same type of shrubbery as a child in Ireland. As she stood watch, she thought about how easy it had been to track these poor excuses of humanity. All she'd had to do was follow the carnage. The ten men had left a trail of dead bodies and destroyed refugee camps behind them everywhere they went.

Fifty-two hours. Finding their trail, then using every skill she had to keep from being discovered made her grateful for the sadistic training she'd endured so long ago. Fifty-two hours to watch, plot, and hate the bastards ever more deeply.

At least three of them seemed to have some military experience, based on their recent actions, most likely much of it in the stockade. She had total confidence that she could take care of the other seven with little effort.

She could have picked them off one by one on the trail once she'd caught up to them, but she wanted to make sure that this would be the last time she'd have to deal with them. She needed to know that there were only ten. She'd travelled a course parallel to theirs and when they had made camp the night before, she listened, gathering intel and information along with the boasting and bragging that turned her stomach. When the subject turned to Szabo, it had taken every ounce of her self-discipline to stay where she was hidden.

Now she watched them lounging around their fire, eating something that smelled truly disgusting and grousing amongst themselves. The apparent leader walked over to his rucksack and pulled out Szabo's laptop case. Back at his spot, he settled in and then removed the computer from its case and flipped it open.

"Nice of that li'l girl to leave this for us." His voice was smoother than Maguire had expected. "All I got to do is figure out how to get in."

"Nice of that li'l girl to spread her legs for us, too," a voice to his left said, and they all laughed.

"She was a fine piece. Nice tits, you know," another commented wistfully.

"Yeah, too bad we had to mark 'em up," another one of the group added. "We should've brought her with us, at least until we find the others. Who knows how many more split-tails are in that group. We could still be havin' us a fine ol' time."

"Steiger ruined that. I swear she was about to come until Steiger opened his fat mouth," the man left of the leader said.

"Yep. Too bad about Steiger, though. He was a damned good lookout."

"They were both lessons for y'all." The leader pressed some keys on the laptop, sighed in frustration and then tried again. "We had to kill Steiger for goin' against us. If he didn't want to join in, he should've just walked away. Any of y'all don't like how I'm leadin' this group and don't want to take orders from me, you're welcome to leave. If you openly defy me, you'll get what Steiger got or worse."

"Worse?"

He looked up from the laptop. "A man's got needs. I didn't realize how much coming inside a woman improves our concentration. We can't always wait until we find us another woman to pass around, though. Sometimes a hole is a hole, and the tighter, the better."

The man immediately lost the budding erection the memory of the blonde had provoked. "I don't want to defy you, Donovan, but I ain't no fag."

Donovan glared at him. "You calling me a fag, Becker?"

"No, but—"

"This is war, Becker! Remember that. Certain rules don't apply anymore. Steiger found that out. You be a good little soldier, and you won't have to worry about bending over for anyone unless you want to. After being inside that tight bitch, more than a few of us realized that it's much nicer to enjoy warm flesh that isn't your own hand." He looked around at the others. "If there are more spinners in that gal's group, good for us, but we had to kill her as a warning that they shouldn't come after us. If they aren't already dead, we'll find them."

"Kill the men and take the women," said the man leaning against a tree.

"Donovan, you want a guard tonight?"

It was one of the men Maguire had tagged as having military experience.

Donovan didn't take his eyes from the computer screen. "We're home, so just set out Mutt and Jeff. They ain't worth much on the trail, so they can go without sleep."

"How long we gonna rest up?" another asked around a mouthful of food.

"I figure a week, then we'll forage to the west, where that group is headed. Map says there's a small town about thirty miles out. That's probably where they're going. We can see what's left there, too, killing two birds with one stone. Maybe do some recruiting. I want more outlying scouts. Our scouts are the reason we found them women in the first place," Donovan added.

Waiting for full darkness, Maguire watched as the two appointed guards began their rounds as the others went off to their tents. The one called Donovan entered the only building, a one-room log cabin that, like most every structure now, had seen better days. She waited for another two hours until she was sure that the resting men were truly asleep.

Quietly slipping out of her hiding spot, Maguire kept her senses attuned to everything around her. Keeping to the deep shadows provided by the surrounding foliage, she carefully navigated the circumference of the camp. It covered roughly fifty yards total with cut back trees and booby traps that were almost too easy to notice. She silently thanked the powers that be for stupid people with an abundance of arrogance.

After completing her first circuit, Maguire went looking for the guards. She only had to follow her nose. They smelled of sweat, grease, and blood. She stalked the first one, waiting until he had to relieve himself. When he unzipped and began to urinate, she made her move. She wrapped her arm around his neck and cross-braced her other arm behind his head, applying pressure against his carotid. It took very little time to choke him out. She checked his pulse and eased him down to the ground. A grim smile crossed her face. She wanted them all alive, at least for now. His armband was shoved into his mouth as a makeshift gag, and she used his shoelaces to secure his hands.

The second guard took slightly longer. He fought just enough for her to consider snapping his neck, but he finally slumped to the ground. She tied him in the same manner as the first guard, then dragged him and laid him beside his friend. She checked both for a pulse. She was going to kill them, but she didn't want them dead just yet.

Maguire checked the moon's position in the sky. She had quite a bit to do and not a lot of time. Moving quickly but carefully from claymore to claymore took all of her nerve. She had never really liked working with things that could blow one all over the landscape, but if she did it correctly, these bastards would get one hell of a surprise in the morning.

***

When the very last moments of night were disappearing, she dropped the bloody body parts into the fire pit and covered them with ashes, then stole a shovel, took it to her sheltering shrub and quietly scraped out a depression deep enough for a concussion wave to pass over it. Maguire set the shovel aside, then stretched out in the shallow trench as much as possible and took the opportunity to rest. She wiped sweat and grime from her forehead and watched the camp slowly come awake.

The first lowlife to come out of his tent walked over to the fire pit, stirred the glowing embers and added logs to the dying fire to rejuvenate it, then laid a grill top down on the round of rocks. Then he walked towards the woods, unbuttoning his filthy jeans.

They filtered out by ones and twos, Donovan included, and he put the camp coffeepot on the fire. Apparently he was the keeper of everything that could be considered a luxury.

It was not long before the smell of cooking meat filled the air. Most of the men began looking around, then focused towards the fire. Maguire enjoyed their confused expressions when they realized that there was no meat on the grill. Donovan, ever the leader, scanned the perimeter of the camp with suspicion. He rose quickly, kicked the coffeepot from its perch, and risked his boots to flip the grill top away from the flames. He grabbed a thick branch that lay nearby and raked through the firewood. It wasn't long before he found Maguire's breakfast offering.

"Mutt! Jeff!" His voice had a dangerous edge to it. "Goddamn it, men, answer me."

There was no response from the guards, but one of his men was retching at the up-close sight of the cooking body parts.

"Get out there and find those two," Donovan ordered, and then dashed back into his shelter.

After a long moment, four men reluctantly rose to follow his order, their eyes clearly showing their reluctance to go.

Donovan returned with a holstered sidearm lashed to his thigh and carrying a firing device trailed by thick brown wire. He walked back to the remaining men.

The four men returned in twosomes, each pair dragging the corpse of one of the overnight guards. The deceased were naked from the waist down, their legs crimson with drying blood. The men who had retrieved the bodies were visibly relieved to drop their former compatriots alongside the fire pit.

Donovan gave one of the bodies a contemptuous kick, then glared toward the woods. "Whoever you are, when I'm done with you, you are going to beg me to kill you," he bellowed at the top of his lungs.

"I wouldn't make threats I can't carry out, if I were you," Maguire called, knowing that the foliage would disguise the origin of her voice. As she'd expected, the men began looking in several directions to locate the speaker. "And please spare me the 'we're going to rape you 'til you die' bit. It's old news." She reached into her pocket and took out a worn but usable earplug, which she placed in her right ear.

"It's the truth, you fucking bitch!" Donovan roared. "We're gonna show you what you're good for."

She moved deeper into the foliage, knowing even a small change in her location would make her voice appear to be coming from somewhere else. "You'll have to find me before I kill each of you. You're already two men down." She stretched out in the depression again.

"Why would you want to do that?" The unnerved voice that asked the question was not Donovan.

When no one answered, Donovan bellowed, "Who the fuck are you?"

"Chestnuts roasting on an open fire," Maguire sang, then fell silent. She saw another man puke up his guts as he caught the reference to the cooking meat. She silently watched them as they stood dumbly in a circle for a few minutes more; she relished the various shades of pale on their faces and the fear she could see creeping over them. She slowly tugged on the string next to her. If she had gauged things correctly, she was going to have to plug her left ear very quickly.

A split second after a low branch moved ever so slightly to his left, Donovan closed his fist on the firing device.

Even through her attempted protecting of her ears, Maguire heard the boom and felt the concussion, and reflexively closed her eyes. When she opened them again, most of the band was either dead or unconscious, but three were rolling on the ground in serious pain. She moved swiftly.

***

Donovan rolled from his side onto his stomach, nearly deafened by the explosion. His attention was drawn away from his pain to the scuffed, filthy boots that came to a halt a foot from him. When he looked up, he saw something out of his nightmares. The face that came into view was matted with a mixture of camouflage paint, mud, and blood. The eyes blazed with hate.

"You were saying something about me beggin' you?" the woman stated flatly.

Donovan could barely hear her with the ringing in his ears. He groaned as new pain washed over him.

"Music to my ears," the woman muttered, "Hurts, doesn't it? Hold that thought, I've a few things to take care of. But don't worry, I'll be comin' back for you." She slammed her open hand down on the back of his head.

***

Donovan slowly opened his eyes to the sound of screaming. He found that he was sitting with his back against the porch brace of his cabin, his wrists tied tightly behind him. He heard a sound to his right and snapped his head in that direction, immediately regretting it. His nightmare was sitting there, watching him. She had shed her uniform jacket and the black tank top was dripping blood. She tossed a bulky object at his feet.

"Mine, fragmentation, anti-personnel, M18A1. Plastic shell casing, C-4 explosive with approximately 700 steel balls." She stood up deliberately and moved toward him. "Works better when you don't have a piss poor night watch to make sure some nasty bastard like me doesn't use their incompetence against you."

He struggled against his bonds, but they held tight. Her calm, even tone sent a chill down his back. "When the rest of my men get here—"

"Please don't insult my intelligence, *Mister* Donovan."

She reached behind her back and Donovan flinched, but what she brought out was his logbook. She opened it to an earmarked page.

"I don't know what kind of joke God is playing on me," she read, "but some of these men are worse than idiots. I started out with fifteen men, now I am down to ten. Four got themselves killed on the road and one traitorous bastard I shot myself when he didn't have the stomach for doing what had to be done. He actually tried to stop us from fucking that little bitch." She closed the book. "It's hard to find competent help these days, isn't it?"

He jutted out his chin in a show of bravado. "Go ahead. Do your worst, I won't beg."

"The rest of your bunch are dead. I saved one last scumbag so you can hear what happens to him and be worrying about what I have in store for you. After he's gone, well then, it's just you an' me."

She turned her back on him and walked out of his view. He

could hear one of his men whimpering, begging for something more than his life. When it came, the scream went on for what seemed like forever. Donovan could hear a ragged intake of breath and then another gut-wrenching scream. He tried not to wonder what could cause a scream like that. In between the continual screams, he could hear a tune being hummed, but he could not place it. A horrendous scream crescendoed and then trailed into nothing, and he waited for it to start up again. Instead he heard what sounded like water splashing.

The walking nightmare came into view again. The water that dripped in her wake was tinged red. She was carrying the compound bow that had been in his cabin. She rested it against the porch.

She walked toward him and despite his determination to bear up, no matter what, he flinched when she reached for his shoulder. Still, he did not see the expected gloating face, just a sudden void. She wasn't there. A spike of fear formed in his gut.

Between pushing his shoulder and kicking the shredded remnants of his lower legs, he was forced to turn. He pissed himself. Five of his men hung suspended from trees, naked, with pools of blood gathered under their bodies. The last of them was still alive, barely, and twitching weakly. Each of them was missing his dick.

"You're of Irish blood, are you not, Mr. Donovan?" she asked calmly.

He tried to nod as he ran his tongue over his lips. "I am."

"Then you know what a blood oath is."

He nodded again, very slowly.

"I swore a blood oath. I swore to my comrade that I would cut the beating hearts out of the men who did that to her." She cocked her head to the side appraisingly. "But while I was tracking you, I had time to think about it. Fifty-two hours, to be exact.

"It's a long time to think about what could be more fitting." The woman stared up into the sky. "She had quite the sense of humor. Even in this god-awful new world, nothing could keep her from looking at the good in life. Given her background, I can only wonder how she kept her sense of humor. Her family came from Moscow, poor as dirt when they arrived, eight family members shoved into a tiny three-room apartment. She used to say that family togetherness took on a whole new meaning. You and your men took away the one person in this life that deserved to live to a ripe old age. She made me laugh again."

The flat tone in her voice unnerved him, and despite himself he started to beg. "Please…you can't…"

"Oh yes, I can. I swore her a blood oath. You an' yours, you've had a right grand time of it, haven't you? The killing, the taking of any woman you come across, the feeling of being absolutely powerful. How's that power feel to you now?"

She went and picked up the bow, then deliberated before selecting an arrow from the box-shaped metal frame quiver. The steel, fixed blade broad head tip shone in the sunlight as she came back. This time she halted at his feet, and then took five deliberate steps backward.

"I was protecting my territory."

The woman shook her head. "I might believe that if I hadn't read your little book. When you commit murder and mayhem, you really shouldn't write those things down."

"*This* is murder," he stammered as she fitted the arrow to the bowstring.

Her eyes narrowed in judgment. "So is what you did, but you went one further, did you not? You and yours raped her, over and over." She took a deep breath. "When I was in Ireland, I used to go to this little church every Sunday. Father Tim always ended his sermon with this: Thou shalt give life for life," she drew back the bowstring, "…eye for eye, tooth for tooth, hand for hand," the nock of the arrow reached her right ear, "…foot for foot, burning for burning, stripe for stripe. Odd little man, Father Tim."

She released the bowstring and the arrow caught him in the right lung with a reverberant thud. Donovan stared in shock at the woman's impassivity just before the bolt impaled him to the cabin.

Donovan tried to scream but could not find the breath for it. He did scream when the woman's knife cut into his chest. She kept forcing his chin up to look her in the eyes as she worked.

Donovan felt her hand slide into his chest as he identified the tune she was humming. "Slinky."

"I promised her a beating heart," he heard her say just as he took his last breath.

***

When Maguire was finished, her blood still boiled. Nothing had changed. She stalked over to the campfire and dropped the heart into the flames. "I have fulfilled the promise, *moi drug*." She dropped to her knees. "Father Tim, please forgive me."

Chapter Seventeen

The first day Maguire was gone, no one talked about it. It was clearly thought about, as exhibited by Prescott's occasional frustrated sighs, but no one said anything. In fact, all conversation was kept to a minimum as they moved under the cover of darkness to make it to their next camping destination.

They had settled into a higher area where mountainous rocks and dense foliage camouflaged them. They'd had another bland MRE dinner. The food didn't fill them up, but it was sustenance. They were saving their larger meal for just before they started out again.

They were sitting around the tents as the sun came up, each lost in her own thoughts. Baumer was sure that Maguire could track them, if she survived, but wanted to ensure the resourceful staff sergeant found them, in the event something unforeseeable took them off course. She knew Maguire would follow the ATV tracks but if, God forbid, they were killed or taken hostage, she wanted a means of warning Maguire she might be walking into a trap.

"We need to leave markers," she said suddenly.

"For what?" Prescott asked.

"Maguire." Baumer explained her plan to the group.

"Do you honestly think we'll ever see her again?" Prescott growled.

"If I didn't, I wouldn't waste my breath or my time talking about it," Baumer snapped. She ran her hand through her dirty hair, wistfully wishing for a shower and soap. "Jesus, Prescott, your constant grousing about Maguire and Anna is really getting on my nerves. You used to play well with others. What the hell happened to you?"

The three others stared at the normally congenial Baumer, who had not lost her cool until that moment.

Prescott looked like she was about to bite Baumer's head off. "You know damned well what happened to me!"

"I'm sorry about Nancy and Bethany, but we all lost loved ones! Every one of us here, including Maguire, and we all just lost Szabo! I'm tired of the attitude, Prescott. Could you just give us all a break?"

Baumer knew she needed to stop. She had already said too much and Prescott's expression indicated that she agreed.

"Fine!" Prescott stood up. "I'll give you a break. I'll take first watch." She checked her weapon for ammunition. Before she walked to her lookout position, she said, "If Maguire is so all that, she won't need us to play Hansel and Gretel so she can find her way here. Just keep in mind that we could be leading others to us, too." Prescott spun on her heel and moved to her post.

Baumer watched her stomp off and then looked at Doc and Anna. "Sorry. I guess I'm just tired."

"I think you're allowed," Doc said. "A little bit of her can go a long way."

Baumer immediately became defensive. Even though she knew Doc was right, Baumer didn't want anyone else criticizing her people.

"Who are Nancy and Bethany?" Anna asked, saving Baumer from barking at Doc, who didn't deserve it.

"They were Prescott's wife and daughter."

"She had a wife?" Anna sounded curious rather than offended. "Legally? I didn't think the military allowed that."

"It didn't. Prescott left the Army just before Bethany was born. She made a lateral move by joining a government contractor. That way, she could be honest about who she was *and* make a ton more money." Baumer lowered her head. "Damn. I shouldn't have said what I did to her. She lived for Nance and Bethie."

"You were right, though," Doc reassured her with a gentle touch on her forearm. "We all lost people in the attack."

"I know," Baumer acknowledged. "I still shouldn't have said it."

"How old was her little girl?" Anna asked.

"Bethie had just turned four." Baumer smiled fondly in

recollection. "Prescott's brother was the sperm donor. That way Bethie had traits from both families. She was such a little character, and Prescott just doted on her. Nance and Bethie got nailed by a drunk driver with two priors. They never had a chance. Damn it! I should go apologize to her."

Doc placed a restraining hand on her arm. "She'll be fine. It was something she needed to hear. I was very close to my family, and I lost all of them plus a fiancée. You must've lost someone, too."

"Of course, but I had pretty much cut everyone close to me out of my life already."

Anna looked surprised. "Why?"

"Long story, most of which you've already heard in bits and pieces since you've been with us." Baumer rested her cheek on her knee and looked at Anna. "What about you?"

"My family, though we weren't close, and my friends. But I shared my life with two dogs and two cats. I hope they died right away. I can't stand the thought of them having suffered."

Anna's eyes welled at the thought, and Baumer instinctively put a comforting arm around her shoulder. Anna leaned into Baumer, apparently grateful for the contact.

"Okay, let's all get some sleep. Doc, you've got next watch, I'll go after you, and Anna, you're last."

"I'd better go to sleep now then. I hate that 'middle of sleeping, wake up thing' you guys do."

Anna stood up and walked towards the tents. Baumer and Doc watched her go.

"She's a good young woman," Porras observed.

"Yeah, she is."

"So are you, Lieutenant Baumer."

"Not good enough, Doc." After a second, she laughed. "You know, in the Army we call our medics Doc. Sometimes I wonder if you're okay with that demotion."

"My nephew was a Navy corpsman, a medic as you Army types call them. I'm okay with Doc." There was a wistful tone to his voice. "But you want to ask something else."

Baumer nodded. "Szabo."

"Her neck was broken," he answered bluntly. "Which I guess you already knew."

"Now I know why Maguire was so…unreachable. I guessed, but honestly, Doc, I was hoping I was wrong." Baumer stared into the night.

"That young lady was going to die, and in a much more painful way. Some of the blood was from her lungs," he added. "If those small holes around her ribs extended into her lungs, it was going to take her hours to die. Maguire did the only thing she could to ease Szabo's suffering." His eyes welled with tears, which he mopped with his ratty sleeve.

"Doesn't make it any easier on Maguire."

"None of this is easy anymore." He sighed. "I was taught to save lives, but in my more bloodthirsty moments I can't help but wish that those that did this to us get it back tenfold."

Baumer thought about his words for a very long moment. "You know, Doc, I can relate to that. But what good does it do? Man brought this upon himself."

"Maybe some men, but not this one. We're all paying for what someone else did." He brushed his hands on his pants. "I'll go get ready for my watch."

***

Baumer rose just as Anna started making breakfast. She watched as Anna used a minimal amount of water for mixing up the powdered eggs, then browned the Spam, using a can of Sterno, which produced decent heat but little glow.

"Jess, we're down to our last container of canned heat," Anna said. "Not sure if you knew that or not."

"Great," Baumer said unenthusiastically. She moved to a group of bushes and relieved herself, then used the last of her hand sanitizer for a minimal clean up. She woke the other two just after sunset.

The group ate in silence, then Anna cleaned up while Baumer, Prescott, and Doc packed up. As they stowed the supplies on the dirt bike and ATV, Baumer touched Prescott's arm.

"Pres, about this morning—"

"No, you were right. I thought about it a lot while I was on watch. I've been lost in my own grief, and I know I have been acting as though I'm the only one who is hurting. I'll try to do better, but I can't promise whatever I say or do won't come out angry," her voice broke, "because I am still so fucking angry."

Baumer pulled Prescott into a hug. "You need to cry, Pres. You need to release your grief in ways other than anger."

Prescott gave Baumer a quick squeeze then pulled away. "Not now. Not here. Not until we're someplace safe. Once I fall apart, I may not be able to get it back together." Her voice was shaking.

"I don't believe that, Pres. Once a soldier, always a soldier. You won't allow your emotions to get the best of you."

"God, Jess, I'm just so…empty." Prescott balled up her fist and squeezed, clearly waiting until the impulse to cry had passed. One deep breath later, she managed a smile. "We need to start looking for gasoline. The tanks on both our vehicles are running low."

"I know. What I wouldn't give for a working cellphone right now to help us find the nearest town."

***

They continued north, their path lighted by the full moon. Just before dusk, the dirt bike ran out of gas and they reluctantly left it where it fell. Doc and Prescott walked alongside the ATV, which they estimated wouldn't make it much beyond their next campsite.

After their sparse meal, they relaxed. Not much conversation had been exchanged during their night trek, for which they were all grateful. Talking seemed to zap whatever reserve energy they had when they were on the move.

They all missed Szabo, and only the hope that Maguire had found and gotten revenge against the lot that tortured, raped, and murdered their amiable comrade gave them the emotional fuel to keep going. Exhaustion began to overtake them, regardless of how much sleep they got.

"How much longer to Noble's?" Baumer asked as she absentmindedly drew in the dirt with a stick.

"It would help if I knew exactly where we are," Prescott said. "Given the landscape, I'd say we're somewhere in

Wyoming. If that's true, we should start heading northwest. We need to reach Afton and then try to travel parallel with Highway 26 without getting too close to the actual road. Once we get to Idaho Falls, we cross the Snake River Plain to the Bitterroot Range to Salmon. Then we follow the Salmon River to the Salmon River Mountains, where Noble said she'd leave a sign."

"What kind of sign?" Doc asked.

Prescott shrugged. "She said I'd recognize it."

"So, how many more days traveling? Approximately," Baumer asked.

"Another two weeks maybe. Ten days?" Prescott cocked her head. "Best I can guesstimate."

Anna looked eastward. "It's starting to cloud up," she noted.

They followed Anna's gaze and saw dark storm clouds blowing their way.

"Great. We're going to get soaked. Everybody start digging trenches around your tent," Baumer ordered.

"Better idea. One of us will be lookout, so there will always only be three of us sleeping. The big tent can easily fit three, and that way we can keep the other tents dry. We'll put all supplies and rucks in with us, and dig one big moat," Prescott suggested. She looked at Doc. "You'll just have to exert all your willpower to keep your hands to yourself." She winked and smiled at him.

He smiled back. "I'll be too busy sleeping to have anything else on my mind."

They took down the other tents and stashed everything inside the big tent just before the wind picked up.

"Anna," Baumer nodded toward the sentry position, "you take first watch."

"Me? But—b—"

"Just do it, please."

Anna and Prescott both stared at Baumer. "Okay," Anna finally said, bewildered.

Prescott checked the ammunition and handed Anna the rifle and night vision binoculars. The young woman accepted the weapon with a nod and walked to her post.

"What are you doing?" Prescott asked. "I always have first

watch."

"So, you can take another watch. I doubt Anna will be much good in the raging storm it looks like we're in for. If she has first watch, she should only be minimally exposed, yet she'll have done her part for the team."

Prescott shook her head. "The things you do to accommodate that little princess."

"The mark of a good leader is logical improvisation," Baumer said with a grin.

***

When Doc woke Baumer for last watch, she had to untangle herself from Anna, who had burrowed into her at some point while she slept. Slow recall brought back a misty memory of a loud thunderstorm and Anna latching onto her for dear life. Baumer moved stealthily in order to not wake the young woman, donning a thermal top before she put on her shirt and jacket. The rain had stopped, but it had left the air damp and chilly.

Baumer knew it would be about another hour before the sun rose. Her eyes quickly adjusted to her surroundings, and she kept her thermo night goggles mostly pointed southeast, hoping for a glimpse of Maguire. She couldn't hide her disappointment when it came time to get the others up and moving and there was still no sign of her good friend.

"We're almost out of powdered eggs," Anna announced as she inventoried the food supplies.

Baumer yawned and rubbed her eyes. She had strained them with her vigilance, watching for Maguire. "What do we have left?"

Anna rummaged through the sack. "We have four red beans and rice meals and three meat loaf with gravy meals. There are some individual packets of, like, crackers, cheese spread, and peanut butter."

"That's not much if we have another ten days or more ahead of us."

Anna frowned in thought. "There has to be towns or stores or abandoned homes we can forage from, right?"

"I'm sure there are, but we have to be careful," Baumer reminded her. "The route we've been traveling has kept us away from most civilization...if there is any left. Even if we did run across some buildings, that doesn't mean they haven't already been looted. We also have to watch out for survivors who are protecting what they have left or what they've found."

She pointed to the boxes of rice and beans. "Take two of those and ration them out to make four meals. Divide the cheddar cheese pretzels and give everyone an equal amount. Put the crackers, cheese spread, and chocolate sports bar with the individual packets. We'll need those for energy when we run out of food. How are we on water?"

"We're getting low on that, too."

Baumer nodded. "Prescott said we'd be crossing a river. We can use our handy dandy water purifier and process some river water, if we don't come across some other source before that. We need to make sure the water isn't contaminated, though. There are some things these filters can't protect us from."

"How can we tell?"

"Maguire left us her tester kit."

"No sign of her yet?" Anna asked hesitantly.

Baumer's smile was both weary and disappointed. "No, but we need to give her a chance to catch up." She placed a reassuring hand on Anna's shoulder and squeezed it gently.

Anna returned Baumer's smile before opening the boxes and separating the supplies. "Why rice and beans? I would think meatloaf would be better for our main meal."

"Let me ask you a question. If we have to spend another night crammed in a tent with each other, which would you rather we have eaten just before bedtime—beans or mashed potatoes?"

Realization of what Baumer was asking made a blush crawl up Anna's cheeks. "Oh. Right. Got it." Anna cleared her throat and continued to apportion the food. "Jessica?"

"Yes?"

"I really miss Szabo." Anna's voice choked with emotion.

Baumer pulled Anna to her. "I know, sweetie. I really miss her, too." She released the younger woman when Doc approached.

"Just to lower your spirits a little further," Prescott said, "we have about an eighth of a tank of gas left in the ATV. After that, we're down to whatever we can carry on our backs."

Knowing that Anna and Doc wouldn't be able to carry as much weight as Prescott and Baumer, who were trained to haul necessary items for long distances, they packed the rucksacks and tested them for weight, and then loaded them onto the ATV.

Chapter Eighteen

The ATV sputtered through its last bit of fuel a quarter of the way into their night journey. With the vehicle no longer useful, each member of the team shrugged into their pack and continued on foot.

Anna constantly stopped to adjust the weight on her back, which put her behind the others. The heavy rain that caused their muddy climb to be even more challenging made the trek to the summit sluggish at best, even for the two experienced backpackers.

"I'm not sure I can make it to the top," Anna shouted from below the other three.

"Sure you can, princess. Just keep putting one foot in front of the other. That's how Jess and I learned to not give up," Prescott coached.

Baumer walked back to Anna and offered her a hand. "We're almost there. Maybe we can stop for a bit and get our bearings. Believe me, if it's as steep and muddy on the other side, we'll all probably be sliding down the mountain on our butts." She pulled Anna over the difficult patches as they hiked higher.

At the peak, the landscape leveled out. Baumer, Anna, and Doc removed their packs and stretched, while Prescott used the night vision binoculars to scan the area.

"Huh," Prescott grunted.

"See anything interesting?" Baumer asked.

Prescott removed the glasses. "We're closer to Idaho than I initially thought. I just saw a sign for Highway 26. So that's some incentive, at least. Other than that, the only thing out there with warm blood is sparse wildlife. I think we can stay close to the road without any problem. We just need to stay alert." She looked at Anna. "How're you doing there, princess?"

Anna peered at Prescott, caution in her expression. "I'm okay. I just need to get used to it."

Prescott nodded acknowledgement and moved over to Baumer. She lowered her voice and said, "We could leave the princess behind as a marker for Maguire."

"I heard that," Anna said loudly, a hint of sarcasm wrapped around her usually sweet voice. "It might be bear country. Prescott, you want to walk point?"

Baumer gave Prescott a sharp jab to the ribs. "Behave, Pres."

Prescott snickered and rubbed her side. "That was a good one. Actually, I'm surprised she's done as well as she has," Prescott admitted. "But seriously, are you leaving a trail for Maguire, or have you given up on her?"

"I haven't given up on Maguire and, yes, I have left some clues along the way and, no, it's not breadcrumbs."

Prescott grinned.

Baumer looked around. "Jesus, Pres, it's raining like a bitch, my legs are killing me from climbing what feels like the Matterhorn, we're probably going to be sleeping in freezing cold mud when we make camp, we're running out of food, and you're finally in a good mood. What the hell is wrong with you?"

"Don't you get it? We're almost there." Prescott was still smiling. "We've traveled for months, we've crossed four states, and we've survived—"

"Don't jinx us, Pres! Damn! We're not there yet, and we don't know what will be waiting for us when we get there."

"Party pooper," Prescott said amiably.

They walked another mile or two before seeing a road sign. It indicated there were three towns not too far ahead of them. The closest was five miles away.

"We might be able to get some additional supplies there," Doc said hopefully.

Prescott turned to him. "Doc, do you think you could handle my pack for the next mile?"

"A mile? Sure, I think so. Why?"

"I need to go ahead and check out what we might be walking into." She removed her rucksack and handed it to Doc, then turned to Baumer. "Now is when I really miss Maguire. She's a better scout than I am. More precise."

"Don't doubt yourself, Pres. Just make sure you come back to us. No heroics," Baumer ordered.

"I'm not the crazy one, remember?" She slung her rifle over her shoulder and held up the night vision glasses. "I'll meet you up the road. Stop at the next mile marker and wait for me. If the town is occupied, they'll have roadblocks and guards about three miles out."

"What then?" Doc asked, as Anna caught up to them.

"Then we figure out an alternate route, around the problem," Prescott said.

"And add another couple days to our journey," Anna said unhappily.

***

Baumer, Doc, and Anna had been at the rendezvous point for over an hour by the time Prescott returned.

"You want the good news first or the bad news?"

"You mean there actually is some good news?" Baumer asked. At Prescott's nod, she said, "What's the bad news?"

"The town is definitely occupied. I can't tell you the size of the group, because it's night and most are probably asleep. There are two civilian vehicles blocking the road into town, and three men with weapons standing guard."

"What kind of weapons?"

"All I could see was what they had in their hands, Mac 10s. No way of knowing what they could have in the vehicles. There was razor wire too, so we have to assume they have the town completely cordoned off. We won't be able to get anywhere near there."

"And the good news?"

"I located an abandoned house on the far side of town, two and a half miles beyond their razor wire. It's well off the road, and it has amenities. There's no electricity, but there is a generator with gas in it. We could all get hot showers and sleep in real beds, and best of all, there is a storm cellar with a ton of canned goods and a dual battery powered freezer, still running,

147

with actual meat in it."

Doc's skepticism showed on his face. "Are you sure it's safe?"

"As sure as I can be. I'm pretty sure we'd be safe there, at least until we get rested up."

"Are you sure it's not a bait trap?" Baumer asked.

"I can't be positive, Jess, but it's been months since Day Zero. My guess is that whoever is in charge is going to be pretty conservative with their fuel, if they have any left at all. If I were in charge, I'd lock down the town and stay there. If I forced people to come to me, I'd have all the power."

"Why do you think they missed this house? I would have sent out recon teams to gather every inch of uncontaminated supplies I could," Baumer said.

"Not sure. It's possible they just missed it. It is kind of in the middle of nowhere. But I scanned the area really well, and I saw nothing to indicate any recent activity. No broken branches or stepped down grass, or fresh tracks of any kind that I could see. It looks okay." Prescott looked at each of the other three in turn. "Well?"

"Well, let's go," Baumer said.

***

Doc was the last one to revel in the luxury of a working shower. Regardless of all that had happened, he was still a gentleman and he had insisted all the ladies go first.

He spent his time in the shower thinking about the situation he was now in—a post-apocalyptic world where his saviors and only friends were a traumatized rape victim and four lesbians…well, three now, and possibly just two. He had to laugh at the irony of having been raised in a Baptist household and brainwashed that homosexuality was a sin and that gays and lesbians were perverted miscreants who preyed on straight men and women, trying to convert them. And yet, as his throat was about to be slashed in his own clinic, his assailant was shot, and it turned out that it was gays who had saved his life. It wasn't lesbians who rescued him, it was four very brave soldiers who stepped into an impossible situation and eliminated the threat.

They gave him sanctuary with their group, so they clearly didn't hate men, and they took a young straight woman under their collective wing and never once—to his knowledge—tried to seduce her. Nor did any of them appear to be interested in hooking up with one another. They had one mission in mind, to survive, and they took that seriously.

By the time Doc got out of the shower, the sun was rising. Feeling pounds lighter, he toweled off, actually able to stand the smell of himself again. He raided the closet in the master bedroom and was delighted to find a selection of men's clothing. The original owner of the clothes might have been the same shirt size as Doc, but a pair of jeans he tried on proved to be bigger in the waist and shorter in length. He took the belt off his raggedy pair of slacks and threaded it through the loops of a pair of denims, shrugging at the hem of the trousers that stopped at his lower calf. Next, he rummaged through the footwear on the closet floor and found several pair of well-worn work boots. They were a little large, but nothing several pairs of socks couldn't fix.

He found Baumer sitting by the front window in the living room, the blinds cracked just enough so that she could see out.

"What are you still doing up?" he whispered as he drew close and eased his way to the floor.

"Watching." She looked at him, then back out the window. "Why are you up?"

He smiled. "Appreciating the joys of a shower, as you well know." He took in a breath and let it out again. "I haven't said it officially, but thank you. You all saved my life." He swallowed. "How do I pay that back?"

"You don't, Doc. We aren't keeping count here. Someday we'll need your skills for more than we do now. End of story. Honestly, I thought we were beyond all that."

"We are and we aren't," Porras said. "I'm alive because of you four—" He dropped his eyes.

"We were four when we showed up at your office," Baumer said softly. "You don't have to censor yourself with me. Prescott maybe, but not with me."

He nodded. "I have tried to live my life as the gentleman I was raised to be. My grandfather was a simple country doctor, and I wanted nothing more than to be like him. I'd like to think I am." He took a deep breath. "You might not want payment for what you all did, but I swear to you, no one who needs help will ever be passed over by me."

"I don't doubt that at all. But just from the time I've known you, I think that was always the case." Baumer sounded choked up.

"Maybe." His face broke out in a slow smile. "My corpsman nephew had a tattoo of his unit crest on his shoulder blade. Maybe I'll have 'Baumer's Bitch' inked on my bicep."

Baumer nearly choked on a spurt of laughter.

"Breathe, Lieutenant." Doc's smile grew in the dark. "Anna told me about that day. And I'm incredibly impressed enough to actually think about getting a tattoo to commemorate it. My grandfather would spin in his grave."

ChapterNineteen

After her evening shower, Anna searched through a couple of closets looking for clean clothes and now looked adorable in what appeared to be the attire of a teenage boy. She was dressed in black parachute pants and a light grey, long-sleeved t-shirt under a zip-up dark blue hoodie. She wore a Denver Broncos baseball cap with her hair pulled through the back in a ponytail, and black high-top canvas sneakers that were too big for her.

When she bounced into the kitchen, more energetic than she had felt in months, she surveyed the cans of vegetables that had been brought up from the basement. "What do you want me to make for supper?" she asked Baumer.

The lieutenant couldn't help but grin at Anna's appearance. "Why, don't you look like just the cutest fifteen-year-old boy!"

"Shut up!" Anna gave her a playful push and then leaned in close. "How do men stand to wear boxer shorts?" She pulled gingerly at the crotch of her pants.

"Are you borrowing some undies from that boy's dresser?"

"I had to. And Jessica? I started my period," Anna said with a broad smile.

"Oh, that's going to be a—" Then it hit her what that meant. "Oh, Anna, that's great!"

Anna grinned as Baumer pulled her into a happy hug. "It means I didn't get pregnant, right?"

She released the younger woman. "Let's hope that's what it means, sweetie. It certainly is a good sign."

"When I missed my period last month, I was sure I was pregnant. I don't know if I could have survived that."

"Your cycle might have been disrupted because of the extreme emotional upheaval. My last period was barely there, which is unusual for me," Baumer said. "And not to burst your bubble, but it's not uncommon to spot when you're pregnant."

Anna's smile faded. "Really?"

"Really." Baumer reached over and tapped the bill of Anna's cap. "Listen, we're a team now, right?" She waited until Anna gave her a slight nod. "Until we get a sign that you are pregnant, we'll hope you aren't. If it turns out that you are pregnant, we'll handle that, too. If bearing your rapists' baby is something you cannot do, I am sure Doc or Noble, once we get there, knows how to safely take care of that. Or, if you decide to have the baby, at least you should be able to raise it in a safe environment. It will be up to you."

"I hope I don't have to make that decision."

"Me, too. Whichever way it goes, we'll be here for you, Anna. You're family now," Baumer said warmly.

Tears sprang to Anna's eyes. "Thank you, Jess. You're more family to me than my own flesh and blood."

***

Anna dried the last of the dishes and listened to the rain beating out a tempo on the glass of the kitchen window. If she tried hard, she could imagine that this was home and nothing bad had happened. The pretense did not last long. The absence of Szabo's soft laughter was still too close to her heart. Closing her eyes, she wished she could pray for the woman who sometimes intentionally made them smile by acting like a goofball, but she no longer believed in God.

She did hope that Maguire had killed them in their turn.

Them.

It was the only term she was willing to use. Everyone understood who she meant when she used the word. She walked from the kitchen into the living room. Prescott had her map spread out over the table that had recently held their dinner. Dr. Porras was inventorying the meager medical supplies, and she recalled his joy at having found peroxide in the bathroom of their refuge.

Baumer stood at the open front door, peering into the darkness. Each time they'd made camp in the last five days, she kept an eye out for Maguire until she'd been forced to rest before her watch.

"Standing there like a jilted lover isn't going to conjure her up," Prescott said without looking up from her map.

"And acting like a horse's ass is really only going to fucking piss me off," Baumer shot back sharply. She sighed and took a deep breath. "You made me cuss. Again. My mama would be turning over in her grave." Baumer rolled her eyes. "What am I saying? With the way my language has been the past couple of months, I might as well call mama Pinwheel Emily."

Prescott actually laughed. "Okay, Jess, I know I'm harping. That was the last one for the night."

Baumer turned her gaze on Prescott, then nodded. "Thanks for cooking, Anna, and for doing the dishes."

Anna flushed as the other two looked at her. "You're welcome. I can't help with the maps or medicine, but I can…"

Dr. Porras looked away from the medicine bottles and took off his glasses. "I'm sorry, Anna, I am grateful. I got distracted again." He smiled gently. "If you like, I can start teaching you some basic medicine."

Anna laughed flatly. It was not a pleasant sound. "Sorry, Doc, but you would most likely be wasting your time. My brother got the good looks, my sister the brains. I couldn't learn."

"That's bullshit," Prescott snapped in a grating tone. "You've got brains, princess. Prove it. We might need what the doc is willing to teach you."

For a long moment, everyone was shocked into silence, and three sets of eyes stared at Prescott.

"What? I'm not a complete asshole all the time." She turned back to her map and resumed scribbling calculations.

Dr. Porras raised an eyebrow in amazement at the other two women. Anna tried to think of something to say to thank Prescott for her vote of confidence. Baumer smiled softly. She opened her mouth, but whatever she was about to say was forgotten at the sound of a rough engine coming down the road.

"Defensive positions!" Baumer barked, grabbing her own M4 from beside the door.

Prescott bolted up the stairs and into the bedroom that faced the road. The doctor nervously kept watch at the back. Anna knew neither she nor Doc was very good with a firearm, and there was simply not enough ammunition to spare on rookies. She stayed by the front door, next to Baumer.

Given the rain, neither woman could clearly see the driver of what appeared to be a Vietnam War Era Army Jeep. She blinked in disbelief. She'd only seen them in photographs and museums. The driver slowed slightly to turn into the driveway, then slammed on the brakes.

"Don't shoot," Prescott shouted from above. "It's Maguire."

Rifle in hand, Baumer opened the door and rushed out.

***

Maguire stepped out of the Jeep, soaked to the bone and beyond. Her gait was jerky as she moved toward her lieutenant, water streaming off the brim of her patrol cap. When she was three feet from Baumer, she halted, came to a swaying attention, and snapped a salute. "Sergeant Maguire returning from duty, Ma'am. Mission accomplished."

"Mags?" Baumer returned the salute, then slung the weapon over her shoulder.

"I would have been here sooner, but I ran out of gas and it took a while to find some." She was rambling. "I almost missed your last directional. Oh, and I picked up some of our weapons and gear. They're in the vehicle—"

"Come in out of the rain, Mags," Baumer coaxed. Even from three feet away, she could see that Maguire had not slept in days and she'd lost weight she couldn't afford to drop. Very slowly, she took two steps forward. "Mags, come on in out of the rain," she repeated quietly.

Maguire looked at her with a confused expression. "I found a Jeep." She tried to say more but she couldn't seem to find the words, and then she listed forward. She tried to right herself and failed.

Baumer caught her as she fell. Even with the weight loss, Maguire was a handful. "Pres!" she shouted, but it was Anna who helped shift the weight balance. Together they managed to half drag, half carry Maguire into the house.

"Put her down," Doc Porras ordered, beginning his examination with three women hovering behind him. When he turned to them, his expression was grim. "Get a warm bath running, lukewarm, not hot. She's hypothermic and dehydrated. Not a good combination. Anna, would you please warm some water and add half a cup of sugar?"

"What will that do?" Prescott asked as she moved toward the bathroom.

"Folk remedy for dehydration. Now quick. Jessica, if you'll help me get her out of these soaked clothes, we can get her in the tub."

They worked as a team without noticing. All that mattered was making sure Maguire made it past the danger point. Once she was in the warm water, Baumer fed her spoons of sugar water. When it looked like the process was going to last most of the night, Prescott relieved her, then Anna took a turn, with Baumer returning to check any progress. When Maguire stopped acting like a zombie and began shaking, she was lifted out of the tub, dried off quickly, and put into a bed with several blankets over her. Baumer took off her shoes, pants, and shirt and crawled in next to Maguire.

Prescott could not hold back the smirk, but did at least hold her tongue.

"Keep that thought to yourself, Pres." Baumer tried to smile.

"I'm beyond thinking, Jess. I'll take the watch. We can all try to catch up on rest tomorrow."

"I think it is tomorrow." Baumer sighed as she snuggled close to Maguire.

"I'll send the others to bed." Prescott started out of the room, then turned back. "Did she get them, Jess?" Her voice was soft.

"She," Baumer swallowed, "she said 'mission accomplished.' I think she got them."

Prescott bowed her head for a moment. "Good."

Baumer closed her eyes and listened to Prescott walk out of the room. "But at what cost?" She had five minutes for contemplation before Dr. Porras tapped on the doorframe.

He checked his patient's vitals as best he could without

proper equipment. "Keep her warm, and as often as possible, get some of that solution into her. A little at a time, we don't want to hydrate her too quickly. I'll set my alarm for two hours, then I'll check on her again."

Anna walked into the room with another glass of sugar water. "Doc, you get some sleep. I'll come get you if she needs you."

"I'll be fine," he objected.

"Not if you're dead on your feet, too. I didn't do much today, and I can doze. Jessica can wake me up if something happens." She cut him off in a tone that no one was willing to argue with as she placed the water on the table next to Maguire.

He crumbled. "Wake me when you need to." And he walked out of the room.

Baumer watched her young friend close the door and find a comfortable spot to sit on the floor. "Well now, that sounded like some backbone there, Anna." Her words were not teasing in the least.

"I have one, I just don't use it very often," Anna answered honestly. "No one listened to me much at home."

"Maybe they should have."

They fell into a comfortable silence, listening to Prescott's footsteps as she patrolled the upstairs areas and the squeak of bedsprings as Dr. Porras settled into sleep. It was a long while before the silence was broken by Maguire mumbling something that neither woman could make out.

Baumer rubbed what she hoped were soothing circles on Maguire's back. The woman seemed to calm as long as the contact was light.

"Jessica?" Anna asked softly.

"Yes?"

"Do you think she did what she said she was going to?"

Baumer did not have to think twice, and she would not sugarcoat the truth for Anna. "Yeah, I think she did." She tried to figure out how to explain it to the young woman. "Maguire is a special kind of soldier, Anna."

"You mean because of that commando school she talked about?"

"No. I think what she is, part of who she is, started in

Korea. She doesn't talk about it much, but I looked into what happened there. It was terrible, even by the standards of war. The unit she ended up with was nearly out of ammunition, so was the enemy. The fighting was medieval. And she wasn't even supposed to be there." She fell silent.

"You've been to war. Why aren't you...?" Anna struggled for the words.

"It was a different situation. My men lost me on purpose. I was responsible only for myself after that. Making a mistake while getting back to my lines would kill only me. Due to her rank, if Maguire made a mistake other soldiers could die. That kind of pressure will break you or make you very angry after the fact. Maguire gets angry."

"Did she love Szab, do you think?" Anna's voice was hesitant.

Baumer smiled softly. "I think that Maguire hasn't had a lot to laugh about in quite a while, and Szabo was able to give her that gift." She kept to herself what she and Dr. Porras had discussed about Szabo's death.

"Have you ever loved someone, Jess?"

"Oh yeah. I've loved a few times. Now the one I really wanted to marry...James Darren Williamson. We met when I was five and he was three." She thought about him for a very long moment, and smiled at the memory. "My only younger man."

"But...but..." Anna sputtered and sat up quickly. "I thought..."

"Breathe, sweetie." She laughed gently. "Just because I hang out with lesbians, doesn't mean I am one."

"But...you've never corrected anyone who assumes you are."

"Why? Correcting people would make it seem like I thought it was a bad thing that I should separate myself from. My parents were extremely wonderful people. They taught me that human beings should be taken for their inner worth and not some label that's stuck to them for whatever reason." She watched as Anna absorbed those words. "And James? Well, James had the cutest smile on the face of this earth."

Anna resettled in a comfortable position, resting her back

against the wall. "What was he like?"

Baumer smiled. "Well, aside from his 'eating dirt' phase, he was great. He went from being this clumsy, shy, gangly kid into a smart, funny man. He took life seriously, but he had fun with it, too. Almost everything could be a joke. And damned if he wasn't right most of the time." She sighed. "We dated all through school, even college and Army training. He wanted to be a helicopter pilot. He got attack helicopters right off the bat, but he wanted all his ratings, so we waited." She sniffled as the tears began.

"You never got married?"

Baumer shook her head. "No." Her voice was sad. "The dumbass got himself shot down. It was his first tour in Iraq, my second. He was killed instantly, or so they said." She wiped away her tears. "He was bingo fuel, I mean low on gas, and he probably should have taken himself out of the fight, but he wouldn't leave his troops. He was like that, loyal to a fault. I swear I still love him. The brass told me he was banking left to take out the enemy when a Stinger missile t-boned him." There was a measure of pride in her tone. "What about you? Any sweethearts in your life?"

"Not really. Everyone I was interested in zeroed in on my sister or my other friends," Anna answered quietly.

Baumer smiled. "Don't worry. Someone will see you for who you are one of these days, and then you'll discover how nice love is."

For several minutes they fell silent. "He really ate dirt?"

Baumer snorted. The question surprised her. She nodded. "He really ate dirt. A lot. It's kind of funny now. But he was six when he did it." Baumer chuckled then sobered. "He was my beautiful everything." She sighed. "He still is. I don't know if anyone else will ever measure up to him."

Whatever else she might have said was lost as Maguire began to thrash under the sheets. Baumer was hard pressed to hold her in place.

Anna pushed off the floor and lay on the bed beside the Irish woman who was burning with fever, then began to murmur to her in low tones. After a few minutes, the patient slowly relaxed.

"What did you just do?" Baumer asked in a whisper.

Anna brushed her hand over Maguire's hair in a soothing manner. "I just did what I used to do with our dogs and horses when they were restless or tossing a baby. You just talk to them like a small kid."

"You can do that?"

Anna did not take her eyes off Maguire. "Well, yeah. It's easy. She's a lot like a beat dog right now—too skinny, and skittish as hell. You just talk to her in a low voice, let her know you want to take away what is making her hurt, and she won't bite your face off."

A light went on in Baumer's head. "Anna, can you do this with horses that are okay, I mean horses that are in the corral or grazing around?"

Anna smiled easily even as she continued to soothe Maguire. "Sure. They just need to know you need and want them. Give 'em a treat and sweet talk 'em, and they're like puppies that'll follow you home. They're really nothing but big dogs."

"How many horses have we seen in the last fifteen or so miles?"

Anna thought about it. "I dunno, twenty-five or so."

Baumer leaned over and kissed the top of Anna's head. "You, my dear, are a genius. Horses. I didn't even think about that, because I have the worst luck with them."

"What walks down stairs, alone..." Maguire murmured her song "or in pairs...odd little man...Father Tim...please, Father, forgive me."

Baumer shifted slightly but Anna stopped her. "Rest, my soldier," she whispered as she wiped Maguire's forehead with a cool, wet cloth.

Sweat beaded up again. "Forgive me, Father...I killed them. I liked it...Szab, my sweet Szab, I'm sorry...forgive me, Father. I gave her a beating heart." She thrashed weakly in the bed, then her voice turned harsh. "Kearney, try your boys again, mine are for shit...here they come again...single shots, pick your targets."

Baumer whispered "Korea" to Anna and wrapped her arms around Maguire without constraining her, while Anna continued to stroke the damp forehead.

"Kearney…oh Jaysus man…" She took in a shuddering breath. "I'll give back three for you. When I have a son, I'll name him Rory," she rasped around a low sob. "Hail Mary, Mother of God, pray for us sinners…" She took another shaky breath. "With no respect at all, Sir, take your medal… and place the pointed ends for maximum pain somewhere…give it to the likes of my men who died…and give one each to my Irish soldiers as well…Eight days," she ground out harshly, then she took a deep breath, the fight almost gone out of her. "I'm cold."

Baumer slid off the bed and grabbed another blanket to toss over Maguire, then laid down again, sharing her warmth, her heart nearly breaking. "Mission accomplished, Sergeant," she said in her best command whisper. "Better than outstanding…outfuckingstanding."

Maguire licked her lips. "Request permission to stand down, Ma'am."

Baumer leaned in close and whispered into Maguire's ear. "Stand down, Staff Sergeant."

Maguire's body suddenly relaxed and lay still.

Chapter Twenty

Prescott finished placing the usable items from Maguire's acquired Jeep on the table and wiped sweat from her head with a towel. The night's downpour had given way to a hot and humid day, but if the clouds in the distance were any indication, it was going to be another wet night. She looked over the inventory; Maguire had managed to scrounge some good stuff. The compound bow was in great condition, and the three dozen arrows were tipped with steel heads. They would be excellent for hunting.

There were two hundred fully loaded magazines of ammo for the M4s. It would be a bitch to haul around, but at least it replaced some of what had been stolen from them. There were two rucksacks filled with their own clothing, so they wouldn't have to depend on borrowed underwear any longer. Unfortunately, Anna's only spare pair of shoes was not in the batch.

She slid three bottles of alcohol towards the far end of the table. They went nicely with the two full economy size bottles of aspirin. She shook her head at the five bottles of prescription antibiotics. Finding them had been a shock. Who could ever have known that these simple things would make a doctor cry with joy. Doc had quickly volunteered to haul those in his own rucksack.

"She did good," Baumer said as she passed Prescott on the way to the kitchen for a cup of coffee.

"Yeah. She did," Prescott admitted grudgingly. "The Jeep's got nearly a full tank. I wish she'd managed to get some spare fuel, though. After this tank is gone, we're back to hoofing it."

Baumer came back with two cups and set one on the table. "About that." She took a sip and savored it. "It seems Anna has a skill set that we weren't aware of. She has a thing for horses."

"That's nice," Prescott dismissed absently as she opened Szabo's laptop, which Maguire had protected above everything else. The rain poncho Maguire should have been wearing had been double wrapped around the computer. Then Baumer's words sank in, and she looked up in astonishment. "She what?"

"She told me that working with tame horses is relatively easy, you just have to know what you're doing. Apparently she knows what to do." Baumer smiled.

Prescott was instantly suspicious and edging towards anger. "And we're just learning this, why?"

Baumer laughed. "Because we never connected the dots. She told us where she grew up, she gave us everything we needed to know, and we didn't make the connection. So much for smart soldiers and intel geeks."

"Huh?"

"We ignored soft intel because she's 'just a princess, just a little girl.' Plain and simple, Pres, we blew her off and made it harder on ourselves. We could have ridden here." Baumer wrapped her hands around her cup. "Any idea how far we've all walked since Szab died?"

"Fuck me," Prescott muttered as she considered the truth of it.

"Exactly. I want you to go with her to scout for horses today. I'm thinking you shouldn't have to go any further than a mile in any direction. Nothing further out. I don't want anyone to know we're here."

"Why don't you go with her?"

"Afraid of a little girl?" Baumer sounded like an eight-year-old bully.

Prescott bristled instantly. "I'm not afraid of anything."

"Then you'll be her cover. I won't even tell you to behave. But you better," Baumer teased. "We need this, Pres. The fuel in the Jeep won't last, and just think of how much further we have to go. If we can eliminate two or three days of travel time by riding the horses rather than walking, we'll be much better off."

Prescott relented. "I get it. I'll go, I'll cover her. This better work."

"I knew you would see it my way." Baumer sounded smug.

"Maguire is still running a fever. Doc and I are going to keep an eye on her."

"She bad?" Prescott felt compelled to ask.

Baumer sobered. "It could turn bad. Doc's hearing a lot of fluid in her lungs. She should have stopped and taken shelter, but she didn't. I don't know what kept her going."

"I've known soldiers like that, drive on at all costs. Most of the time the downside isn't worth it." Prescott lifted the laptop. "She brought us back our method of communication, though. I checked, and this house had satellite connectivity through their cable company. A little tweaking and I can get us back up so we can contact Noble." She touched the laptop gently. "And I can go to the pictures on this and see Szab." Her voice cracked. "Don't you ever tell Maguire this, but I'm glad she got the bastards, and I hope to everything evil that she made it hurt."

"Pres, I'll never say this out loud again and I hope to God she never tells me in detail 'cause I will puke—she castrated everyone but the leader." She took a seriously deep breath, "From what I pieced together from Maguire's nightmare ramblings, she pinned him down with an arrow from that bow, and then cut his heart out while he was still alive." She shivered.

Prescott was silent for a long time after the gruesome details sank in. "Jesus, God. I wish I could feel sorry for them, but I can't." She took a breath. "Maguire's insane."

Baumer's head snapped up. "Belay that. She is not insane. She's very good at killing people who kill those she cares about. What do you still want to do to the man who killed your family?"

"Point taken," Prescott muttered. "I still don't like her."

"You don't have to. I'm not asking you to. I'm just glad she's on our side," Baumer said fervently.

"That makes two of us." Prescott ran her fingers over the laptop and blinked her eyes to hold back the tears. "Just for bringing me pictures of Szab, I'll try not to piss her off any more than is absolutely necessary."

***

Baumer closed the bedroom door softly behind her, but nevertheless, Maguire slowly opened one eye. "What time is it?" she rasped.

"Time for meds and some water, it sounds like." Baumer tried to smile as she walked to the side of the bed, but couldn't. "You scared me, us, you know. What were you thinking, traveling in the rain like that?"

Maguire blinked. "What rain?"

Baumer's hand stilled on the water jug. "The torrential storm you drove straight through."

"I don't recall," Maguire managed weakly as she tried to get up. When her muscles failed to respond, she gave up. "What's the damage?"

Baumer poured a glass of water and shoved a straw into it, then sat on the bed and held it for Maguire to drink. "Hypothermia, lungs filled with fluid, four episodes of tachycardia. I thought you were having heart attacks, but Doc assured me you weren't. Frightening, though, because it felt as if your heart was going to beat right out of your chest." She was not sugarcoating a thing. "A few more hours out there, and you'd be dying right about now."

"Might have been for the best," Maguire murmured. After a long sip of water, she fell silent.

"Want to explain that?"

She shook her head. "You really don't want to know." Her voice was barely a whisper.

"You talk in your sleep. I know some of it." Baumer set the glass of water down and faced her friend. "When I was stuck out in the desert by myself, I killed two men eyeball to eyeball. I did what I had to do, so did you."

Maguire looked at Baumer. "Did your heart sing with joy when you killed them?"

"I don't think so, but I was extremely dehydrated, so I can't tell you what I was thinking or feeling at the time. They were blocking my access to water," she answered directly.

Maguire looked away from Baumer. "I reveled in every bloody moment of it—each slice of the blade, every single scream, every fucking second of begging. And they *fucking begged*," she ground out. "And all I could think of was, how much did Szab beg?" The tears fell then, but Maguire showed no embarrassment. She didn't even wipe them away.

"After seeing what they did to Szab, I can't feel sorry for them." Baumer thought for a long moment. "I'm not a shrink, and I can't give you absolution or whatever it is you're looking for, Mags. What I can tell you is that I'm damned glad they're dead, and I hope it hurt. If that makes me a bad person, then so be it." She took a breath. "In all honesty, I can't say that I wouldn't have done what you did."

"You couldn't be what I am. You actually have a heart, I think," Maguire said.

"So do you, Mags. The rest of you is trained to compartmentalize. If you didn't have a heart, I don't think Szab's death would have gotten to you so personally."

"How much longer before we move on?" Maguire asked after another sip of water.

"Doc wants your lungs clear. We have time, Mags. We push too hard or too fast, you die. I don't want to go to your funeral. Besides, Anna has a new job." She barely contained her smile.

"Share," Maguire rasped.

"How do you feel about horses?"

"That they're too high off the ground," Maguire admitted.

***

Maguire's legs were shaky as she stepped out of the first actual shower she'd taken in many weeks. Although she luxuriated for less than five minutes so that she could conserve the same opportunity for the others, the feel of real soap and heated water were heavenly. She grabbed a thick bath towel and wiped the steam off the mirror. Studying her reflection, she noted new marks and scars that scored her skin, mapping out a new chapter in her life's story. She shook herself out of her reverie and began to dry herself. She was still weak, but weak she could work with.

***

Doc Porras turned from the kitchen window at the sound of shuffling. He looked down at Maguire's feet and saw that she was wearing fluffy bunny slippers that were way too big for her.

Maguire saw the direction of Doc's stare and shrugged. "My feet were cold." She moved over to the coffee pot and poured herself a cup. When she turned around, Doc was still gaping. "What?"

"I…it's just…well, they just aren't *you,*" he told her.

"Did you miss that part where my feet are cold?" She shrugged. "Desperate times, and all that. At least they're not pink." She took a sip of the black coffee. "Not bad. Did you make this?"

"No. I prefer coffee you don't have to cut with a knife. Jessica made it."

"Speaking of that, where are the others?"

"Prescott and Anna just got back with three horses." He turned to the window and pointed.

Maguire joined him there to look outside. "Holy shit, those puppies are huge!" she croaked.

***

"These were all we could find without getting too close to the outer perimeter of the town." Prescott was holding a rope that was attached to a makeshift halter around one horse's head. "They aren't in great shape."

"They are plow horses," Anna added. "I'm not sure how long they've been foraging to stay alive." She ran her hand along a once-muscled, broad chest of a black Shire. "Their coats and bodies told us they were starving, so I lured them closer with apples. They came right to us. I think they're all sick," she said sadly. "I don't think they will do us much good, a day, maybe two, on the terrain we have to cross."

"The other thing we have to consider is that they may have escaped from the town, which means someone might be searching for them. That wouldn't be good for us either," Prescott added.

Baumer gently rubbed the velvety nose of one of the horses as she looked at Anna. "You don't think they could at least get us a few days closer Noble's?"

Anna ran a hand along the horse's hind leg. "I think it would be a disaster in the making. They'd need nourishment and water, and we're not even sure we'll have enough of that for ourselves."

"Princess is right, Jess," Prescott chimed in. "I don't know how they've survived this long with the limited natural water resources. Plus, for all we know, they've been grazing on contaminated grass. Doesn't seem that moving out with sick animals would be of any more benefit than traveling without them."

Anna nodded. "Their stomachs are extremely delicate. If they eat something that is poisonous or disagrees with their typical diet, it could easily kill them. Horses don't have the capacity to vomit, so colic would always be a huge risk. My guess is these horses have not been out on their own since Day Zero. They would have been dead long before now if they were. Somebody was caring for them until recently, the people who lived here, or maybe the people in town." She shrugged. "As much as I would love for them to be with us, I think they would be more hindrance than help," Anna concluded.

Baumer studied Anna's expression and saw the disappointment and despair in it. "Great," she responded in a deflated voice. "So what do we do with them?"

"Shoot them, I guess," Prescott suggested. "Put them out of their misery so they don't have to face the inevitable."

"Not a good idea," Maguire said from the doorway.

The trio was startled at hearing her voice, and then amused by her attire. Even Prescott cracked a smile.

"Why not?" Jess asked. "Good to see you up and about, by the way."

Maguire drew in a deep, clearly painful breath. "First, unless we have silencers, the shots will echo. No matter how far we are from town, we can't take the chance of the people there hearing. In all likelihood, they have horses too, and could catch up with us long before we could get out of Dodge. Even if they don't hear the shots, if they have horses and if these did originally come from town, the townsfolk might come looking for these strays. If they find the carcasses, it will alert them that someone has been here. It wouldn't take long for them to be on our tail."

"I hate it when she makes sense," Prescott grumbled.

"Then we're back to square one," Baumer said. "Damn it. Do we dare risk one more night of rest, or should we pack up what we can carry again and hit the road?"

"I vote for hitting the road," Maguire said.

Anna looked at her appraisingly. "Are you up to it?"

"She was probably born up to it," Prescott said, removing the rope harnesses from two of the horses.

"Doc, if you feed me aspirin and a couple of those antibiotics per day, will that help me?" When he nodded, she continued. "Then double up all the dosages, and we can get going." She stifled a cough. "Don't worry, I won't cough and give us away."

Chapter Twenty-One

It had been almost three days since they had departed from the abandoned house, and two and a half days since the Jeep ran out of gas. The quintet had traveled quite a distance, with Prescott in the lead and Maguire covering their tracks as best she could. Maguire checked around and behind her for signs of being pursued. So far, no sign of any pursuit, but she knew it would be folly to let their guard down.

Anna had started limping, and so had fallen behind the others.

"Please...I can't walk anymore. My feet are bleeding," Anna said reluctantly.

Prescott looked skyward in exasperation as she blew out a sigh, then she looked over at Maguire. "We need to make tracks. If our presence at the house has been discovered and we are being followed, our pursuers might not be that far behind us. And we have at least another day's travel, even if we don't run into any difficult terrain."

Maguire nodded. "And?"

"We're not leaving her." Baumer's command tone invited no argument.

"She can't walk!" Prescott barked. She indicated the open area through which they had been hiking. "We cannot make camp here. We're sitting ducks. We'd be better off shooting ourselves rather than waiting for the alternatives."

Baumer stepped closer and got into Prescott's face. "We are not leaving her. I still outrank everyone here, and we aren't leaving her. That's an order!"

"And how many times do I have to remind you that there is no military anymore! There's no ranking system anymore. We agreed to be a team, you are not in charge!" Prescott argued.

"That's right, we're a team, and Anna is a part of that

team."

Maguire looked around, keeping watch for movement in front, behind, and off to the sides. "Could we manage to walk and talk? Even standing here is making us an easy target."

"She just said she can't walk," Baumer reiterated.

"I'll carry her."

Baumer, Maguire, and Prescott turned to look at Porras. He was crouched beside Anna, removing her torn canvas sneakers to look at her blistered, bloody feet.

Prescott spoke up. "That means you will be unable to shoot or defend yourself if we get ambushed."

"I'll carry her piggyback. She can carry my rifle and—"

"No," Prescott said firmly. "We may need your muscle in other areas. Do you think you can carry her, as well as both backpacks and both rifles?"

"I don't think that'll be a problem, but she needs to take the pressure off her feet. She'll be lucky if they don't get re-infected," Porras said in a tone that brooked no naysaying as he stared into Prescott's eyes as if daring her to object.

Prescott blinked and walked back to Anna. She extended her hand as she blew out an angry breath. "C'mon. I can carry you piggyback."

Everyone, including Anna, looked at Prescott as if she'd finally lost her mind.

Prescott noticed their expressions. "What? Look, I'm tired of being slowed down and I'm tired of Baumer freaking out every time we say anything about her little princess here." Prescott waggled her fingers at Anna. "Come on, let's go. Last offer, or I'm out of here without any of you."

Anna stood, and Porras helped her onto Prescott's back. "Damn, girl, don't you eat?" Prescott said. "You're lighter than my duffel."

Anna remained silent as they resumed their trek.

"I'll tell you what, though…we come under fire, and I'm dropping you on your skinny little ass, got it?"

Anna gripped Prescott's neck tightly. "Will it shut you up if I say yes? Because I am so tired of being your whipping girl."

Prescott grunted and continued walking. Without a word, Doc grabbed Anna's bag and fell into line. Maguire looked at

Baumer and rolled her eyes. It was going to be a very long day.

***

Anna had actually fallen asleep and that made her a bit heavier, but that didn't bother Prescott, as it also kept her quiet. Prescott carried Anna approximately a mile before trading with Baumer, who toted Anna another three-quarters of a mile before they came upon a densely covered area in which to make camp.

Baumer and Prescott set up the tent while Maguire laid out a perimeter trap. When their meager amenities had been set up, Porras tended to Anna's feet. He cleaned and disinfected them, then wrapped them up and left her seated on her sleeping bag.

The only other meal they'd had that day was jerky, nuts, and dried fruit. Still, they decided not to risk having a fire, so dinner entailed handing out one of the last two MREs, which they shared. Three of the four settled to eat while the fifth stood sentry.

"I'll take first watch," Anna volunteered.

"You normally have last watch," Baumer countered.

"I know, but that's when we have to make breakfast. Besides, I got a chance to doze earlier, so I'm more rested," Anna reasoned.

"Doze? Christ, you were out," Prescott griped.

"Fine! I slept!" Anna stood up and painfully hobbled off to her post.

Baumer glared at Prescott. "Why are you so hard on her?"

"Why are you so easy on her? This isn't Girl Scout camp! We're in this for our lives, and you handle her with kid gloves." Prescott leaned back against a boulder.

"Look, Prescott, so she's had a hard time keeping up. We are well aware that she doesn't have our training, and there was no way we could leave her on her own," Maguire said.

"It's not like she's had an easy time of it. Jesus, Pres, she was gang raped for four days and in shock when we found her," Baumer reminded.

"You know I never would have left her there, but it pissed me off that she thought we were as bad as the guys who raped her."

"She wasn't wrong. We *are* as bad as those guys," Baumer said emphatically. "In our own way, we are. She was right to be wary of us."

"If we hadn't come along, she would have died. Either they'd have killed her when they were done with her, or the wilderness would have claimed her. She has absolutely no survival skills. Hell, she doesn't even have street smarts. Sure the little princess can cook, but that's only useful as long as she's provided with something to prepare. I'm sorry you think I'm so rough on her, but so far she hasn't proven that she's an asset. Everybody here has a skill we need, except for the princess." Prescott's tirade ended abruptly, then continued more softly. "Is it so hard to forget that we went from the 21st Century back into the Stone Age in a matter of minutes? It's survival of the fittest. It has to be."

Maguire was breaking down her weapon to clean it, an unlit cigarette dangled from her lips. "Fine, so she wasn't prepared for anything like this. Neither were we. Yeah, we were trained, but really, who of us here ever saw anything like this happening in our lifetime? 9/11 was one thing, but this was another entirely. Not everyone we run into is going to have the training and combat skills we have. We can't fault the kid for not knowing what to do, any more than she could fault us for not knowing how to act at a fucking cotillion…or something equally as debutante."

Prescott was silent as she absorbed Maguire's words.

Porras scratched the back of his neck. "I know I'm not a part of your elite trio, but I have to tell you, for what she's been through and the condition her feet are in? She's pretty amazing."

"Come on, Doc. You're a guy and she's attractive. She and Jess may be the last straight women you meet, so of course you'd think she's pretty amazing," Prescott said.

"He's right, Pres. You really need to back off," Maguire warned.

"We've got another day, two at the most," Baumer said. "Once we get to Noble's, you won't ever have to deal with her again."

Prescott shook her head. "Look, I know she's not a bad kid.

I know this situation has been horrible for her. I'm not that much of a hard-ass bitch. My concern is that she'll inadvertently get us killed. I know she's trying, but these aren't war games. We don't get back up if we lose the fight. We don't get to go out and slam back a beer and talk about how we can do better next time. It's hard enough to watch my own ass, you know?"

"I'll watch her ass," Baumer said seriously.

"Of course you will," Prescott said with a smirk. "You've been doing a pretty good job so far. When did you turn to the fairer sex, Jess?"

"I haven't!" Baumer snapped.

"Waste of time, anyway. No one will be getting in those pants anytime soon. Even if she was into women, she's probably been scared away from any kind of intimacy for a long while," Prescott offered.

"Prescott, I understand where your thinking is coming from, but I do have to ask—would you like to die today?" Maguire's voice was quiet, controlled but dangerous. "I can make that happen. Drop your body in a ditch right now and not feel a fecking thing. Just keep walking down that road you're pounding. Just say one more undeserved word about that young lady."

"Okay, well, this is where I go take my nap." Porras rose to his feet. "Will I still be fourth watch?"

"We'll wake you when it's your turn," Maguire said. "Try to get some rest."

He nodded at her, and then squinted at Prescott. "I understand what makes you so bitter, and also unnecessarily crude, but speaking for myself, I could do with less of it." Porras crawled into the tent.

Maguire and Baumer watched him close the flap and then looked at Prescott.

She shrugged and sighed. "Whatever."

Maguire turned and invaded Prescott's personal space. "Care to test that *whatever*?"

"Back up, shithead."

Maguire stood stock still. "Make me."

Prescott reached for Maguire's collar, then suddenly froze and looked down. The point of Maguire's blade was playing along her ribcage.

"Back the fuck up on that girl and give her a bit more credit, or I will gut you like a fish and not feel a thing about it." Maguire sheathed her blade, spun on her heel, and walked away without looking back.

***

"Maguire. Pssssssst. Maguire, wake up," Porras whispered urgently from his guard post. The little hairs on the back of his neck were standing up. "Mag—"

"I'm right here," she said as she knelt beside him.

"Where'd… I thought you were over there, asleep."

"I was, until I heard your heart rate go up." Maguire's voice was hushed.

Porras stared at her. "You can't hear my heart rate." He studied her as her eyebrow shot up near her hairline. "Never mind." He returned his attention to the valley behind them. "I heard voices. They sound distant but close enough, you know?"

"Like you hear them louder with every wave of wind?"

"Yeah. I'm not trained like you. They could be anyone going anywhere." Porras shrugged.

"Better to be prepared."

Prescott slid up on the other side of the doc. "What are you thinking, Maguire? Think it's people from the town?"

"I'm thinking they would have to be unduly obsessed to follow us this far. However, I do believe a scouting mission is in order. I want to know for sure whether we should be concerned."

"And you want to find out how many there are," Porras said.

Maguire shook her head. "Not necessarily. If they aren't after us or they're not coming our way, their number doesn't matter."

"How 'bout I do the recon, and you get Jess and Anna ready to move out?" Prescott offered.

"Why you?" Porras asked before Maguire could answer.

"Because if I get caught, it's not as big a loss to the team as Maguire would be," Prescott admitted. "My skills are not as sharp as they used to be. Maguire is a born survivor and can think on her feet a lot faster. You all need someone like that. Jess can think for herself, but these split-second decisions cannot be left to chance. With Maguire, you can be certain that none of what happens will be by chance."

Maguire nodded. "So, what's your signal?"

Prescott tapped the LED flashlight with the red lens. "You're going to have to keep eyes on me. Every hundred feet I get, I'll send you one flash so you'll know where to look for my signal. Once I get close enough, I'll send you three short flashes. If they are moving toward us, I'll send you a single ten second flash. If they are moving away, I'll send you two five second flashes and then return to camp."

Maguire nodded and looked at Porras. "Do you have the night vision glasses?"

He held them up. "Yes, but I didn't see anything."

"She'll need those more than you will." Maguire took them and gave them to Prescott, and then handed Porras the regular field glasses. "All you have to do is stay on her red light. I'll go wake up Jess and Anna. We'll be ready to move on your signal."

***

Prescott moved out, and Porras followed her movement with startling clarity. He had been concerned that he would lose her, that he would somehow do something to cause harm to Prescott or the rest of his group. He could not stand the thought that he could be the cause of Anna reliving what she had endured at the hands of scavengers, or any of the women experiencing a death like Szabo's. That would be too much for him to bear. He had been very fortunate to have been rescued by them. They were a team and, although he lacked their skill and training, they made him feel like an equal member. He couldn't, wouldn't, let them down.

Finally Prescott sent the three short flashes to indicate her proximity to the brigade of unknown travelers. "She's there," he whispered, loudly enough to be heard a short distance away.

Without responding, Maguire helped Anna and Baumer

The End

finish packing up their campsite as quietly as possible, while Porras watched and waited.

Chapter Twenty-Two

Prescott settled herself in a thicket about a hundred yards away from what appeared to be a disorganized contingent of survivors. She studied the group, first and foremost, to determine their direction. They were moving slowly, but definitely toward the southeast. She decided to keep watching them long enough to be sure they were not going to reverse their route. Prescott could hear the rumble of several voices blending, but there were two voices that rose above the rest. They were arguing about whether to continue moving or make camp. The disagreement persisted, even as they kept moving further away. After another five minutes of surveillance, Prescott felt safe enough to signal Doc that the group was not a threat. She waited until they were out of sight before she returned to her own campsite.

When Prescott reached their perimeter, she saw Maguire smoking a cigarette, making sure the glow from the ash was behind her hand. As Prescott drew level with Maguire, Porras rose and accompanied her the rest of the way.

***

Baumer and Anna were seated on the ground, backs leaning against the same rock. "What'd you see?" Baumer asked as Prescott approached.

"Unknown." Prescott shrugged. "There were maybe thirty in the group. I saw a few weapons, shotguns and M16s. They may have had more, but if so, they weren't obvious. They seemed to be dazed civilians, as there was no order to their movement."

"Looking for sanctuary," Anna commented.

"Probably," Prescott agreed. "Their current concern seems

to be to find a place to camp."

"Moving under the cover of darkness won't help them if they have no real strategy about finding whatever it is they are looking for in the long run," Baumer said.

"One thing you've got to say for them," Maguire stabbed out her cigarette and then fieldstripped it, "thirty of them are still alive, so they must be doing something right. Or…they just haven't yet run into what we have."

"I don't think they would have been a threat if they had come upon us. My gut tells me they probably would have just acknowledged us and moved on."

"Fortunately, we didn't have to rely on your gut," Maguire said. "I'm surprised that after all we've been through, you can still be so naïve."

Prescott rolled her eyes. "And I'm surprised that after all we've been through, you still think I have a naïve bone in my body. The general demeanor of the group appeared to be non-confrontational. They are traveling at night; they have no transportation other than their feet, and no means, other than on their persons, to carry any kind of arsenal. They were loud. They had kids with them. Everything about them screamed survivors, not mercenaries. You're not the only one with instincts, Maguire."

"Shut it. Both of you," Baumer said, weary of their pissing contest. "Okay then, since we're all up and packed, we might as well start moving, too." She stood up, extended a hand to Anna, and helped her up. "Which way, Pres?"

Prescott flipped open her old-fashioned compass, read it, and pointed to her left. "That way."

***

Prescott read aloud a sign that was nailed to a tree: "You will never know how much it has cost my generation to preserve your freedom. I hope you will use it wisely."

"Is that sign from Noble?" Baumer asked, as they all stopped to catch their breath. They had been walking since before dawn, and it seemed that every mile was marked by Prescott claiming they were getting closer.

"Yes, Ma'am."

"Noble said that? Was she in the Wars of 9/11?" Anna asked innocently.

"No," Prescott said. "I mean, yes, she was still employed by the government at that time. She warned them that something was up. Hell, she was the intercept analyst who got the FBI agent's memo about the flight schools in Florida. She shoved it up the line and was ignored. But no, those are the words of John Adams, our second U.S. President." Prescott counted the words on the sign. "Twenty-two words, twenty-two more miles."

Anna's shoulders slumped. It might as well have been twenty-two hundred more miles. "That's another day, at least."

"We'll be by there midday tomorrow," Prescott said. "There should be another sign at the nineteen-mile mark and the fifteen mile mark. Noble said if we need it, there is a secluded area to make camp for the night at the fifteen-mile mark."

"So, seven more miles, mostly uphill, 'til we make camp." Porras surveyed the mountains before them. "Hopefully most of tomorrow is downhill."

"We're in the Salmon Mountain range, so once we go the seven miles, we'll see. Depending on the direction the sign tells us to go, we may not be going downhill but at least we could be on level ground." Prescott said. "I know nothing about this compound, other than that it exists."

"Let's get moving," Maguire said, taking the lead. "We need to step it up if we're going to reach mile fifteen before dark." She turned to Anna. "You up to it?"

Anna's feet were still tender, but at least they had begun to heal. "If it means finally getting to where we're going and that we'll be able to rest, I'll walk on stumps if I have to."

***

By the time they had reached the fifteen-mile sign, the sun had set and darkness almost completely surrounded them.

Maguire stood the closest to the post, so she read the words aloud: "Cowards die many times before their deaths; the valiant never taste of death but once."

"Another John Adams quote?" Anna asked.

"No," Maguire said. "William Shakespeare. It's a quote from Julius Caesar. Fifteen words, fifteen miles."

"I think I like Noble already, Pres. She's not only clever, she's clearly well read," Baumer noted. "Come on, troops, let's make camp."

They searched for the secluded area in which they were to set up and discovered it was a cave. There were two chambers—an outer section, with several natural rock chimneys to release smoke, and a large inner section. They settled in the second alcove. Baumer gathered twigs and branches for a fire, grateful that they could build one without being afraid that someone would track them from its glow. This night, they would be warm when they hunkered down in their sleeping bags.

While Anna and Baumer got the fire started, Doc stood guard at the mouth of the cave.

Maguire and Prescott, who had gone hunting for their supper, returned about half an hour later. Maguire was carrying a marmot carcass.

"Oh my God!" Anna pointed at the dead animal. "Look at the size of that squirrel! Did radiation do that?"

"It's not a squirrel, although I think it's from the same family," Prescott said. "But it's about a ten pounder, so we should all be able to have a decent meal tonight."

"Is it safe to eat?" Doc asked.

"Noble said the radiation has dissipated and they've been doing fine with area game. I'm assuming anything within a certain radius should also be okay," Prescott said.

"Kind of a big assumption to take for all of us," Doc said.

Maguire set the carcass on the ground. "Seriously, Doc, if I didn't think we'd be okay, I'd say so." She removed her knife from one of her utility pockets and was about to start skinning the animal when Baumer stopped her.

"Do not do that in here, Mags. I'm not going to sleep in a confined area and have to smell guts all night long. Take it outside."

Maguire put her knife away and grinned at Baumer. "Yes, Mom." She picked up the marmot and exited the chamber.

"Doc, there's a stream about five minutes from here. Help me top up our water supply, would you?" Prescott asked.

Porras nodded. "I hope your friend's place has their own filtration system. I'm not so sure our filters are good anymore."

"At this point, any filter is better than no filter," Prescott said as she collected the water containers.

***

When they hit the one mile marker, it was distinguished by a standard "No Trespassing" sign. In the upper right hand corner was an Army unit insignia—crossed daggers with lightning bolts for blades behind a chess piece knight, for Psychological Operations.

"This is it," Prescott said. "That's Noble's PsyOps crest. Just a mile in, and we're there."

"Fecking mindbenders," Maguire grunted, then grinned. "I love those guys."

"What do they do?" Anna asked as she adjusted her rucksack.

Baumer beat Prescott to the explanation. "Psychological Operations is an Army unit whose job is to get into the mind of the enemy."

"Noble was recruited right out of high school. PsyOps was just starting up and her test scores from her college entrance exam showed an aptitude toward a tactical, operational, and strategic mindset. So the military sent her to a post-affiliated college to study psychology. While she was there, they found that she had a great mind for intelligence analysis, too. She did four more years on the Army's dime, getting her Masters. A military think tank recognized her potential, so they hired her. She really is amazing," Prescott added.

"Jaysus, Prescott, could ya just have an orgasm already so we can get moving?" Maguire wiped sweat from her sunglasses.

Prescott flashed Maguire her middle finger as Anna giggled. Doc just smirked and shook his head.

"It does sound like you're in love with her, Pres," Baumer joked.

"Nah, not love. But a whole lot of admiration." Prescott's

grin was genuine.

Baumer arched an eyebrow. "And a little history there, maybe?"

"Yes, but way before Nance. Nothing more than a frowned-upon fling, because we risked fraternization charges as well as being bounced out under Don't Ask, Don't Tell. We were better friends than lovers anyway." Prescott looked up at the dark clouds gathering in the sky. "Damn! It's hot now, but looks like we're going to get a nasty storm soon. We better move. One mile, people."

Chapter Twenty-Three

The skies opened up and they were thoroughly drenched by the time they approached the outer perimeter of the compound. The walls were high, with spikes affixed atop the huge, concrete barricades. There was razor wire coiled around the spikes and barbed wire soldered to the sides in a pattern that would discourage even the most ambitious challenger from trying to scale the exterior of the fortress' enclosure. The estate walls appeared to extend for miles, and it seemed that every quarter mile, an impenetrable watchtower stood menacingly, as though a steel reinforced, cement sentry was guarding the periphery.

When they were less than a quarter mile from the entrance, the group was braced by four heavily armed women.

One woman took two steps ahead of the rest. "You Prescott?" she asked. "I'm Carrie." Her eyes locked on Doc, and her M16 was immediately raised and aimed; the other three followed suit.

With Carrie's rifle sights trained on the doctor, Prescott didn't immediately notice that the other guards had weapons pointed at her and her company.

"Yeah, I'm Prescott. What the fuck's going on here? Why are you drawing down on us? Noble is expecting us."

"You said nothing about bringing a man with you," Carrie accused.

"Actually, I did. He's a doctor. He will be extremely useful—"

"He's a man," Carrie snarled.

Baumer took a step forward. "He's a part of our team!"

"We have our own medical team, and men aren't allowed in the compound," Carrie retorted. "Noble's orders."

"Fuck her." Maguire's hand twitched above her holstered sidearm.

"That'll never happen," Carrie said with a sneer.

"Okay, let's all stand down here," Prescott said. "Let's call a truce. Noble knows me."

Finally, Doc said, "Look, I…I can stay outside while you get this straightened out."

"Not gonna happen, Doc," Maguire growled.

"It'll happen if Noble commands it," Carrie corrected smugly.

"Look…Carrie, is it?" Baumer asked.

Prescott knew that Jess was trying to keep her voice civil, though she was clearly chewing on the inside of her cheek to prevent herself from screaming at the woman.

"Yes, Carrie," she answered, acknowledging Baumer as the leader of her group.

"Carrie, I'm Lieutenant Jess Baumer. Can you please contact Noble and advise her of the situation? We've come a long way, and we'd like to get off our feet and get dry."

***

The group was marched into the inner compound, with Dr. Porras blindfolded and Anna and Baumer each with a hand on his arms to guide him. Maguire walked behind him, ready to catch him if he took a spill. Her guts churned with an anger that was beginning to boil over into hate. She never would have surrendered her weapons if Baumer hadn't quietly ordered her to. As angry as she was, she took in every detail about the layout and armament of the compound without being obvious. If this all went to shit, she was going to know where to shoot once she got her rifle back, and she would start with the bitch that'd pulled a gutting knife out of a sheath on her belt and held it on the doctor while another guard blindfolded him.

Prescott kept trying to talk some sense into Carrie, who was leading them, but her words fell on deaf ears.

They reached a well-put-together ranch-style house, where they were halted. Carrie pulled Dr. Porras away from the group. "Take those four inside. He'll wait out here," she barked to the sentry.

"It's pissing down rain. At least let him stand on the

porch," Maguire ground out between gnashing teeth.

"He'll stand where I tell him to," Carrie snapped back. "And you will shut the fuck up."

Maguire's face went blank. "Like hell," she growled.

Carrie turned and swung her knife in one smooth motion, and Maguire smiled evilly as she sidestepped and moved in. A split second later, the guard squealed as her knee exploded with pain.

Maguire ripped the knife out of the woman's hand, then with a twist of her own body was suddenly holding Carrie as a shield, with the knife to her throat.

"See now, you, me, and him are going to stand on the porch while the others unfeck this situation." Maguire was in full Irish mode. "If any of the fools standing around out here decide to try to rescue you, you'll be gurgling your good-byes." She pressed the blade against the woman's throat with just enough pressure to reinforce her threat. "Move."

Carrie signaled her crew to stay where they were, and Maguire slowly walked her captive up the porch steps. With each step, the pressure Carrie put on her knee elicited a grunt of pain.

"You good out here, Mags?" Baumer asked quietly, as one of the compound women opened the screen door.

"Oh, just grand." Maguire flashed a smile that did not reach her eyes. She tightened her hold on Carrie's throat. "Quit yer bitching. Yer knee's only dislocated. At least yer out of the rain. Doc, take off that damned blindfold." She watched as he slowly complied, then dropped it to the ground.

Maguire and Doc watched the group disappear through the doorway. He tried to speak, had to swallow, and then swallow again. "Maguire, thank you." Then he turned to the other woman. "Miss, would you be okay with me taking a look at your knee?"

"Excuse me?" Carrie sputtered, despite the chokehold. "Men."

Maguire pulled her arm a touch tighter. "He's a doctor, you addle brained eejit." She glanced at Porras. "You can fix her up later, Doc, if I feel generous."

***

The three new arrivals waited as Carrie's second-in-command knocked once on the office door. A soft "enter" was barely audible, but the woman opened the door and stepped inside.

Rachel Noble was, as Prescott remembered her, a stern-looking woman in her mid-sixties, whose personality and manner of speaking would tolerate no disorder. She was physically fit and her older-style, tailored military camo fatigues showed off her athletic frame. She had always been a force to be reckoned with, and now was no different.

Noble sat behind her desk, reading a ledger. She looked up, obviously expecting to see her captain. "Where's Carrie?"

Prescott pushed her way past the escort and glared into the grey-green eyes. "Carrie is on the porch nursing a probable busted knee, with our resident psychotic mick holding a knife to her throat. And for once, I actually agree with the nutcase."

Noble maintained her calm demeanor, but barely. "Nice to see you finally made it, Pres. And what the hell are you talking about?"

"Did you or did you not get our last message? The one where I specifically told you we would be coming in with five total, including a male doctor?" Prescott demanded.

"Yes, I did. I specifically instructed my guards to follow my protocol."

Prescott was seething, and she did not try to hide her anger. "Does your protocol include disarming us, insulting the doctor, blindfolding him, pulling a knife on him, and making him stand out in the rain while we catch up on old times?"

Noble processed the words quickly. "They blindfolded him? I never told them to do that."

"Well then, your little Nazi is micromanaging," Prescott spat.

"I'm not inclined to allow strangers who won't be living here, especially male strangers, to learn our layout. That's also why my office is close to the gate, so there was no need to blindfold him. The rest of the 'welcome' will also be dealt with." Her voice was flat with anger.

"Oh, I think hell will freeze over before your Carrie does anything like this again." Baumer stepped into the room. "Baumer, Jessica. The wallflower behind me is Anna."

"You were right, Pres. She is a spitfire. Good to meet you, Lieutenant."

"I wish I could return the sentiment. The greeting at the gate left me feeling a little…unwelcome." Baumer was bluntly honest. "I get that you don't trust the doc, but we've never met either and you didn't blindfold me."

"And I told you that would be dealt with." Noble stared back at Baumer. "Almost all of my women have been horribly abused by men. I'm not going to change the way we do things just because someone is feeling butt hurt," she answered just as bluntly.

"Noble, I love you in so many ways, but this is more than hurt feelings. Carrie drew a knife and put it to Doc's throat. One misinterpreted move, and our doctor would be dead, and then, quite honestly, so would your entire guard. Maguire would have killed them. I would have helped her."

Noble blinked in clear surprise. "From the messages we've exchanged, I got the distinct impression that you hate that particular member of your party." When Prescott didn't respond, Noble sighed. "On the porch?" Four head nods answered her. "All right then, let's go sort this out."

Without another word, she circled around her desk and stalked out of the office, the others trailing behind her like a row of ducklings.

She pushed the porch door open with great care and then stepped outside. The situation hadn't changed. The captain of Noble's guard was being held with a knife to her throat while standing awkwardly with all of her weight on one leg.

A lanky, rain-soaked man was quietly pleading with one very intense woman. "Maguire, you really have to let me look at her knee."

"I said I'd think about it, Doc. Perhaps."

Noble cleared her throat as the others from the house joined her on the porch. "Carrie, I don't recall my orders including any blindfolds," she looked pointedly at the knife, "or you being held hostage."

"Noble, I was just..." Carrie's hesitation made her sound like a disobedient child who was about to make up an excuse.

"Ah no. You were a right bitch when your boss wasn't here to see it, so just own up to it." Maguire flicked the blade against skin.

"I apologize to you all for this...misunderstanding." Noble was clearly choosing her words carefully. "Especially to you, Doctor." Her tone was sincere, and Noble met his eyes steadily.

"I know you probably won't believe me, but I truly understand," Porras responded with a wry expression. "Now may I please take a look at Carrie's knee, Maguire?"

Maguire released her chokehold and watched with disinterest as the woman dropped to the ground. She totally ignored the grunted "fuck" that followed the thumping sound.

"Oh, that's mature, Maguire," Prescott growled.

"Smitty, you and Dora help Carrie inside. Take her into the study so the doctor can check her knee and do whatever it is he needs to."

"I don't want him touching me!" Carrie yelled as she was assisted into the house.

"Carrie, enough." Noble's voice wasn't loud, but it was firm.

Porras turned his head to look at Noble. "You can put a guard on me, if you'd like."

"Doctor..."

"Porras."

"Doctor Porras, I wish it were not a condition, but..." Noble shrugged as she held the door open.

"My fiancée was an OB/GYN. We both worked in women's clinics and saw our share of abused women," he explained with quiet dignity. "If being guarded helps put others at ease, I have no objection."

"Smitty, keep an eye on the doctor. Dora, get him whatever supplies he asks for," Noble called after the two women escorting the injured Carrie. She stepped aside to let Porras enter the house.

Noble turned to Maguire and held out her hand. "The knife, if you please."

Maguire contemplated the weapon and then smiled.

"Surely." She drove the point of the knife deep into the porch railing and stared at Noble in challenge.

Noble repressed a smile. Her eyes went from the embedded knife, back to Maguire. "Color me intimidated, Sergeant Maguire," Noble said with a chuckle. "Now, if we can go to my office to sort out this cluster?"

Chapter Twenty-Four

Following a brief meeting with the new arrivals and some of her guards, Noble sent everyone but Prescott to get some sleep or go back to duty. Noble took the comfortable looking chair nearest Prescott and looked her in the eye. "Now, how are you really?" There was true concern in her voice.

"I'll let you know after I decompress." Prescott rolled her glass between her hands. "It's been a motherfuck getting here, and the reception was not at all what I expected."

"Nor I," Noble admitted as she averted her eyes. "I'm very disappointed in Carrie, and I will be letting her know that in private. She was just promoted to Captain of the Guard, and I think it's gone to her head."

"My advice is to smack her down while she still *has* a head. Maguire takes no prisoners." Prescott took a deep breath. "As far as your Carrie is concerned, I'm giving you fair warning that she is also on my shit list. She was wrong, so very wrong, Rachel."

"I understand. It will be addressed ASAP."

"That would be appreciated." Prescott nodded. "I do think that our group can bring something to the table here that will benefit all of us."

"I actually pulled Baumer's record. She has excellent officer evaluation reports. She'll make a fine leader, I think."

Prescott grinned. "Yeah. Jess was a damn good NCO. I think that's what made her a fine officer. And you know how hard I am on those people." She chuckled. "I have yet to see her leave a soldier behind, but she also picks up strays, if you get my meaning."

"The doctor was a good stray to pick up. Young Miss Anna?" Noble prodded.

"Smart, not much backbone, but she'll eventually get there.

She's had a lifetime of being stepped on, but she's done okay after she had a little time to get used to all this insanity. I pushed her hard, every button I could think of. She bent a few times, but she did not break. Don't tell the others I said this, but she even made MREs taste good." Prescott took a sip of her drink. "Nice beer, by the way."

"Thank you. We have a small microbrewery. It helps take the edge off the tension of being cooped up together during the long winters," Noble said proudly. Prescott knew the sanctuary was her third pride and joy. "Maguire?"

Prescott groaned. "I'll be honest, I waver between hating her and being grateful that she's here. I don't have a clue as to what makes her tick, other than that she's completely loyal to Baumer. I told you she was nuts, and I don't think I'm too far wrong."

Noble laughed softly. "Oh, Devon, you have been traveling with one highly trained, extremely jacked-up individual."

Prescott blinked. "You got access to her full record, didn't you? I tried, but only got the 'way too clean' record on file."

"You, my dear, have the keys to the information kingdom. I, on the other hand, helped build that kingdom. Let me ask you something. Why would a soldier's record be so sanitized that you could not get *all* of it?"

"She's an operator, or she screwed the pooch incredibly bad," Prescott answered automatically.

Noble's eyes twinkled. "Or both."

"Or both," Prescott agreed.

"Korea. She and four of her team ended up executing a delaying action that helped the rest of her company escape to attempt a quick retreat and re-supply. When they couldn't rejoin their unit, she and her team then went on several hit-and-run missions. During one of those missions, they hooked up with an Irish Defense Force team getting its backside kicked. The tide was turned, but it was eight days before anyone could get to them." Noble sipped her beer. "Eighty percent walking wounded, twenty percent killed in action. When they were evac'd, she was running around with a through-and-through to her left side."

Prescott snorted. "So, she's superwoman?"

"No. She is, however, very pissed off when she loses a soldier, especially when those soldiers die for no good reason. The elements were in place, honestly, they should have sent help, but they were too busy trying to figure out who screwed the pooch on that one. I think she knew all their excuses were bull." Noble paused to let that sink in. "The Irish government pinned its highest medal on her and, once she was back in shape, invited her to the Fianoglach. Unlike most countries, Ireland opened their commando school to women years ago. In its entire history, they've had two Irish women attempt it and one American. Maguire was ten years older than most of their candidates, and she aced the damn school."

Finally, some things were starting to click for Prescott. "She has said they were trained by U.S. Army Rangers."

Noble nodded. "Originally. And just for shits and giggles, a number of their instructors went through Ranger school before the damn world ended. Our government was going to pin the DSC on her."

Prescott nearly choked on her beer. "The Distinguished Service Cross? As in, the second highest medal for bravery in combat?"

"That would be the one. She declined, told the committee to give it to the men who died while they waited eight days for help that never came. In not so polite terms. The president was fit to be tied. He couldn't force her to take the medal, but he could command the Army to make her life miserable as punishment for her 'insubordination.' It didn't help that she took a baseball bat to her CO's car. And, no, even I don't know the reason for that particular outburst."

"So, she's not really crazy, she just basically doesn't give a flying fuck."

"Oh, I think she does, but only when she feels like it. I think she can do a lot to improve our forces and defenses, but..." Noble searched for the wording.

"We have to give her a reason to give a fuck. I'll talk to Jess, see what we can come up with," Prescott offered.

***

That afternoon, after everything had calmed down to a semi-reasonable tempestuousness, everyone rested and was fed a warm meal. Noble left the clean-up work to whoever's turn it was so that she could concentrate on her new guests. She was sure Prescott would stay and possibly Baumer, but was not so sure about the rest. Young Anna seemed very loyal to Maguire, as well as to Doctor Porras. The doc did, indeed, seem like a very nice man, as men went. It was unfortunate that he had to be under restriction, but if she bent the rules for one… Well, if Prescott trusted him, there was no harm in showing him around before she evicted him. Why be proud of what she had built if she couldn't show it off? And maybe seeing what she had done, how well she had prepared for the inevitable, would change the mercurial Maguire's mind. Noble wouldn't usually have stooped to courting anyone, but Maguire wasn't just anyone. Maguire was, to use a cliché, an army of one. Noble might not like Maguire's attitude, but she knew talent when she saw it, and she would rather have Maguire on her side than on someone else's.

"So, how about a tour?" Noble offered to the group of newcomers.

"I'll pass," Maguire said with authentic disinterest.

"I would think you would want to see the set-up, see exactly what's going on here and what we have to offer rather than denying yourself visual intel." Just as she thought it might, the challenge piqued Maguire's interest.

"Prescott told us all about this place. Imaginative and intuitive, but I wouldn't expect less from anyone of your training and nature."

"I didn't tell you the half of it," Prescott said. "You really should see it before you pass judgment."

"I'm not passing judgment, numbnuts," Maguire flared, "I just don't—"

"Mags!" Baumer interrupted. "Come with, as a favor to me, okay?"

Maguire stared Prescott down before she turned her gaze to Baumer. She snapped to attention. "Ma'am, yes, Ma'am."

Baumer rolled her eyes. "Come on, Mags." There was frustration in her voice.

"Is Doc allowed on the tour?" Maguire asked.

"Of course," Noble said amiably. "I personally have nothing against your doctor. He seems like a well-mannered, intelligent, capable gentleman. I can't just change the canon of the compound. You being a person of order can certainly understand regulations."

"All the order in the world didn't stop a third world war. Sometimes rules can be changed, should be changed." Maguire sounded a little less like a petulant child.

Noble rose from her chair. "Not that rule." She gestured toward the door. "Shall we?"

All but Maguire stood, and Baumer tilted her head toward Maguire in a silent plea. Maguire sighed, but followed everyone out of the dining cabin.

"Just do me a favor," Maguire said to Noble, as they all headed for the cabin that served as a dayroom. "Talk *to* Doc, not about him. He is right here with us." She gave Porras a playful swat on the arm. He smiled at her and nodded his thanks.

Noble led them to a building that looked like a mountain chalet retreat. The interior was an open space with kitchen facilities, a refrigerator/freezer equipped with dry ice, and a precursory communication system that included a HAM radio. Several flat screen televisions were all dark, indicating no connectivity to the outside world, and an open pit fireplace was surrounded by couches and chairs. It looked like a student lounge on a college campus, complete with bar, pool table, and even old pinball machines.

Next to the door that led to the garage was another ordinary looking door. When Noble opened it, a 2,000-pound iron blast door was revealed. She inserted what looked like an old metal jail key into a slot, turned it, and pulled back on a handle. The sound of seven massive bars sliding into different positions ended in an echoing thud. Noble put a little muscle into swinging the door away from her, and it opened on to a stone-tiled sally port and a second door as thick as the first. Noble repeated the same action with the second blast door. After they walked through that one, they found themselves in an entranceway to a stairwell.

"Holy shit! This is a silo," Maguire said in wonder.

Noble smiled. "Well...not yet. When our country was all about fighting, and staying safe during the Cold War, as you know, the government constructed hundreds of Atlas-F missile silos, preparing for an attack that never came. In the 70s and 80s, they began to abandon the silos. I heard about this one and negotiated to buy it, and the land, at a relatively cheap price. After all, the ones they just deserted, they filled with water. I had a better plan."

"How many acres do you have here?" Baumer asked.

"One hundred and ten. That includes a forest that sustained little damage and an underground water storage tank that initially held 1.5 million gallons. Since Day Zero, we've used about seven hundred thousand gallons. Any rainwater we get now, we run through an extensive filtering system and add to our storage."

"What do you do for power down here?" Doc asked.

"In the beginning, we had to rely on generators and whatever solar power we could harness. Then, thanks to the effects of the pulse, everything went dark for about two weeks. Fortunately, we didn't get hit too badly in the Northwest Territories, of which we now consider ourselves a part, so we are able to harness solar power again, which is good because our gas reserve was getting critical."

Noble led them to a spiral staircase that, after twenty-six winding steps down, opened into a two-level state of the art communication center. It was staffed by four women monitoring a surveillance system with several above ground cameras, operated by a digital system that gave them a 360-degree view of the compound and beyond the reinforced, razor-wired, spiked, exterior walls.

"This used to be the launch control center. Most of the equipment was left behind, so all we had to do was tweak and calibrate. We have highly trained former military personnel who constantly watch all movement on the grounds and around us. There isn't anything that goes on in or around our perimeter that we don't know about."

"What about from the air?" Baumer asked.

"We have radar and Doppler capabilities. Any change in air

density immediately registers there." She pointed to a bank of screens. "We also have the exclusive code to the microwave towers, and access to military and commercial satellites."

"How the hell did you manage that?" Maguire asked, clearly impressed.

"It pays to play nice with people in power and in the Intelligence community. Of course, the towers-to-satellite communication is spotty at best. It will improve in time. When we—and by 'we' I mean the world—can re-establish continuous electricity, we'll be on the boards pretty much before anyone else. We also use advanced fiber optics, which is beneficial because it uses light and electromagnetic waves and is less likely to be susceptible to any electromagnetic interference. Plus, it gives us higher bandwidth and more transmission distance."

Prescott's focus was drawn to one of the workers exiting a clearly marked restroom. "What about septic?"

"Four replenishing wells and an eighteen hundred gallon, in-ground drainage system. Below, we have more for the dorms."

"Is this...climate controlled?" Maguire asked. When Noble nodded, Maguire followed up with, "How did you do that?"

"Natural earth ground temperature. It's almost always 68 degrees."

"What material was used to build this?" Baumer asked.

"As far as we know, it was the standard three-foot-thick epoxy resin infused concrete reinforced with stainless steel mesh."

"Venting?"

"Vent tubes—high circulating, three feet each."

Noble completed the tour of the bi-level Operations area, and when she felt the group was sufficiently impressed, she moved on to another staircase that led to a long tunnel. Noble opened another standard door and escorted the group into the living area. She looked at Maguire. "*This* is the silo."

"How many levels?" Doc asked.

"Ten levels, twelve thousand square feet." She guided them into an area that resembled the above-ground open living space. It had a large screen television, living room, game room, and kitchen area that resembled a mess hall. "Below we have a food storage and prep area. Next floors down are two levels of four-person bedrooms with shared latrine and shower facilities. There are ten two-person rooms for privacy. They are used on a rotating schedule. We have an underground hydroponic grow room for herbs, vegetables, and fruits."

"I thought you said it was safe above ground," Prescott said.

"It is, but we continue to test the soil, mostly out of habit but also from an abundance of caution. Because we weren't a direct hit, we didn't suffer the concentrated radiation so many other areas did. While others are looking at decades before it is safe to grow again, we determined that we were okay to replant within months. In the meantime, we'd been growing underground for years, almost since this compound opened."

"What about meat?" Doc asked.

"We have dairy cows and chickens that we were able to house in a prepared area two floors beneath the barn. They are for milk and eggs only. Since Day Zero, we have all become vegetarians. We were only able to bring the livestock above ground recently, because the air quality checked out and they should be breathing fresh air. We're tapering off feeding them from our reserve and slowly reintroducing them to their natural diets. We are being overly cautious, because our most recent tests indicate the surface soil does hold trace amounts of contaminants. Not much, but even so, we don't want it showing up in our dairy products."

"Why wasn't this area targeted in the strikes?" Anna asked.

"Because this was a site that was decommissioned and pretty much obsolete before the Strategic Arms Limitation Treaty came about, and our enemies had that information. Why waste a nuke on an unpopulated, disarmed area? Fortunately, it can still withstand a direct nuclear hit."

"You had all this and you didn't save any men?" Doc asked. "How do you propose to continue life? Unless you've found a way to create artificial sperm along with your other accomplishments."

Noble smirked. "Even though there are scientists on my staff, we are not that advanced. Men did survive locally, mostly because of what they learned here before they were moved off the compound. All sons of the women on this property are banished on their twelfth birthday. If they reach puberty before that, they are banished then."

Astonished at the idea, Anna asked, "Where do they go?"

"It's not as barbaric as it sounds. There is an old military camp about a mile from town. That's where a majority of the town went when word of the attack came. There are several underground bunkers there. The camp is run by a retired Jarhead general and an Army National Guard two-star and their families. Years ago, when the camp was abandoned by the military, they decided to move onto the property and squat. The government didn't expend any time, money, or energy to remove them so, like me, they cultivated the land and used what was there to create their own compound. The boys go there until they get old enough to decide for themselves where they want to be for their adult life. Some stay, some leave. Their families who live here get to see them any time they want. So, Doctor Porras, to answer your question, good old-fashioned procreation does take place and will continue to take place. Just not on this property."

"Is that camp where I will go?" Doc asked.

"You will be taken into town, which is about two miles from here. You can spend one night at the main boarding house there, and tomorrow, if you'd like, I'm sure someone will arrange to take you to the camp. You will decide whether you want to live there or in town. You cannot stay or live here."

Maguire barked, "That's bullshit."

Doc placed a calming hand on her arm. "No, it's okay. I understand. I don't think I'd be comfortable here anyway."

"Maybe I should go with Doc," Maguire grumbled.

"You could," Noble said affably, "but I would advise against it. The town works with us, but they really don't like 'our kind' living among them. Sooner or later you'd be driven away or end up back here anyway."

Chapter Twenty-Five

Seated in the back of one of the compound's horse-drawn wagons, Maguire accompanied Doc and Lisa, the driver, on the furrowed road into town. It was dark by the time they reached the borough limits. Candles in light posts and hanging paraffin lanterns were the principal illumination for the main street. As the wagon pulled to a stop in front of a big wooden homestead, Maguire could see that flames from a stone fireplace lighted the interior of what she surmised was the boarding house.

An older couple came outside to meet the wagon. "Hello, young lady," the silver-haired man greeted. "Good to see you again. And who have we here?"

"Hi, Mr. and Mrs. Cameron," Lisa said with a warm smile. "This is Sergeant Maguire of the U.S. Army, and this gentleman is Doctor Porras. They and a few others arrived at the compound today from Texas via other states, and the good doctor here needs lodging."

"Are you a real doctor?" Mrs. Cameron asked.

She reminded Maguire of the traditional image of Mrs. Santa Claus—plump and matronly, with white hair, twinkling eyes, and rosy cheeks.

"Yes, I am a full-fledged doctor, Mrs. Cameron. I'm a general practitioner." He extended his hand, which Mr. Cameron grasped. "Nice to meet you both." He shook Mrs. Cameron's hand.

"Is Sergeant Maguire staying, too? Are you two..." Mr. Cameron hesitated, "...together?"

Maguire and Doc exchanged glances. She wanted to burst out laughing at the implied question. Not that Doc was unthinkable as husband or boyfriend material, she had become rather fond of him, but she was sure she was the very image of a stereotypical lesbian. Then again, maybe not, as the Camerons were still waiting for a response.

"No, Ma'am," Maguire said. "Just Doc is staying with you, at least for now. I haven't made up my mind whether or not I will be staying at the compound."

"You will always be welcome here, Sergeant," Mrs. Cameron said warmly. "Rachel Noble has been good to us through all of this. Anything we can do to return the favor, we will gladly do."

Maguire was surprised to hear that. She had somehow gotten the impression that Noble and her crew had a prickly relationship with everybody who wasn't housed at the sanctuary. She nodded at Mrs. Cameron. "Good to know." She watched Doc as he retrieved his few belongings from the wagon. "You'll be okay, Doc?"

His smile seemed sad. "Sure. I'm looking forward to acquainting myself with the Camerons and getting settled. You two," he inclined his head toward Lisa, "should probably start back. It's been a long day."

"That it has, Doc," Maguire agreed.

Lisa climbed back up on the bench seat of the wagon and Maguire was about to join her when Mr. Cameron spoke.

"Sergeant? Lisa said you are in the U.S. Army. I'm—" He glanced at his wife, then back at Maguire. "I mean, we're wondering, is there an Army anymore? Any organized armed services?"

Maguire considered a moment before she answered. "That's a good question, Sir. Right now, we aren't sure ourselves. There are those of us who survived who still consider ourselves bound by our oath, but if you are asking who's in charge of anything, I'm sorry, Sir, I just don't have an answer for you."

Mr. Cameron bowed his head briefly, then sighed as he looked at Maguire. "That's pretty much what we figured. It's just that we haven't had anyone new to ask in a while."

"I wish I had better information for you, Sir." She hauled herself up onto the seat beside Lisa. "Thank you for taking in our doctor. He's a good man." She looked at Doc. "Going to miss seeing your pretty face every day. Don't ever tell anyone I said that. It'll ruin my street cred." She grinned and winked at him.

"We'll make sure Doctor Porras feels right at home here," Mrs. Cameron said. "Please come back and visit any time."

"Thank you, Mr. and Mrs. Cameron," Lisa said. "I'll be in later this week to see if you need anything."

"Thank you, Lisa. Goodbye, Sergeant." The Camerons waved as the wagon lurched forward toward the main road.

Despite Lisa's good-natured attempt at conversation, Maguire was not the best company on the ride back to the compound. She felt fragmented, frustrated, and irritable. As far as she could see, nothing in the immediate future gave any indication that there was a solution for the chaos they all faced.

***

"Did you get Doc settled in?" Baumer asked as Maguire entered the cabin they were to share with Anna.

"Well, I don't know if he's exactly settled, but he's at the boarding house Noble suggested. The owners seem like nice people, and they are thrilled that he is a doctor. The town has no gas or fuel resources, so they're living like the Amish."

"We'll work on Noble. In the meantime, Doc isn't that far away," Baumer said soothingly.

"Two miles…on a horse. You should have seen the look on his face. You should have seen the look on mine."

"Mags, we're guests here and we need to abide by Noble's rules until we can prove to her that she has nothing to fear from Doc and, I'm sure, others."

"She has given every indication that she is going to be pretty rigid as far as her rules are concerned."

"But she's never been faced with what we're actually living now," Anna commented quietly from the doorway. "Maybe things will change."

Maguire snorted derisively. "And maybe angels will fly out me arse."

***

A week later Maguire found herself standing in Noble's

office, watching the woman rifle through a very thick file. Finally Noble slid her glasses from her nose and looked up at Maguire. She pulled another file to the top of her pile.

"I apologize for keeping you waiting," she said evenly. "Please take a seat."

Maguire watched her for a moment more before doing as asked. She sat, but she didn't relax.

"You confound me, Sergeant Maguire." Noble leaned back and her fingertips brushed the file folder. "You have an amazingly full and messed up career. Despite the missteps, you became a fully trained, special operations soldier during a time when that was extremely rare." She sighed. "I haven't decided whether or not I like you, but I am smart enough to realize that I need you."

"To do what?" Maguire's voice was noncommittal.

"I have been advised that a standing militia and special operations group of our own would be beneficial. I've thought about it in the past, but I haven't had the personnel to organize it," Noble explained.

"You've had the personnel available to you," Maguire pointed out. "At your men's camp."

Noble nodded. "Yes. But most of my women have a history with men, and not a good one, mind you." She didn't exactly sigh, but the sound she made was close. "I don't expect you to understand. I've read your record, Maguire. Every unit you served with, officers and enlisted alike characterized you as 'one of the guys.' Most of my women were victims of the guys." She leaned back in her chair. "That is not a negative characterization either of you or of the women who are here. It simply is a fact. I now have the pieces in place here to run a training program to forge volunteers into a militia and special operations force."

"To what end?"

Noble blinked. "Excuse me?"

"To what end? I can see a militia, a self-defense home guard so to speak, but a special operations force?"

Noble thought about the question for a long moment. "I spent my entire career studying seemingly small events, analyzing them and finding the patterns that connected them.

For some reason I am hard wired to see everything, big and small, and put those thin lines together." At last she came to the crux of her answer. "Things here have been on an even keel lately, but it was definitely not easy during the early days. We were accepted by the locals only after the recovery from the destruction began. I don't believe that this war, or whatever it is, is finished. You've seen some of what I've been getting reports about. I still have connectivity to communications. We stay passive but we are listening, so to speak. I am going to need scouts, pathfinders, and yes, special ops to stop threats before they reach us. I'm not disingenuous enough to claim that I won't use aggressive force if I need to." She maintained eye contact with Maguire without blinking.

Maguire took a deep breath. "I don't know whether I like you or not, either. But so far, you have been honest with me." She looked over Noble's shoulder to a view of the compound.

"Everyone here contributes, even you, if you decide to stay."

Maguire chuckled. "So my good looks and charm won't be enough."

"Not by a long shot," Noble answered without cracking a smile. "If you decide to accept my offer, which is room, board, and protection in exchange for taking the lead on training both elements of the future military that will serve this community."

Maguire laughed out loud. "Ms. Noble, I am the last person alive that *needs* protection. I will, however, concede that room and board are an enticement." Her humor gave way to a more serious demeanor. "If I decide to take your offer, what will I have to work with?"

"You will have Prescott, whose title would be NCOIC of the basic training. I have eight women who have experience as drill instructors or drill sergeants, none over the rank of sergeant, but a combined thirty-two years of experience. I have fifteen more with military experience. You will be Training Command. You would answer only to yourself. I will not interfere in training issues. My only response to those who complain or whine about training is to hand the complainant a tissue and order her back to training. Don't kill anyone on purpose, but be hard on them. To do otherwise would only get them killed should they ever be in combat. All your trainees will be volunteers. They will know what they are getting into." She pushed the large pile of files towards Maguire. "If you say yes, the files of those who will become the core of your cadre will be yours to examine."

Maguire stood abruptly, pushing her chair back. "I'll get back to you with an answer after lunch."

Maguire strolled around the compound, eating a sandwich she'd liberated from the mess. She took a slow walk around as much of the perimeter as she could, just watching. When she came to her decision, she started back towards Noble's office, taking mental notes as she went along.

When Noble offered her a chair, Maguire opted to stand at the window instead of sitting. For a very long minute, she said nothing. "I'll do it, but you'll have to modify things."

Noble understood what Maguire was doing. "Talk, I'll listen. That way we'll figure out what will work for both of us."

"First off, I won't be in charge of basic training. You have qualified instructors for that, and you have one hell of a fine officer who can lead them. Use the right people for the right job." It wasn't a criticism. "I suggest a basic training of no less than two months, not including a week's orientation time."

Noble considered the suggestions and nodded her agreement. "And what will you be doing?"

Maguire turned to Noble and tilted her head in the direction of the window. "I'll be out there, training ten women for three months how to be Fionaglagh. In turn, they will become the instructors of your Special Operations Force."

It did not take Noble long to decide. "Done. I'll schedule a meeting with Prescott and Baumer. We can hash out the details and logistics together."

***

Through the daily messenger between the town and Noble's fortress, Doc sent word that he would love to have dinner with his former traveling companions. They agreed on a day and time, and when the appointed date arrived, Baumer, Anna, and Maguire took a horse-drawn wagon into town.

On high alert, Maguire was sitting backwards, gripping a Cobra submachine gun and scanning what was behind them. Armed with an Ingram MAC-10, Baumer paid attention to what was ahead while Anna kept the horse on the right path.

"This must have been what it was like in the Old West," Anna said, sitting between Baumer and Maguire, holding the reins.

"Well," Baumer muttered, looking down at her weapon, "not exactly like the Old West."

Anna glanced at Baumer and then at the weapon that looked like the offspring of a machine gun that had mated with an automatic pistol. Baumer didn't seem uncomfortable with firearms, but she didn't appear to be totally at ease, either. Unlike Maguire who, as Prescott once suggested, might have been born with a gun in her hand. Anna shot a quick glance at the vigilant Maguire and grinned. Maguire was unconsciously stroking the fore end of the carbine in an almost intimate manner.

"Jeez, Mags, I hope you're going to make an honest woman out of it," Anna joked.

That caused Baumer to turn around. Catching Anna's reference, she started laughing.

Maguire scowled, then becoming aware of how reverently she seemed to be caressing the sturdy weapon, she stopped all movement and glowered at Anna. "Eyes front, missy," she said. "Give a lass some privacy."

Proud of herself for having gotten one over on the dour Maguire, Anna obediently turned around. She nudged Baumer, who squeezed Anna's shoulder in a brief hug.

"I can't wait to see Doc. I know it hasn't been that long, but it feels like forever," Anna said.

"It will be interesting to see the town and how he is settling in," Baumer observed.

***

When they entered the town proper, Doc was outside waiting for them. Clearly, he had the same sentiments as Anna because when the horse drew to a stop, Doc bounded to the wagon and helped Baumer down, instantly wrapping her in a bear hug. He repeated the hug with Anna, and then opened his arms to Maguire, grinning.

"Doc, you know I adore ya, but if ya hug me like that, I'll hurt ya," Maguire warned with a raised eyebrow. She hopped out of the wagon and found herself enveloped in a secure embrace.

"Careful, Doc," Baumer said dryly. "She's stealth. Make sure you have the same number of testicles as you did before you hugged her."

"I'm sorry. I'm just so damned happy to see you." Doc hugged Maguire then quickly released her, but he kept his arm around her shoulders. "Where's Prescott?"

"Noble wouldn't let her off the leash," Maguire grumbled.

"Mags." Baumer's tone held warning. "Pres wasn't feeling up to par, and she didn't want to risk bringing any germs to you or the town."

"Much appreciated, but I have antibiotics for that."

Maguire raised an eyebrow. "Who did you have to kill to get those?"

Doc smiled. "No one. When everything hit the fan, the Camerons cleaned out the four drugstores in town and packed all the pharmaceuticals in dry ice. Most of the medications are still within the expiration date."

"That was pretty smart. But why haven't they shared them with Noble?" Baumer asked.

"They offered. Noble told them they already had what they needed. They offered some to the men's camp, too, but they said they would come calling if they needed anything else. When they found out I was a doctor, I inherited the pharmacy."

"Have you had any patients yet?" Anna asked.

"Well, the Camerons and a few other people who are still in town have stopped by. We're working on a barter system. I check them out, and they supply me with food, water, and whatever necessities I might need. It's not a bad set up." He took Anna's arm gently. "Come on in and see my new home and office." He escorted them through the entrance to a brick building.

Doc's home was well furnished, yet seemed quaint without

electricity. The table was ready with five place settings, but he removed the extra plate and silverware now that he only had three guests. The aroma of spices and simmering vegetables filtered through the room. The women saw a cast iron pot suspended over an open flame in the fireplace.

"Wow, Doc, whatever you've concocted smells wonderful," Baumer said, inhaling deeply.

"Mrs. Cameron made a creamy corn pudding-type dish but what you're smelling is a barley, green bean, asparagus, carrot and onion stew with garlic and cilantro. I tossed in some beef bouillon, too."

"Oh my sweet lord Jesus," Maguire said, her mouth almost watering. "Where'd you get cilantro?"

"One of the townspeople, Lee Curtis, grows it as well as garlic. He also built a mill so that he can grind roots and grains for flour. He actually trades with Noble—flour for dairy."

He led them through the house, detailing the use of each room. What was once a large sun porch had been turned into an office. The windows had shades so that when privacy was called for, it was available, and when it wasn't needed, Doc had a bright room in which to relax.

"What happened to the people who owned this house?" Maguire asked.

"According to the Camerons, most everyone who left town after Day Zero went to search for relatives they hoped had survived. This area was barely touched by radiation and destruction, but of course there still is no power. Some of the long-time residents toughed it out. Looting was minimal, and the people who stayed were able to stockpile a lot of supplies scavenged from abandoned homes and businesses."

Anna was paying rapt attention. "How many original townspeople are still here, Doc?"

He shrugged as he led them back through the house to the hearth, where he stirred the stew. "Just a handful. I guess this wasn't a big place to begin with. According to the Camerons, this area has been spared from the roving bands of mercenaries and survivalists foraging for surplus or more power. They think it's due to the reputation of Noble and the two generals who manage the camp on the other side of the county." He drew the ladle from the kettle. "Looks about done. Anyone want to taste?"

***

Dinner had been consumed, the dishes were done, and it was time for the trio of women to head back to the compound. As Baumer hooked the horse up to the wagon, Doc pulled Anna to the side.

"How are your feet?"

"Not bad, Doc. I've been soaking them in heated salt water and Prescott brought me some aloe vera from Noble's healers, which has helped soothe the pain and burning and mostly dried up the skin."

"Good, good. I noticed you were walking better, but I just wanted to check."

"You're sweet. Thank you, Doc." Anna stood on her tiptoes and gave him a friendly peck on the cheek.

He smiled shyly and followed her to the wagon, where he helped Anna and Baumer back up to the bench as Maguire hopped up on her own.

"Thank you so much for coming into town," Doc said. "I didn't realize how lonesome I was until I saw you."

Baumer nodded. "Same here. We wish you could stay out with us, Doc."

"And I still haven't decided whether I'm staying there or coming in here to hang out with you for a while," Maguire said.

"Well, you'd be more than welcome. As would all of you," he said with a sincere smile.

"Thank you, Doc. We really enjoyed ourselves. We'll have to do this again soon." Baumer handed the reins to Anna.

"Anytime. Really. Tell Prescott to get her butt in here next time."

"Will do," Baumer said before Maguire could say anything. "We'll tell her you said hi."

"Thanks. Be careful on the way back." He waved as Anna turned the horse around to head back to the compound, and then watched until they were out of sight.

Chapter Twenty-Six

Reverting to her drill sergeant days, Prescott woke all the women who had signed up for training by banging loudly on a metal trashcan as she strode through the sleeping quarters of what was now designated as a Defense Corps area. Some of the women, those who were retired or ex-military, seemed to get a kick out of the ritual, but the younger ones appeared to instantly regret volunteering for Noble's fighting forces.

"Get your asses out of those racks. You have things to learn and things to do. Move it, people." Prescott's voice bellowed up and down the two rows, each with twenty-five bunks. "You have fifteen minutes to make your racks, get dressed in your PT uniforms, and get your asses out on the quad. PT uniform consists of shorts, t-shirt, tennis shoes. Move it, people, you are too slow. You now have thirteen minutes to get your shit together. I am not seeing any purpose in you. You will learn purpose, or you will regret it." She dropped the trashcan to the floor with a boom and a clatter. She looked around at the other instructors, "Cadre, get 'em moving."

The dazed collection of women struggled to line up in groups of four on the newly designated practice field. Even such a seemingly simple activity was by no means an easy process. The novices were hounded incessantly by the instructors filling their ears with shouts, screams, and curses. Missteps were rewarded with aggressive verbal attacks. Finally the instructors were more or less satisfied with the formation. They exchanged glances with one another, then turned and faced Prescott and Baumer who stood waiting.

"I am Senior Drill Instructor, Staff Sergeant Prescott. You are trainees. Your instructors are here to teach you, correct you, and generally ensure that you do not get yourselves killed." She assessed the group as she spoke, mentally taking notes. "The officer to my right is Lieutenant Baumer. She is the Training Company Commander. Do not let her kind face and gentle demeanor fool you. This is your only warning." She did a quarter turn and saluted. "Ma'am."

Baumer stepped forward, returned Prescott's salute, and let her gaze sweep left and right. "You are volunteers. If you did not understand what you were signing on for, you will be given the opportunity to drop out of this program without repercussions. For the next two months, those that stay will learn to be soldiers. At the end of the two months, you will know how to work as a team in order to defend this sanctuary. This training regimen will not be easy. Your instructors all have experience in the military, and they know what they are doing. They also know when someone is not giving their best effort. If you stay in the program, I suggest you give it everything you've got." She turned away from the training company. "All yours, Senior Drill Sergeant."

As Baumer strode back to her newly appointed office, she turned at the doorway and watched Prescott work.

"My name is Devon Prescott. I am a former staff sergeant with the U.S. Army. Among other things, I have been trained as a combat soldier and a drill instructor. I will get you started with formation and headcount every morning and then turn you over to your instructors. I know you're all anxious to kill shit, and we're going to get to weapons training in a bit. First, you need to know that a ready group means they are performance ready at a moment's notice. And a ready group uses guns only as a last resort. We are going to learn core behavior first. If your mind isn't trained, your body won't be either. Before we begin practical instruction in drill, order, marksmanship or any of the rest, we will be doing PT. For all you civilians, that's physical training. For those of you civilians who don't know what physical training is, you call it exercise.

"You've already done a good job of living off the land, so I think we can skip that particular subject. For now. Those of you who make it through the basics of this course will be instructed in how to survive in a hostile situation. This is not a program for the weak or faint-hearted. You heard Lieutenant Baumer, we will not take it easy on any of you. Those who are prior service understand that the severity of the training exercises is for your own safety as well as the safety of your team members. If you get singled out for criticism, it isn't personal, it's for your own good. The team needs to know the weakest link in its chain. If you can't cut the program, you will be dropped, so if this is not what you believe you signed up for, leave now."

Prescott surveyed the group, waiting for their reactions. A few expressions were startled, but no one left the ranks.

"You will get up at 0520 every morning. That's twenty minutes after five AM. No exceptions. Getting your period will not be an excuse to miss training. Conflicts don't initiate a ceasefire just to wait until you get off the rag."

Prescott looked back at the rest of the instructors with a smirk. "Although in some cases, maybe they should."

She was surprised to see an actual grin appear on some faces. "Oh, Lord," Prescott muttered, shaking her head. She refocused on the group. "Okay, ladies, let's start with some exercise before I turn you over to your new worst nightmares."

***

The subtle change in the lieutenant's posture let Maguire know that Baumer had felt her presence even before the sergeant stopped and leaned against the doorframe near her.

"What do you think?" Baumer asked, then her nose crinkled. "You stink, by the way." The smile on her lips took the sting out of the insult.

Maguire had been training the first group of candidates for the last month. It was *not* the kind of training you could do in a classroom.

Maguire didn't waste any energy on taking offence. She knew how bad she smelled and looked. She also knew that her corps candidates were a lot worse off than she was.

"I remember my first day of basic training," Maguire said. "Our senior drill sergeant yelled that if there wasn't a brown stain on the butt of our trousers at the end of the day, then clearly they hadn't *motivated* us enough."

Baumer's face scrunched up. "Ew. That's disgusting."

Maguire chuckled. "Yeah, but he had a point." She took out

a cigarette, struck a match, and lit it. Her personalized lighter had long since run out of butane.

"You vetted all these women. Good group?" Baumer asked.

"I hope. They certainly have the drive and determination. It's also a plus that one-third is prior service, so there are no surprises about what they're getting into."

"What's Noble's objective in all this? I mean, other than a cohesive militia."

"She would like me to turn some of them into an elite group, like Special Forces. She'd like those who were chosen and those who were dumb enough to volunteer to be so well trained that everything they need to do has become second nature by the time any more shit hits the fan, if it ever does. And we've seen what it's like out there, so we know it will."

"What's your plan?"

"Same thing we talked about initially—teach them how to protect themselves, each other, and the compound, train them on stealth movement, reconnaissance, and surveillance. We have seasoned instructors lined up to teach them in all weaponry available to us, and Prescott and I will personally train them in unarmed combat."

"I've seen you fight. Won't you be asking the impossible by expecting a recruit to defeat either of you?"

"They won't have to beat us, they'll have to demonstrate specific movements and skills that will let us know they've got what it takes. If someone is foolish enough to actually challenge me? Well…more power to them. Who knows? I might be pleasantly surprised. But we won't do it like the Army did."

Baumer smirked. "You mean showing them just enough to get them killed and then not practicing those moves ever again?"

"Exactly. Once they pass the test, they will have a bi-weekly refresher to keep their skills honed and their instincts sharp. They will also have recon missions when we get negative intel from the surrounding villages."

"The good thing, Mags, is that the women who volunteered, even the non-vets, have had fundamental survival courses and realize why this is necessary. And that mindset is as important as the training. You know as well as I do that if they aren't psychologically schooled, all the training in the world won't help them in situations for which they aren't mentally prepared."

Maguire nodded. "True that."

They watched in companionable silence as Prescott wound down the regimented body conditioning. There appeared to be a number of women ready to collapse from the strenuous workout.

Maguire took a last puff of her cigarette, field stripped it, and placed the rest in her pocket. "Prescott's actually pretty feckin' good at this." She looked Baumer in the eye. "Don't ever tell her I said that. Not that she'd believe you anyway." Maguire winked.

"You big softie," Baumer whispered as Maguire walked toward the sweaty, heavy-breathing group of recruits.

"Okay, ladies," Prescott announced, "it's time to meet your new best friend. Watch her. Listen to what she tells you. Remember that what she teaches *will* save your life."

Standing at parade rest next to her, Maguire arched an eyebrow at the irony. It probably annoyed Prescott to say anything positive about Maguire as much as it annoyed her to compliment Prescott. Prescott was being a true soldier and thinking of the mission first, and she couldn't fault the Senior Drill Sergeant for that.

"Staff Sergeant Branna Maguire," Prescott announced. "You will refer to her as either Sergeant or Top. Top is a nickname usually reserved for someone of a much higher enlisted rank, usually a First Sergeant, or Top Sergeant of the company. We don't have one of those. Sergeant Maguire will be the senior enlisted soldier in our limited chain of command totem pole, so she will be our Top. I can tell you from personal experience that her brain fires on entirely different pistons than yours or mine. Never, ever take anything for granted with her." Prescott stepped aside and then took one step back to allow Maguire to take command.

While passing each other, Maguire mumbled so only Prescott could hear, "Top? Really?"

Prescott grinned. "Better than being a bottom."

"Guess that all depends on whose bed you're in," Maguire

replied in a hushed tone.

Prescott shook her head and executed a perfect about-face. She stood directly behind Maguire. "They're all yours, Top."

Maguire didn't even blink but did think that it was too bad she and Prescott mixed like oil and water, because when it counted, they worked well together. She returned her focus to the new "troops" in front of her.

"I will not wish you a good morning. Until you actually graduate, there will be no such thing. At least half of you will fail. I am Staff Sergeant Maguire. I am a fully trained United States Army Military Police Officer. I am combat tested. I have personally killed human beings who have been actively trying to kill me or mine. Some of you have seen the unusual tab on my shoulder. I earned the right to wear the commando patch of the Fianoglagh, Irish Army Ranger Wing. I am the only woman to have earned that right."

Her eyes tracked the group and found one candidate who rolled her eyes. She memorized her face. "I will not blow smoke up your backsides and tell you that this will be fun. It will not be anything approaching fun."

Their response, looking like six-year-olds who'd just found out the truth about the Easter Bunny, did not disappoint. With a smile that remarkably resembled that of Hansel and Gretel's witch, Maguire's stare stopped on the eye-roller as she said, "Now, who's up for a short run?"

That "short run" turned into five laps around the interior perimeter of the compound. Maguire was sure that a majority of the recruits wondered just what level of fresh hell they had volunteered for. That's what she would have thought if she'd never done any of this kind of training. She was also pretty sure the only reason they didn't dare complain out loud was that she and Prescott completed the run wearing full rucksacks and combat boots.

The women entered a metal-reinforced Quonset hut turned classroom, gasping for breath, some only coming through the door after they had heaved last night's meal outside.

***

A month passed, which seemed like too short a time to Maguire, Prescott, and the instructors, but felt like years to the trainees. Baumer and her two comrades had little time to socialize or commiserate, because the kind of program they were putting the troops through was a 24/7 endeavor. They saw Anna only briefly, when they returned to their cabins after training and before they fell into bed. They took turns getting up in the middle of the night and waking the trainees for cleaning, runs, exercise, or drill.

Baumer openly expressed surprise that at the halfway mark of basic training, they had only lost two women—one who dropped out, and one who broke an ankle by stepping into a hole while running at night. Stef, the injured trainee, was not deterred. When she was physically able, she was ready to be cycled into the next batch of inductees. All in all, the women were shaping up to be damned good soldiers, which seemed to surprise Noble more than Maguire during their week six meeting.

Noble sat at her desk, Maguire occupying the chair opposite her. "Pres tells me things are going well."

As much as Maguire was wary of Noble, she had to admit that the woman had a powerful presence. She wasn't sure whether she liked the woman, but, the situation with Doc aside, she grudgingly respected her.

"The program is actually going better than expected. A majority of the women you suggested made the cut. That tells me you know your people. Jennings is a pretty dedicated standout. She's going to be a real asset. Unusual in one so young."

Noble chuckled. "One so young? Like you're ancient?" Maguire shrugged. "Lisa Jennings is a military brat, so she is well versed in attempting the impossible in order to please. Her father was a base commander at NAS Whidbey Island, so she has the attitude and the wherewithal to be quite good." Noble opened a desk drawer, and pulled out a bottle of Jameson's Gold Reserve Irish Whiskey.

Maguire's eyes widened and she almost started to salivate. "You've been in possession of Jameson's and this is the first I've learned of it? Do you have a death wish, woman?"

Noble snorted as she turned around and retrieved two brandy snifters from a shelf behind her. "Don't get your booty in a bunch, Maguire. I just got this from my last trade market with Mugnier, the commandant of the boy's camp. I didn't ask where he got his hands on it because I really don't care. But rest assured, Sergeant, you will be the first and only to share this particularly fine spirit with me."

Maguire tilted her head in question. "You don't even like me. Why would you do that?" Her words were not harsh, more an expression of disbelief.

"First, that's not true. I neither like nor dislike you. You have not allowed me close enough to you for me to form an opinion based on a personal relationship. But I admire your experience and skills, and whether you think so or not, you are a really good fit here."

Noble poured an equal amount of the aromatic libation into the two glasses, recapped the bottle, and put it back in her drawer. Then she picked up both snifters and handed one to Maguire. "Cheers."

"*Sláinte*," Maguire responded. As she savored the first swallow, Maguire closed her eyes as the smooth, malted sweetness coated her throat. In her thickest brogue, she said, "Aye, it be like an angel peeing down me gullet."

Noble smiled. "Can't argue with that assessment." She set her drink down. "I'm curious. Now that you've spent a month and a half here, what's your take on us?"

Maguire took another sip and set her glass on the small stand next to her chair. "You still won't let Doc on the property. Why would you think my opinion would change?"

"Seriously? *That's* your compass? Everything you've seen, everything we can do and have done, all the ways we're surviving and thriving, and your response is based on not allowing one man in our compound?" Noble seemed more curious than angry. "We don't need your doctor. We have our own medical team."

"You have healers, nurses, and practitioners. I'm not trying to take away from their experience or training, but they aren't doctors."

"It has always been my understanding that nurses run all

hospitals. Doctors are just the final word in prescribing treatment," Noble taunted.

"Doc isn't like that."

"I'll take your word for it," Noble said, her tone indicating the opposite.

"And that little condescension right there is why my opinion won't change." She swallowed the last of her whiskey and stood up.

Noble shook her head. "You puzzle me. You are a lesbian to the core, yet you continue to defend this straight man."

Maguire stopped at the door but didn't turn around. "I'm a lesbian, not a manhater. I know when men can bring something positive to the table. I don't trust easily, but I trust Doc. He's part of our team. As long as he is barred from this property, I will never belong here either." She strode out, letting the spring door slam behind her.

Chapter Twenty-Seven

Ten weeks later, the newly graduated troops moved on to the second phase of their training. Surprisingly, the excessive eye-roller had made the cut in basic and volunteered for Special Ops school. The first morning of the new session, thirty women entered the training classroom. There were envelopes on the tables, each of which held the name of an applicant. Those with prior military experience or an analytic brain cell did not relax, did not take their time getting situated. They stood behind their nameplate and waited warily. Others took their time in finding their assigned seat. Having had five days off since the end of basic training, they were relaxed. They actually felt comfortable enough to chat and joke with each other, as no one seemed to be watching every move or chewing them out or telling them what to do. Most of them took it as a nice change in operating procedure.

So it was almost a surprise to them when suddenly Maguire was standing behind a table podium and the classroom door shut behind the last instructor. The closing of the door caused silence to break out.

Without warning, Maguire bellowed, "On your feet!"

The entire group responded quickly. Maguire took notice of the instant change from the casual demeanor she had observed from the other room to the professional bearing now that she was in the room with them.

"In front of you is an envelope. You will take off your newly earned rank and you will place it inside the envelope. Now, people! You will learn that, unlike basic training, orders are rarely repeated here."

The volunteers did as they were told, some looking at their rank sadly before exiling it to the envelope as ordered.

"For those of you with military experience, let me assure

you that this will suck even worse than the first time around. You will stay focused and learn from the training cadre, or you will be gone. There will be no slack given. You will learn to pay attention to detail. You will learn what it means to be exhausted, you will learn what it means to be truly hungry, and you will learn how to kill another human being.

"There will be other things you will learn. You will learn what fear is. Before we teach you to kill, you will learn who you are." She took a breath and exhaled sharply.

"First, I'm sure you all remember Senior Drill Sergeant Prescott mentioning that your primary weapon in any situation is your brain, your wits. If you are mentally prepared, you have already won half your battle. Control and compartmentalize your fear before it becomes panic, and then rely on your instinct and training to get you the rest of the way. Before we are through with you, action and reaction will be instinctual, thought will be secondary. Your training will keep you alive. Look around you, all around you." As the trainees followed her order, she continued, "The faces of those around you are your battle buddies. Everyone will be assigned a battle buddy. I don't care if you don't like each other. I don't care if you are waging a blood feud. You will learn to work together at a higher level, or you will be gone. As of right now, you depend on them, they depend on you." She motioned to the women at the back of the room to come forward.

"These women are your new cadre. While you have been dealing with basic training in a nice controlled environment, they have spent the last three months working their asses off out in Mother Nature. If you whine, you will find no sympathy from them. They have been there and already done it. Just to give you an idea of the attrition rate for this school, these women are the only survivors from a candidate class of twenty-three."

As the cadre stood in the more relaxed position of "at ease," Maguire gestured toward them. "All of these women, with the exception of Sergeant Prescott, you are very familiar with. You've shared responsibilities with them in this compound since Day Zero, some of you, way before that.

"Until training is over, these women are no longer your

friends. They are your handlers, your lifeline to success, so don't expect any of them to give you a break. Whatever current or prior relationship you have had with them, it won't help you here. Everyone, individually, will graduate this training on her own merit. Not only do I not want, I cannot afford to have slackers or teachers' pets on my team. This goes for them, too. If I find out any one of them has 'helped' any of you along, you will both be out. Am I understood?"

"Yes, Top," they chorused enthusiastically.

"Outstanding," Maguire said. "Cadre, get them and their shit stowed in quarters, then chow 'em. First formation, one hour." She turned her attention back to the new troops.

"But…we graduated," the former eye-roller, said, her voice nearly a whine.

"Welcome to Hell, Part Two, ladies." Maguire turned on her heel and walked away without looking back, even when the onslaught of intimidation began anew.

***

The rain beat down on the candidates standing in a semi-circle, watching Maguire assemble an entrenching tool. Prescott and the rest of the instructors stood by. Several early melons were balanced on a board on top of a sawhorse. "Grab an entrenching tool, assemble it. Now."

They reacted automatically. By this point they understood every order had a reason, even if the reason was not readily apparent. Nearly numb fingers opened, extended the entrenching tools, and then screwed the twist knob tight.

"Every single thing you have can be a weapon if you need it badly enough. Your entrenching tool can be used in the event of hand to hand combat." Maguire spun around and chopped the edge of the spade down on a melon. The melon skin split as the spade buried itself deep in the fruit. "One melon each, one stroke. Go."

The candidates took turns cleaving the melons. As one group was done, the instructors replaced the broken fruit with fresh. Several candidates smiled during the exercise. Maguire took note of who did and did not enjoy themselves. Once they were done, she allowed them a brief time to joke with each other about the task.

"Remember that sound," Maguire intoned. "That's almost what the human head sounds like when you split it open. When you hit bone, there is a dull cracking, as well, otherwise the rest of it is damned accurate."

Suddenly realizing what she meant, two candidates vomited up the contents of their stomachs. The rest lost their smiles.

"It was fun until you learned the lesson," Prescott barked. "Do not ever lose sight of the fact that at some point in time, you *will* have to take a life. None of this is fun and games, ladies."

Maguire stalked over to the two candidates who had puked. She eyeballed them and was pleased when they did not look away. She nodded sharply. "People die in combat. None if it is nice or pretty, and it stinks to high heaven. Blood smells. Brains smell. Cut a man's bowels out and it smells. Leave the corpse there and it smells." She began to walk away. "Cadre, melon on the dinner menu. Road march in two hours. Full rucks and battle rattle," she ordered.

Prescott grinned. "Gotta love this job."

***

It had taken several meetings with Noble to arrange for the trip, but finally Baumer, Maguire, and Prescott were at the men's compound and about to meet the two retired generals. They hoped to discuss the possibility of reaching an agreement concerning a military treaty. For the meeting, all three wore their duty uniforms. Maguire was wearing the beret of the Fianoglagh, hoping it would send a silent message.

In keeping with the faith that was being invested in them, they surrendered their weapons before being asked and pulled the offered blindfolds on themselves. They walked alongside their guards, chatting amiably and even cracking a few jokes. The entire time, however, as previously agreed, each woman was taking mental notes to be discussed later.

They were led into a room and allowed to remove the blindfolds. They were in a nondescript office with a long table and comfortable looking chairs. A young man in a relatively unadorned battle dress uniform offered them refreshments, said that the generals would be with them momentarily, then left the room, leaving the door open behind him.

"Nice digs," Prescott said sincerely.

"Glad you like it," a deep timbred voice offered.

With his one star, General Brendan Barton led the way for General Al Mugnier with his two. All three women snapped to attention and saluted. The generals took their places at the table opposite the women and returned the salutes.

The two men were as different as night and day. Barton was blond and tall with his hair cut at barely regulation level; Mugnier was shorter and stockier, with salt and pepper hair that was worn in a high, tight cut that was almost painful to look at. Each general wore the serious expression of men accustomed to making life changing decisions.

"Take a seat," Mugnier ordered, leaning back in his chair.

"Thank you, Sir." Baumer was crisp and respectful. She sat, then Prescott and Maguire followed.

A soft knock at the office door forestalled any immediate conversation. Two orderlies entered with trays of tea, a short bottle of whiskey, a carafe of water, and five glasses. Once everything was situated, the orderlies snapped to attention and then departed.

"Have at it."

Barton's was the deep timbred voice. He smiled and reached for a glass of iced tea. It took a moment or two before everyone had a glass of whatever they wanted. Only Mugnier and Maguire selected whiskey, and only a small sip was taken.

"Generals, first off, thank you for seeing us," Baumer began. "I'm Lieutenant Jessica Baumer. To my left is former Staff Sergeant Devon Prescott. To my right is Staff Sergeant Branna Maguire." She reached into her BDU pocket and produced a sealed envelope. "This is the proposed treaty from Rachel Noble." She handed the envelope to General Barton.

"And what does Miss Noble propose?" General Mugnier asked in a wry tone. "More interestingly, what did it take to get her to propose any accord with us?"

Baumer smiled. "A great deal of bitching and complaining,

Sir." she answered bluntly.

General Barton barked out a laugh. "I like her, Al." He looked at Baumer. "Which one of you led the bitching brigade? Honest answer, if you please."

Baumer shrugged and all three lifted their hands. "It was a three-pronged assault, Sir."

General Mugnier chuckled. "I can imagine. Miss Noble doesn't entertain the thought of treaty lightly. Without boring me with minutiae, what are we looking at here?"

"Sharing," Baumer answered succinctly. "Intelligence, hard and soft, training of forces, and special operations."

"Power?" Mugnier's question had an edge to it as he opened the envelope.

Maguire chuckled. "No, Sir. Noble is the Queen of Connaught, if you will. She doesn't want your power, and she certainly won't give up hers."

Barton clearly caught the historical reference. "So, if the Queen of Connaught has her own power, why would she be interested in sharing these other things with us and expecting us to do the same?"

"There is no expectation here, Sirs," Baumer leaned forward. "This is a proposal that we put our butts on the line for. Maguire and I came from Fort Hood, Prescott from Fort Huachuca. I don't know if you've seen the outside, but it's been bad, and human nature being what it is, it will get worse." She took a sip of her tea. "Medieval would be an accurate assessment. In many places, it already is."

"So you say." Mugnier scanned the pages of the treaty.

"The L.T. and I watched people being crucified in Las Cruces, New Mexico—nails pounded into flesh and bone, the whole lot, Sir." Maguire maintained eye contact with both generals. "We would like an alliance, but we're not going to lie to you to get it."

"One of our traveling party was raped and murdered by a militarized group of men who took what they wanted, when they wanted. It's happened." Prescott's voice shook with hate. "We have what we need at Noble's, so we don't have to barter anything here. You don't have to give up any power and neither does Noble. It's a win—win situation, if you agree."

"Only one thing wrong with this proposal." General Mugnier's voice held a slightly superior tone. All eyes turned to him. "You don't have Special Ops. I would know if you did."

Maguire shifted in her seat to look at her companions. "Told you I picked the right place for training." She turned to face the general. "Have you ever heard of the Fianoglagh, Sir?"

Mugnier searched his memory for a moment. "European Special Forces?"

"Irish, Sir." Maguire did not suppress the wolfish grin that crossed her face as she held up her beret with the flash facing the two generals. "Irish Army Ranger Wing. Mainly anti-terrorist, but after that boondoggle in Korea they went back to the combat roots. I have a fully trained cadre and now the core operators for a future Special Operations force." She took a satisfying sip of whiskey. "And your boys didn't see any of it happening. I wasn't even trying to hide. I will give your boys credit though. I moved my training grounds twice after I spotted them."

"Holy crap," Barton wheezed. "You're *that* Maguire." It was not a question. "Al, she's the one who pissed off the Joint Chiefs." He started to laugh.

General Mugnier's expression morphed into something close to a smile. "Well damn. I owe you a thank-you, Sergeant. Marine and Navy Joint C's were assholes. Hated both of them." He sat back heavily in his chair, which squeaked in protest. "Paul," he shouted to the young man posted outside the closed door, "get the orderlies to bring in some notepads and coffee. It looks like we have a long session in front of us."

***

Baumer knocked on Noble's office door and waited for permission to enter. When it came, she took a deep breath and breathed a prayer.

She walked in and halted one step from Noble's desk. The expression on the older woman's face was one of hope, expectation, and trepidation. "What's the word?"

"A tentative yes." She placed the proposed treaty in Noble's hand. "There are some suggested revisions, of course, but it looks like we are not far from a done deal, Rachel." She let herself relax.

"I'll look these over. I didn't think Albert Mugnier would agree." She admitted. "He and I grate on each other."

"He doesn't strike me as stupid. And it helped that Mags caught sight of his recon boys when she was training her cadre and moved her training grounds accordingly." She allowed herself a wry grin. "Three times. She saw them three times, and he didn't know that you now have a Special Operations group that apparently is better at it than those recon boys he personally trained."

"Great. Now I owe Maguire another one."

Baumer's smile turned gentle. "I know Mags. She's not keeping count." She took a breath. "You take your time reading over the counterproposal, but I would respectfully advise that you take the deal. Most of the counters are in reference to communication clarification. I didn't get the impression that they would try to grab anything that's not theirs, not after what we described going on in the world. You know that I wouldn't lie to you."

Chapter Twenty-Eight

A deep chime rang out from the center of the property. Baumer, in the west side of the wooded area, turned her head without immediately halting her archery instruction. "Time for the town hall?" She smiled at the adopted phrase for Noble's mandatory meetings.

Lisa Jennings grinned and put away the compound bow that had been raising welts on her forearm for an hour. "Well, I never thought I'd be happy for one of those. No offense, Jess."

"None taken. Get a bracer made and you won't have that problem," Baumer instructed as she pointed at the raw patch of skin.

Lisa groaned. "Now you tell me."

"No pain, no gain." Baumer slid her own arrow into the quiver and quirked a smile at the tall, stout woman. "If I had told you beforehand, would you have listened to me?"

Lisa smiled sheepishly and shook her head. "Probably not."

"How did you graduate Maguire's training with archery skills like yours?"

Lisa grimaced. "Sheer damned luck. I think I was too exhausted to think about failing, I just shot."

"And now with me you're back to being bad? I think I'm insulted."

"You shouldn't be." Lisa grinned. "I'm hitting the target now. Sort of. It'll be better once I pull my head out of my backside and feel comfortable asking questions."

"Sometimes a life lesson comes by way of the copious use of peroxide and Band Aids. C'mon, she hates it when we're late." Baumer turned and started walking.

Lisa caught up to her and shot a glance at her watch. "That's strange. We don't normally have a meeting until later in the day."

Baumer filed the information away. They joined the throng of women who were parading in from various parts of the sanctuary. Fifteen minutes later, nearly the entire population of the refuge had gathered before the building that housed Noble's office.

Noble strode out of the structure with quick steps. She wore a worried expression as she asked, "Have any of you seen my granddaughter, Angel? Anyone?"

Baumer looked around and noticed that Noble was answered with shaking heads and several instances of eyeball rolling.

"She was last seen heading for the stables," someone called.

"She didn't come inside," one of the horse wranglers responded.

"Carrie, break them down into groups and search the entire grounds, woods included," Noble ordered. She looked back to the group. "I know she's done this before, and I'm sorry to have to take you away from your work again."

Baumer followed Lisa as Carrie started shouting orders to various groups. She caught a glimpse of Prescott, who was obviously pissed off. She tapped Lisa's shoulder and pointed to Pres. Lisa nodded, and they joined Prescott's search party.

Prescott was standing with Anna, Maguire, and six others. "You look a little put out, Pres," Baumer teased gently.

"I was just about to have pancakes," Prescott muttered. "Seems her granddaughter does this several times a year."

Lisa snorted. "No shit. You guys were visiting your friend last time she disappeared. I have to say I'd rather face basic training again than deal with this kid."

"I find this juvenile, I'm gonna hang her by her toes." Prescott's pique was undoubtedly fueled by the fact that she had missed breakfast.

"That'll teach her," Maguire deadpanned.

"And you'd do what, parent genius?" Prescott shot back.

"Instead of sending everyone out to get her back, I'd leave her out there until she got hungry enough to come back in."

Prescott snorted. "When you actually have a kid, I'll come to you for parenting advice."

Maguire turned into Prescott, effectively blocking her way. For a long moment the Irish woman appeared much larger than she actually was. "When you learn anything about me that isn't to do with the Army, come see me, otherwise you should most likely keep it to business."

Baumer grabbed Maguire's collar. "C'mon, Captain America, we have a little girl to find." She tugged and was grateful when Maguire stepped back without further comment. After a few paces, she released her grasp.

Anna caught up with them. "You do have a way with women, Maguire."

"A bad way." Maguire took the lead and moved ahead of the rest of the group.

Anna turned in mid step and made sure she caught Prescott's eye. "You know, Pres, sometimes you say things that hurt without meaning to. And you do it well."

For the next hour they searched the surrounding areas until they came to the creek that ran through the back end of the sanctuary. They halted at the tree line to take a short breather.

Anna looked around as she handed her canteen to Baumer, whose own was in need of a refill. "This one might be rough. It's thick brush and a high running creek. If I was a bored kid, this is where I'd go for sure."

"Run away a lot did you, princess?" Prescott jibed.

"Oh yeah. You have no idea," Anna answered. "I had a lot of good reasons, too. Watch out for the creek banks, they can crumble down fast."

"Got it, Anna." Baumer handed the canteen back. "I got point this time. Everyone spread out. There are ten of us, so let's say ten feet between us."

"Roger that." Maguire stepped off the distance. The others quickly followed suit.

"Okay, let's move out." Baumer used a hand signal to move them forward.

They walked into the thick treeline with little difficulty for the first twenty feet, then it got thicker and the pitch got steeper. Baumer slapped her hand on the trunk of a tree to keep her balance. Failing, she slipped to her butt as her feet went out from under her. The pain from jolting down on hard ground drove the air from her lungs. For a moment she felt a stinging sensation on her tailbone and lower back.

Prescott rushed over and latched onto Baumer's collar, then hooked her hand up under her arm and hauled her to her feet. "You okay, Jess?"

"Just perfect," Baumer snapped as she brushed her butt off and then rubbed her back. "I'm pretty sure this is not part of my job description."

Anna moved over to the tree and looked closely at the surrounding foliage. "Jess? You're going to hate this, but you just slid through poison ivy."

Baumer stiffened with anger. "Are you kidding me? Poison Ivy?"

"I'm not kidding. I wish I was." Anna scuttled back into her shell.

Baumer sighed. "I'm sorry I snapped, Anna. I'm not mad at you. Just...I swear I'm gonna kill this kid."

***

The alarm sounded again, two short spurts to signal Angel had been found, and Baumer had to stop and rest as they headed back to the buildings. A wave of nausea overpowered her, then a debilitating cramp, rendering her weak. She sat down on a tree stump and took a few deep breaths.

"Jess?" Anna handed her canteen to Baumer, who waved it away.

"I think I might be coming down with something. I don't want to share the germs."

Anna recapped the canteen. "Maybe you should take rest of the day off. Go back to the cabin and rest."

"I'll be all right in a minute," Baumer insisted unconvincingly.

Anna studied her. "I don't know. You look pretty pale." She placed her hand on Baumer's forehead. "And you're really warm."

"Well, yeah. It's a hundred freakin' degrees out here."

"No, Jess. You are running a fever."

"I'll be fine." Baumer stood up, got dizzy, and immediately

sat back down. "Or not."

***

Prescott hurried into the cabin and nearly ran over Anna, who was fetching another cool washcloth to put on Baumer's forehead. "What's going on? Maguire lit out of here like her ass was on fire to go and get Doc. Said Jess was—"

Anna shook her head vigorously and put her finger to Prescott's mouth. "Shhh. She'll hear you," Anna whispered harshly.

Prescott shrugged in helplessness. "What—?"

"Noreen is in there with her," Anna said, referring to the compound's primary medic. "She thinks it's a spider bite but—"

"But…but what? Maguire said she needs Doc. It's got to be bad if we have to go all the way into town to get him."

"It is bad, Pres. Noreen thinks her diaphragm is paralyzed and—"

"From a spider bite? What the hell kind of spider?"

"Black widow," Noreen had come out of the room and was leaning against the doorway. "They are indigenous to Idaho. We don't know if we have the antibiotics to combat the effects of the venom if it's not treated right away. Most of us who've been here all along know that if anyone experiences anything that feels like a bee sting, they are to come see me right away."

Prescott was still chewing over the need to go for Doc. "What do you use to treat it?"

"What normally works for us is plantain leaf oil applied directly on the bite. But Baumer waited too long before getting help."

Prescott looked from Noreen to Anna, then back to Noreen. She blinked as she tried to process the implications of Noreen's flat statement. "What do you mean she waited too long? You can fix her, right?"

Noreen stared down at the floor. "She waited too long," she repeated helplessly.

Prescott stared, speechless, then looked at Anna for additional information.

"That's why Maguire's gone to get Doc. He might have access to anti-venom and other treatments that might be able to reverse the effects, or at least slow them down."

The hope in Anna's voice was almost enough to make Prescott think there was a chance for Baumer...until Noreen caught her eye and gently shook her head.

"I need to see her." Prescott stepped around Noreen and pushed into the bedroom.

***

Baumer breathing was shallow as her eyes followed Prescott to the chair beside the bed. "Man...th...this...is like a...a big old cup...of suckage," Baumer rasped, each breath labored.

Prescott tried to hold it together. In all the time she had known Jessica Baumer, she had never seen her lieutenant so distressed. "Doc should be here any time now. He'll know what to do."

"I...I...know what to...to do. Send...Maguire on...a search...and de...destroy mission to...find that spider."

"How is that home remedy working for you?"

Baumer shook her head. "Wh...who...knew Idaho...had...so many bananas?" She began to cough.

"Plantains," Prescott corrected and placed her hand over Baumer's. It was ice cold and clammy. "Don't talk, Jess."

"Thought...I'd...been stung...by a bee, or really that damned poison ivy...I'm allergic." She coughed. "N...no soldier stops...work...for that."

"Shhh. Stop using up your strength. You'll need it for later."

"Right," Baumer said.

Even though her voice was weak and laced with pain, her response was said with enough conviction to let Prescott know Baumer didn't believe there would be a "later."

Baumer smiled around her pain. "Do you think James will be waiting for me?"

***

Prescott stood in front of Noble, ready to get down on her knees if necessary. "Damn it, Rachel, he's waiting at the gate. Jess needs him. Please," she begged. "Maguire and I will keep fucking guns on him if that's what you ask, and he'll fucking agree to it."

"There's no need for him," Noble began. "Noreen and the others should be able to handle this. They've done it before."

"Noreen is the reason we need Doc," Prescott's volume raised with every word. "She's admitted she's done all she can!"

Noble looked up, startled by Prescott's words. "If it's beyond Noreen's capabilities, then—"

"You order those assholes at the gate to let him in!" Maguire interrupted, as she burst through the door. "Baumer dies, and our agreement is ended," Maguire said flatly, dripping water on Noble's floor. "And if she dies because Doc was held up, I swear to fecking God, I will hold it against every last one of them that caused it, starting with you."

"Can you back up that threat?" Noble challenged in a tone that had brooked no dissent for twenty years.

"Care to find out?" Maguire asked menacingly.

Noble locked eyes with Maguire. After what seemed like an eternity, she blinked. She picked up her two-way radio. "Gate, when Prescott and Maguire get there with transport, let the doctor in."

There was static, then Carrie's voice. "Please repeat."

"You heard me. When the Jeep gets there to pick him up, let him in."

A muted "Roger" came in answer.

"Go get him," Noble muttered.

Prescott and Maguire raced for the front door. They reached the Jeep at the same time, with Maguire filling the driver's seat first. Prescott's butt hit the passenger seat at the same time Maguire hit the gas. The tires spun in the mud as she directed the vehicle towards the front gate.

"You think it'll make a difference?" Prescott shouted above the engine.

"It better," Maguire shot back.

"And if it doesn't, will you…?"

"You have to ask? She dies, and I'm done here. You lot are on your fecking own," Maguire shouted as she changed gears. In her mind she was counting distance. Wheels hit the first major bump then counted ten seconds, the second major bump, two hundred yards to the front gate. Two hundred yards too long in her opinion. She shoved the pedal to the metal, the Jeep lurched, and she fought the wheel as the tires ate mud.

As the gate came into view she pressed the clutch, tossed the transmission into neutral, and twisted the wheel, a perfect 180 degree turn. Prescott jumped out of the passenger seat.

Covered in mud, Carrie shoved her face next to Maguire's. "You're a fucking asshole."

Maguire looked at Carrie with no emotion and muscled the stickshift into first gear. "We've covered that truth. But I'm the asshole with a gun, so get the feck out of my way."

"And if I don't?" Carrie challenged.

"I'll drag you up to the house."

"And if I stand in front of your Jeep?" Carrie taunted as Doctor Porras tossed his gear in the back.

"If you cost my friend her life, you'll die slowly," Maguire promised.

"Big words."

Maguire gazed at Carrie with dead eyes. "Posture somewhere else but get clear of the wheels, unless you want me to go over you."

Doc jumped into the back and Prescott slid into the passenger seat. "Go!"

Maguire looked at Carrie. "Last warning. Stand clear."

"Fuck you," Carrie shot back.

Maguire stomped on the gas pedal and twisted the wheel to clear Carrie by inches. The woman was pelted with mud and gravel.

"Maguire, you are a fucking asshole," Prescott shouted.

Maguire turned her head slightly. "Must be an echo around here," she shouted back.

***

Maguire and Prescott paced outside the cabin as they waited for Porras to come out. Maguire lit up another cigarette.

"Those things'll kill you, you know," Prescott mumbled.

"Really? Thanks. I've never heard that before," Maguire retorted.

"I'm just saying. I think you sucked down a whole pack in the last forty-five minutes."

Maguire did not reply. She continued to pace and smoke until she heard Porras' footsteps on the porch.

"How is she?" Prescott made it to Doc a split second before Maguire.

"Without the proper equipment here, I can't tell precisely, but I know enough to know the prognosis is not good."

"Define 'not good.'" Maguire blew smoke off to the side, stabbed out the cigarette on the railing, field stripped it, and pocketed the butt.

There were tears in his eyes as Porras took a deep breath. "I'm not going to lie to either one of you. If she makes it, it will be a miracle."

Both women stared at him. "It's an insect bite, Doc!" Maguire protested in disbelief. "You've patched us all up with a lot worse."

"It's venom. It's toxic. And even though they had minimal radiation here, we have no idea what the radioactivity did to whatever lived through it above ground. It could have made the venom stronger. Noreen was right. If we had caught it sooner, I could have treated her with the meds I have available to me in town, and I might have been able to save her, but—"

"No. No, Doc. She is still alive. You can still save her!"

Prescott's voice was desperate, more distraught than either Maguire or Porras had ever heard it.

"Get back in there and make her better! That's your job, Doc! Do it." Now openly crying, Prescott grabbed Porras' shirt and shook him. "Fix her!"

She began to punch at him blindly, and Maguire grabbed her and held her arms at her side.

"Fix her..." Prescott's voice hushed to a whisper as she dissolved into defeated, wracking sobs.

"Pres, I can't." The pain of his inability to help Baumer

was evident in the anguish in his voice.

Maguire released Prescott, who slumped onto the porch step and buried her face in her hands.

Tears glistened in Maguire's eyes, but they didn't fall. "How long?"

Porras blew out a shaky breath and shrugged. "A day or two at the most. You should probably go see her before she slips into a coma."

Maguire shoved her hands into her pockets. "Doc? If you'd had an office here on the compound and access to the supplies you have in town, would it be different? For Jess, I mean."

"It's hard to say," he said honestly. "If she had come to see me when the severe cramping started, maybe. Like I said though…the potency of the venom—"

"If Noreen can heal with banana oil, I would think you could have made a difference," Prescott snapped.

"Maybe," Porras iterated.

Maguire leaned down to Prescott. "Noble and her fucking rules. Remind me when…when this is over, to give her a personal thank-you for killing my friend." Maguire trudged up the steps and disappeared into the cabin.

The End

Chapter Twenty-Nine

When everyone else was asleep, Maguire eased open the door and stole into Baumer's room, then closed the door quietly behind her. She moved the one uncomfortable chair over by the bed, sat down and took Jessica's hand in hers.

"I'm right here, Jess," she whispered close to her L.T.'s ear, then settled back. "I'm right here."

Jessica's eyes opened slowly. "Knew you'd...come back," she gasped. "Tired, Mags. So tired."

"I know, dearlin', I know. Rest now. I've got your six."

Baumer smiled. "You called me Jess," she whispered, then her smile widened. "Can I tell you a secret?"

Maguire swallowed her sadness. "Tell me your secret, Jess."

"I keep seeing James. I think he's waiting," Baumer disclosed. "I'm going to die soon. I know it."

"I think you might be right," Maguire whispered back. "I mean about James waiting for you." She stumbled over her words.

"'S okay..." Baumer mumbled. "We had a time getting...here. I'm sorry you had...to kill," she finished in a wheeze. "Szab...and I will ...be keeping eyes ...on you." She weakly lifted a hand and beckoned her friend closer.

Following the unspoken order, she tilted her ear close to Baumer's mouth and listened. After Baumer had finished speaking, she fell back onto the pillow. Maguire moved the chair back against the wall and slipped out of the room.

***

Anna opened her eyes and stretched. She was surprised to see Maguire sitting next to Jessica, holding her hand. She reached up and turned the lamp on low. Maguire's face was drawn, her eyes hollow with shadows. There were tears running down her cheeks as she lifted Jessica's hand to her lips.

"Mags?" Anna whispered.

"Shh, princess," Maguire answered kindly. She pressed a light kiss on Baumer's hand then settled it by her side. "She's sleeping."

"Are you okay?"

Maguire shook her head. "She'll be leaving us soon, I think." She stroked Baumer's hand. "I'm going to miss my voice of sanity."

Anna sucked in a harsh breath. "I'm going to miss my friend."

"You have been a good friend to her, Anna. Please see that she passes over with a friend at her side. I can't do this again. I think she'll understand," Maguire said as Baumer fought for breath.

"How can you leave her?" Anna asked.

"I'm not leaving her, I just can't be here," Maguire choked out. "I'll be makin' sure she has a proper send off. A warrior should always have a proper send off. And she's been our warrior since this started. She should have been born Irish."

Maguire stood, then leaned down and whispered in Baumer's ear, loudly enough that Anna could hear, "You have earned Tir Na Nog. I'll see you there. I'll count it a favor if you'll be there to welcome me when it's my time. I go now to make sure that you'll be welcomed by my kin. Say hello to my Moira and Rory, will you? My dear friend, I will honor you always. I'll never forget you."

***

Prescott stood outside the cabin and removed her headband. She drew the back of her arm across her forehead to remove the excess perspiration. She submerged the cloth in the rain barrel, pulled it out and retied it, feeling instant relief from the unrelenting heat.

She stepped inside and quietly entered the room where her friend lay motionless on a cot, covered by a sheet. Her stomach lurched, but deep gulps of air settled the contents back where they belonged.

Baumer couldn't be gone. Just three days earlier, they were laughing about old times, and Prescott had told her about the new home brew she and Maguire had cooked up. This tough-as-nails, bright, combat tested woman who had fought in two different Gulf Wars had been taken down by a spider bite. If that wasn't another wake-up call in this new world, Prescott didn't know what was.

"Are you okay?"

Prescott hadn't noticed Anna in the corner, in the same chair where she had sat vigil for the past few days. Prescott was simultaneously annoyed and sympathetic. She'd thought she would have a private moment alone with Baumer, but at the same time she felt grievously sorry for Anna, who had not left Baumer's side since before the lieutenant had slipped into the coma.

"Prescott?"

"Of course I'm not okay," Prescott snapped. "I just lost a dear friend and a respected colleague."

Anna wiped away a tear and dropped her gaze. "I'm sorry. I heard you fighting for air, and I thought you might need some help."

Prescott sighed and inwardly cursed herself for being such a selfish bitch. Anna had been an exceedingly loyal friend to Baumer, was always there for her. She had stepped up when Baumer got sick, before she even knew what Baumer had wasn't contagious and possibly deadly to her. "I apologize, Anna. That was uncalled for."

Anna's head snapped up and she stared at Prescott, shocked. "Who are you, and what have you done with Prescott?"

A slight smile shadowed Prescott's lips. She walked around the bed, over toward Anna. "Were you here when she...passed?"

Anna nodded. "She seemed peaceful, but when someone is in a coma, it is impossible to tell. I only hope she was in a tranquil state, beyond pain."

Prescott looked down at Anna's hand, which still held

Baumer's. "You know, you're going to have to let her go at some point." Prescott's tone was so gentle, she didn't think Anna had heard her.

Anna clutched Baumer's hand more tightly. "I know." She began to weep. "I can't believe she's gone." She leaned against Prescott's side and sobbed uncontrollably.

"Go ahead. Let it out." Prescott placed her hand on Anna's head and smoothed her hair. Anna's weeping continued for a steady ten minutes before it subsided. "When's the last time you were out of this room?"

Anna sniffed. "This morning…sometime, after Dr. Porras came in to check on her. Maguire came by to say goodbye to Jessica and made me take a break. I went to the bathroom and came right back, because Doc told me it wouldn't be long before…" She shook her head and swiped at the tears on her cheeks.

"When was the last time you ate?"

"Maguire brought me a snack bag of dried fruits a couple of days ago, but that's been about it. I haven't had much of an appetite."

"Anna, you need to eat." Prescott's hand fell to Anna's shoulder. "Bau— Jessica wouldn't want anything to happen to you. She didn't insist you come all this way with us and take you under her wing just to have you follow her to the grave. You've spent so much time taking care of her, that you've neglected taking care of yourself."

"Why do you care? You don't even like me." Anna's tone wasn't indignant, it was matter-of-fact.

Prescott squeezed Anna's shoulder. "If I tell you that it wasn't personal, would you believe me?"

"No."

"I can be an asshole. You deserved better from me. I'm sorry." She felt Anna's arm slide around her waist, then a knock on the door broke the mood.

Porras stepped in. "Sorry to interrupt, but—"

"You aren't interrupting," both women chorused.

He nodded. "I need to get her ready for the cremation."

Anna sprang to her feet, clearly upset at the notion. "You're going to burn her?"

"Anna, you know we cremate. It's safer. It's not Baumer anymore, it's just her shell."

Prescott gently took Anna's wrist. "Say your good-byes and let Doc do his work."

She looked into Prescott's eyes. "I've said my good-byes." She slowly released Baumer's hand. "You haven't said yours yet."

"I've said them in my head. I hope she heard them." Prescott tugged on Anna's wrist. "If you're ready, we should go."

Anna reached over and lowered the sheet to reveal Baumer's face. She leaned over and kissed the pale forehead, then lingered a moment and whispered something, then wiped away her tears as she stood up and looked at Prescott. "I'm ready."

***

Anna opened the door of the medical clinic and stopped in her tracks. Out front, six women, including Maguire, stood in two rows of three. A simple wooden coffin rested on the floor between them.

"Anna, we really—" Prescott began. Then Anna stepped out of the way, and Prescott nearly dropped her end of Baumer's litter.

Five of the women were wearing the dress uniform of Noble's Militia. Maguire was wearing her Army uniform, complete with black beret.

"I know she's going to be cremated, but we are going to carry her in the traditional way. She's a warrior, she deserves that much."

Maguire's voice did not invite argument, and Prescott didn't have one anyway. She nodded.

"She really should have a shield, but the coffin was all we could come up with on short notice."

"Hooah," Prescott managed around the lump in her throat.

She stepped forward and halted when Baumer's body was even with the coffin. Maguire and two other women gently lifted the corpse from the litter and lowered it into the wooden box. Two more women quietly settled the lid in place.

All six reached down and lifted the coffin, struggling a little until shoulders on either side of the coffin slid beneath it to bear the burden. A hushed "forward" order from Maguire was all that was needed to propel them towards the pyre. As they marched, residents of the compound and their children stopped what they were doing and paid their respects, even if it was to just lower their heads in acknowledgement of their passage.

Those military personnel who were not otherwise on duty were called to attention. As one, at the order, they presented a final salute, which they maintained until the procession reached the pyre.

At the pyre, the coffin was lowered until it slid into place. Maguire pulled the lid free and shifted it back. She said a silent prayer, her lips moving. She pulled a bottle of Guinness from her cargo pocket and placed it into the coffin, and then dropped in a scrap of cloth as well.

"There now," she said. "That beer is for a special occasion, and the Celt gods will welcome you with open arms. If they give you any shite, tell them which Maguire sent you and they'll shut their gobs." Then in a whisper, she added, "*Moi drug.*"

She took two steps back, snapped a sharp salute, held it, and then lowered it very slowly, rendering final honors. She executed an about-face and marched away from the coffin.

As she came abreast of Prescott, Maguire looked her in the eye. "Noble ready to let Doc live in the compound now? Or is she going to allow more people to die because he lives down the valley?"

"The rule is there for a reason, Mags." Prescott tried not to sound as weary of the argument as she actually was.

"Negative, Prescott. You don't get to call me Mags. That was reserved for Szab, Anna, and the L.T. There are good reasons for rules, and then there are horses' ass rules that defy good reason. If Jessica lying in that fucking box isn't enough to convince you and Noble..." Words failed her.

Prescott pressed her face closer to Maguire. "You think my heart's not breaking right now? I've known Jess since she was a buck sergeant, way before she was your lieutenant. I don't agree with Noble on this, but it's not my compound and not my call."

Maguire gazed at her through callous eyes. "Go say yer good-byes. They'll be putting the flames to her soon."

Prescott held the gaze for a long moment, then nodded. As she walked to the coffin, she wished she had some token that she could send with Jessica Baumer, Lieutenant, United States Army. Taking a last look at her friend and comrade, she also noted the bottle of dark beer and a dark green shoulder tab inscribed in Irish. She closed her eyes as the tears fell. She was hardly aware when an arm snaked around her waist in support. When she looked over, she was surprised to find Anna standing beside her.

***

Maguire opened the door to the communications room and ordered the communications specialist out. The woman looked at her like she had lost her mind. Maguire pulled her pistol from its holster and pointed it at the woman. "I strongly urge you to unass that chair and get the fuck out."

Though her voice was not raised above its normal volume, the woman immediately responded to Maguire's tone. Maguire closed the door, holstered her weapon, and sat down in the chair. She pulled Baumer's notebook from her pocket and flipped it to the page she had earmarked.

Checking the digits on the paper, she readjusted the long-range frequency on the radio system and began to transmit.

"Fort Mescalero from Maguire." She waited for a response.

"Maguire from Fort Mescalero."

"Fort Mescalero, is Red Horse available?" She actually hoped he was busy somewhere.

"Stand by," came the answer she did not want. Her wait seemed to stretch out forever.

"Maguire from Red Horse."

Maguire's forehead broke a sweat. "Red Horse, Maguire here. I wouldn't use this number if it wasn't important." She swallowed hard, hating the message she was about to convey. "I don't have good news." Her voice cracked.

The other receiver of the transmission was quiet for several moments. "Did she suffer?" Red Horse eventually asked in a heavy voice.

"Some." Maguire could not lie to the man about that. "But she went peacefully. She liked you, Apache. And I think you liked her. I thought you should know."

"Understood. Thank you." He was quiet for long enough that Maguire thought he might have closed the transmission, and then his voice came back on. "Is this recorded?"

"Yes."

"My people will have a mourning ceremony for her. You can call anytime, Currahee. I'm sorry."

"I'm sorry, too." With a sigh, Maguire terminated the transmission and flipped the frequency numbers back to those that the communications specialist had been synched to. She stood up and strode to the door. Pulling it open, she let her gaze fall on the woman she had dismissed. "Did you hear all of that?"

"Yes," she answered quietly.

"Good. When you tell Noble about this, you can at least accurately tell her what I said." Maguire didn't bother to look back as she left the communications area.

Chapter Thirty

Maguire stood on the porch, watching the rain pour down in sheets. She recognized the rhythm and gait of the footsteps that sounded behind her. She took another drag, let the smoke run through her lungs, and exhaled. A plume of smoke exited her mouth.

Noble grunted as she looked out at the torrent. "Freak storm."

"Morrigan, the Celt goddess of war, weeps for her warrior," Maguire allowed as she inhaled more smoke. "She always renders her honor and gratitude for a loyal soul."

The older woman sighed. "I hear an unspoken 'unlike you' in there somewhere."

"I am but a humble servant," Maguire answered.

"Bullshit. There's not much humble about you." Noble almost laughed. "And I don't see you as a servant."

"To the right soul, to the right friend, I am," Maguire said tersely.

"And I'm not the right anything." Noble's voice was devoid of judgment.

Maguire jutted her chin in the direction of the smoke from the pyre. "She was."

"She didn't tell us she got bit."

Maguire wheeled on Noble. "She didn't fecking know. She thought it was the poison ivy she went through chasing after your pet child."

"You leave her out of it!" Noble's eyes flashed.

"I can't. If she had been where she was supposed to be, listened when she was supposed to—and you hadn't panicked—this would not have happened," Maguire snapped back. "You crack the rod on everyone else, and yet you let one child run you."

"You don't understand." Noble's voice cracked. "She's all I have left of Jean."

Maguire turned on her again, eyes blazing. "My son's name was Rory Thomas. You know what happened to Ireland when the shite hit the fan. That's where he was. You at least have your granddaughter."

"I'm sorry."

"Save your trite words and teach your granddaughter better," Maguire barked. "She will have to learn to lead these people when you die. And they will be in a sad state indeed if she keeps being spoiled." Maguire took another drag off her smoke. "Neither of you attended Baumer's final journey."

"I couldn't," Noble said, without admitting what Maguire already undoubtedly knew, that she had been with her granddaughter.

"I'll be leaving in the morning. I've trained your women as much as I can. They'll be fine in a fight."

"You could stay."

Maguire snorted. "You are out of your fecking mind if you think I'd stay. You've got Pres. And do yourself, and your troops, a favor—let Dr. Porras live in the compound. He's a good man and he knows his place."

"Men brought us to this condition," Noble said defensively.

"And a few women. Golda Meier, Maggie of the Iron Hand, Elizabeth Two, Rice, Bhuto… Would you like me to go on?" Maguire flicked her dying smoke into the rain.

Noble peered at Maguire. "What do you really want from me?"

"I want Baumer, Jessica, Lieutenant, United States Army. But that's not going to happen because you commanded that the only fecking qualified doctor could not live in this fecking compound. I truly do understand your reasons for restricting men, but he's not an ordinary man, he's a doctor. All of your soldiers live here, all your workers. Why can you not see that you need him here?" Maguire slid another smoke out of her pocket and lit it with a match from a nearly empty book.

"My medics are just as qualified as Doctor Porras if they know what they're treating," Noble insisted.

"And he has the experience and the education to figure out

what they can't!"

"I made a promise and I'm going to have to stick to it—no men in this sanctuary."

"And when men eventually invade here in overwhelming numbers, hurt and kill your women, will you still be so stubborn?" Maguire demanded.

"Will you?" Noble shouted back.

"I won't be here."

"These women can protect and defend themselves! They need no help from any man. You know this, you've trained them. You're the last one who should believe it will take a man to come to our rescue or save us." Noble took a deep breath and released it slowing to calm herself, but got in one more shot. "Who's the man that's going to come and save you, Maguire?"

"If it ended up being someone as honorable as Doc, I wouldn't have a problem with it," Maguire responded around her cigarette.

Noble studied Maguire for many moments. "Take what you need from the stores. If you find women who want sanctuary, send them here."

Maguire nodded. "I'll even turn off the lights as I go."

***

Prescott knocked on the door to the cabin Maguire had been sharing with Baumer and Anna.

"'S open," Maguire called.

The screen door creaked when it opened and closed. Prescott spotted Maguire, supine on the old couch, drinking a deep amber liquid from a bottle with a black label. Prescott smiled. "I'm not even going to ask how you got your hands on a bottle of Irish whiskey."

"It was in the cellar of that house ya found. I figured they weren't ever goin' to drink it, and I sure as hell wasn't goin' to leave it for those townies to find. It's not every day ya find a bottle of Bushmills 21. I thought I'd save it for a special occasion. Celebratin' the short life of a dear friend qualifies."

Prescott sat opposite Maguire in a rocking chair. "What's so special about Bushmills 21?" Maguire lifted an eyebrow in response, as though Prescott was crazy. "What? I don't drink liquor. I'm strictly a beer girl."

"Only so many bottles of this are made each year. They let it mature in three different casks—an oak bourbon cask then a sherry cask, where it stays for nineteen years." Her voice was smooth and wistful, as she relived a memory. "Then it stays in a Madeira drum for another two years before it's bottled. It's very smooth." She extended the bottle toward Prescott.

"No, thanks."

Maguire silently shook the bottle at her. It was clear she wasn't going to take no for an answer.

Prescott cocked her head and took the bottle. "Okay, but if I puke all over you, don't blame me."

"Ya won't puke. Only the cheap stuff makes ya puke."

"Unless you drink the whole damn bottle," Prescott said, as she held the bottle up to the light. "Good lord, Maguire, this is a third gone. When did you start drinking?"

"After my last run-in with Noble about an hour ago. C'mon, drink."

Prescott cautiously lifted the bottle to her lips and took a sip. It didn't burn all the way down like she expected it to. She took a bigger swallow and savored the hints of honey, mint, and vanilla. "This isn't bad," Prescott conceded, handing the bottle back to Maguire.

"Of course not. It's Irish." Maguire sat up, reached over to an end table, and picked up a small water glass. "Here." She tossed it to Prescott. "Let's toast to Baumer."

Prescott held the glass out, and Maguire half-filled it. The two women clinked their containers together. "To Baumer," they chorused, then each took a drink.

"Now, what brings yer sorry arse to my door?" Maguire asked, not unfriendly but not exactly amiably, either.

"I talked to Noble. She's pissed, but mostly at herself. She doesn't like having anything said against her grandkid, but she admitted to me that you were right. Before all...this...happened, they only had to defend themselves against the usual religious fanatics and the Nazi brotherhood. Now they don't know who or what their enemies are. The kids didn't have to worry about where they played or went on the grounds because they had healers if something happened, and they didn't have to worry about medicines they ordered being contaminated. Now it's survival of the fittest. The elderly doc they had died six months ago, but from what I gather, she was more of an advisor than a practitioner. Noreen has been in charge of the medical clinic for a year or two."

She took another swallow of whiskey. "Noble's set in her ways, Maguire, but she's not stupid. She realizes the compound needs changes, but she's afraid. She won't admit that to many people, but she is."

"What the feck is she afraid of?"

"Men. She was raped, had a daughter who was also raped, and now she's got a granddaughter who is the product of a rape. She doesn't want men anywhere near here. When the male children of the women who live here reach puberty, she orders them out. She believes it's for the safety of the women. She actually likes Doc, but she's afraid to let him live here."

"Doc isn't a rapist."

"I told her that. I told her she couldn't find more of a gentleman. I swore I would vouch for him, and she knows you will."

"And?"

"And she's thinking about it, which is a big step for her."

"It won't bring Baumer back." Maguire's tone was bitter. She took a long drink from the bottle.

"I know." Prescott studied Maguire, then focused on the liquid left in her glass. "I'm sorry about your son." She sucked in a breath. "And about all those stupid things I said about you not knowing about kids."

Maguire released a long sigh. "So am I. Ya didn't know, even Jessica didn't know. It's the past."

"If you ever want to talk… I mean, I know the circumstances were different, but I know how it feels to lose a child."

Maguire stared at the ceiling for a moment. "I appreciate that, Prescott."

"Noble said you are leaving."

"Tomorrow. I can't live here, not the way Noble is running' the place."

"Anything I can do to get you to reconsider?"

"Doubt it."

"Listen, Maguire, I know we haven't gotten along very well, but damn it, woman, you belong here. In the short time we've been here, the women have come to look up to you. They admire your experience and your backbone. If you move to town, you'll be looking over your shoulder all the time. If you stay here, you'll only have to be in defensive mode when there's a legitimate threat. You can help make changes, and this place sorely needs changes Noble can't or won't make. Noble isn't a spring chicken. She's going to need people she can trust to appoint to specific positions."

"She's got her minions."

"Her minions don't know any way but hers. You come in here and bring new blood, and it's damned refreshing. It's a new world. They haven't seen it, experienced it. You have."

"So have you."

"I'm not a leader, Maguire. You are. You have no idea how hard that is for me to say." She finished the last of her whiskey. "Noble needs someone who will stand up to her. I do it situationally. You, well let's be honest, you butt heads with her all day long. You and I are the only ones who aren't intimidated by her."

"More power to ya then."

Prescott placed the glass on another end table and leaned forward, resting her elbows on her knees. "I can't do it alone." There was an awkward silence between them, and finally Prescott stood up. "Think about it, okay?"

"I make no guarantees, but I will think about it."

Prescott nodded. "Also, I'm concerned about Anna. She was really emotionally attached to Baumer."

"She'll be okay. She's stronger than you think."

"I know, but she's so, I don't know, vulnerable. She let me hold her hand through the cremation ritual, and she hates me."

"She needed the physical support. And she doesn't hate ya."

"Well, she certainly doesn't like me."

Maguire started to laugh.

Prescott was perplexed. "What?"

"Are ya feckin' blind? Dumb, feckin' Blighty," Maguire shook her head and took a swig.

"What the hell are you talking about?"

"She's crushin' on ya. When ye're in a room, she can't take her eyes off ya. She hounded Baumer about ya. She had to know everythin' Baumer knew about ya. She doesn't think ya like her."

"You're nuts. She's straight, remember? And I've treated her horribly. How could she feel that way?"

"Ya know it yerself—ya can't help who yer heart tells ya to fall in love with."

"There's no way I'd ever get involved with a straight girl. And you've had way too much to drink, my friend."

Maguire raised the bottle in the air and appeared to calculate the remaining whiskey. "Hell, I've only just begun."

Prescott stayed silent, observing Maguire, but it seemed Maguire was done talking. At least to her.

Maguire raised her eyes. "Damn it, L.T., why'd ya have to go and die? I'm still feckin' mad at ya, ya know?" She let out a sigh. "The plan was to get the others to Noble's and then I get out, relying on no one but myself, responsible for no one but myself."

"What?" Prescott asked. When Maguire didn't respond, Prescott thought it must be drunk ramblings. She shook her head and left the cabin.

Jess dead and an actual agreeable, mostly, conversation with Maguire was definitely messing with Prescott's thought process, so she took the long way around the compound, trying to clear her head. With each step, she found a piece of the trip to sanctuary replaying in her brain until it was nearly overwhelming. When she reached the boundary, she turned back.

Prescott strolled in the direction of her cabin. She stopped when she saw Anna talking with Carrie. She considered the body language of both women and didn't like what she saw. Anna stood with her arms folded tightly across her chest, while Carrie was clearly invading Anna's personal space, stroking her arm and— Was she actually licking her lips?

When Anna looked up and saw Prescott, her relieved smile

spoke volumes. She quickly moved around Carrie and ran to Prescott, latching on to her.

"You okay?" Prescott asked gently.

Anna nodded against Prescott's shoulder. "I am now."

Carrie followed Anna, then drew up short. "Oh. So she's with you?"

Thinking about what Maguire had just told her, Prescott put a protective arm around Anna. Still, she didn't want to assume. "Anna's not with anybody, but if and when she decides she wants to be, that will be her decision, Carrie. Not yours or anyone else's."

A predatory smile lit up Carrie's face, and Prescott wanted to slap the grin right off her.

"So, she's still up for grabs?" Carrie confirmed.

"She's right here," Anna said, annoyed.

Prescott brushed her lips against the top of Anna's head in a reassuring gesture that was more solicitous than romantic. "Anna, why don't you go back to the cabin and keep an eye on Maguire?" she suggested. "She's not feeling any pain right now, and I would hate for her to do anything…" she looked directly into Carrie's eyes, "…rash."

"It probably wouldn't hurt if I made her something to eat." Anna left the security of Prescott's embrace and ran toward her cabin.

"That's some hot little—"

Carrie found herself flat on her back, Prescott's foot on her throat.

"A little advice. Just because you don't have a penis you can use as a power tool doesn't mean you don't have the mindset. I don't like you, Carrie, and so far, I haven't found a lot of women who do. Anna, to the best of my knowledge, is straight. She has had a lot happen to her in the past couple of months that I can guarantee you would have never survived. I'm sure she is very confused about a lot of things, and you will *not* add to that confusion. Got me?"

"Let me up," Carrie hissed.

Prescott pressed down a little with her foot, and Carrie coughed and tried to draw in a breath. "What's that? I can't hear you."

"Yes!" she wheezed. "Yes, I got you."

Prescott removed her foot from Carrie's throat and then maintained a defensive stance as Carrie sat up, rubbed her neck and breathed in several deep breaths.

"Noble will hear about this," Carrie sneered.

"And what will you tell her? That I jacked you up because you were cornering an unwilling participant like a potential rapist? That should go over well with Noble's history."

"A rapist! How dare you!"

"Were you too full of what *you* wanted to see how Anna was responding to you? Or was it that you just didn't care?" Prescott glared. "It's women like you who give lesbians a bad name. Stay away from Anna."

"So you can have her?"

"You're kind of a dense bitch, aren't you? If Anna and I were meant to be together, we'd be there by now." She watched Carrie cautiously as the woman got to her feet. "You're lucky it was me that caught you and not Maguire."

"Maguire doesn't scare me," Carrie said.

"No? She should. On our way here, she cut out a man's beating heart because he defiled and murdered one of our team, our friend. She castrated and gutted the others that had participated. She wouldn't think twice about doing the same to you if she thought you were forcing your intentions on anyone who didn't want them, let alone someone as precious to us as Anna."

"Is that a threat?"

Prescott moved toward Carrie, who took an involuntary step backward. "Absolutely," Prescott said with relish. As Carrie turned and walked away, Prescott added, "You may have gotten into Noble's good graces in the past few years, but she and I were warriors together. That bond will always trump your worth to her any day."

***

Anna found Maguire in a state of Bushmill-induced limbo. As she peered at Maguire over the back of the couch, she was surprised when Maguire's eyes popped open and tried to focus on her.

"Hi, Mags," Anna said brightly.

"Anna, me dearlin'! And how are the three of ya?"

Anna grinned, momentarily forgetting about the unpleasantness with Carrie. "How about I cook you some supper?"

"Oh, that would be lovely. Could one of ya stay here, though?"

Anna laughed outright. "Nope. The three of us are needed at the grill."

"I suggest fried eggs, if we've got 'em," Maguire told her cheerfully.

"I went to the big barn this morning, so we've got fresh eggs."

"And fried potatoes? Fried potatoes would be grand." Maguire wasn't exactly slurring her words, but she wasn't speaking clearly either.

"If it's one thing we always have in stock, its potatoes, so you're in luck."

"Will ya eat with me, Anna? I'd love the pleasure of your company."

"The second I smell it cooking, you know I'll have to have some."

"Ye're too good to me, Anna."

"It's just good to finally be able to give back."

"Nah, it's more than that. Ye're special. Ya care about people. Ye're goin' to make someone a splendid wife someday." Maguire looked up at her. "Prescott, maybe?"

Anna flushed. "Why do you say Prescott?"

"I've seen the way ya look at her, even more so since Jess died."

Anna leaned forward and rested her forearms on the back of the couch. "Can I tell you a secret?"

"Sure. I probably won't remember it by tomorrow mornin', so now's a good time."

"I really like Doc, too. I like him and Pres about the same. My heart flutters equally when I see them. You would think that after what I've been through with men, I wouldn't think that way about another one, but Doc is so different. He's so gentlemanly and kind. And handsome."

"That he is," Maguire agreed.

"And then suddenly, I started having feelings for Prescott. They came out of nowhere and I'm puzzled by them, because I've never been attracted to a woman before, especially not one who was as mean to me as Prescott was in the beginning. You would have thought that if I was going to go for any woman, it would have been Jessica or you, but not Prescott."

"Ya can't help who yer heart tells ya to fall in love with," Maguire said.

"Love? I don't think I'm in love, but I'm…definitely attracted," Anna admitted. "I like this feeling of…I don't know…hope, I guess. I'm not ready to act on it yet. With either of them."

The moment was ruined by a very loud hiccup.

Anna looked down at Maguire, who was grinning up at her. "Right. Food. I'll be back."

***

Maguire woke with someone snuggled up against her back. She recognized Anna's lavender scented soap and foggily recalled that the girl had staked out the space beside her in hopes of convincing her to stay. When Maguire said she couldn't, Anna put her arms around her and said, "Then I'll anchor you here so you can't leave." And then Anna fell asleep.

A sad smile touched Maguire's lips. She would miss Anna most of all. If she could be certain that Anna would be safe, or have any kind of a future back at Victoria's in El Paso, she'd take the girl with her.

"Anna, darlin', I have to get up," Maguire said softly. Arms tightened around her, and then Anna's voice vibrated against her back.

"No, you don't." Her words were thick with sleep.

Maguire patted Anna's hands. "Don't think I'm not enjoying this, but I have a lot to do to get ready to go."

"Please, Mags, you can't leave. Who will be my voice of reason?"

Maguire chuckled. "Sweetheart, if I'm your voice of reason, you're in serious trouble. I kill people for a living, for reasons I hope you will never have to understand. Don't look to me for sanity."

"You know what I mean. Who will I talk to about Doc and Pres?"

"Can't say I'm really a big help in that area." Maguire sat up, breaking Anna's grasp on her.

Anna sat up with her. "Sure you are."

Maguire scrubbed her face with her hands, then ran her fingers through her hair. She threw back the covers and got out of bed, stretching as she stood up. She looked back at Anna, who was fully clothed. Tears glistening in her eyes, Anna looked crestfallen and vulnerable. Maguire sat down on the bed and faced her.

"There are certain things I just cannot do," Maguire began. She reached over and took Anna's hand. "Jess was very special to me, and she might have been saved if not for Noble's pigheadedness. The entire way here, all I heard about was Noble this and Noble that, and how she really lived up to her last name. Well, I've seen no evidence of that since I've been here. I cannot live under the command of someone who can't save even one life if it means making a decision that is outside her comfort zone, much less the rest of us, if it comes to that."

Anna said hopefully, "She's going to allow Doc on the compound. Guarded, but still…"

"Too little, too late, I'm afraid."

"But clearly she learns from her mistakes."

"Jess' unnecessary death was an unforgivable mistake," Maguire instantly regretted that her voice had been sharper than she had intended. She didn't want to hurt Anna.

"Mags, you said yourself that we're existing in a whole new world, with a whole different set of rules. We're all learning what's the best way to survive. I think maybe Noble's learning that, too."

Maguire released Anna's hand and stood up. "She's too set in her ways. She won't take advice, she won't accept input from experienced people, she won't—" Maguire sighed in exasperation. "What if her next mistake is you?"

Anna swallowed hard, then said softly, "Then you won't be here to save me."

"I couldn't save Jess. What makes you think I could save you?"

"Jess wasn't your fault, Mags."

"I should have brought Doc directly to the cabin the instant we got him here from town that night. I should have walked him through the front gates and shot anyone who got in my way."

Anna knelt on the bed and reached out, her fingers closing around Maguire's wrist. "Jess wasn't your fault," she repeated more firmly. "And walking through the front gate like the Terminator probably would have gotten you and Doc both dead too. Mags, we're the only ones in this entire compound who have been outside these walls since Day Zero, other than just going into town. We've seen what's going on out there, none of these women have. All they know is what they saw and heard on the internet and cable before most of the communications stopped. We're their link to the new reality—you, me, Pres, and Doc. If you go, that means it'll just be the three of us. You know they won't listen to Doc because he's a man, and they won't listen to me because I'm, well, me. But you and Pres have the experience and background and training to make the rest listen."

"Noble doesn't listen to me, she barely listens to Prescott. If she is going to put this entire compound in harm's way, I cannot stand by and watch it happen. I am not going to die because of someone else's stupidity; I'll die from my own mistakes, thank you very much."

"You're going to go regardless of what I say, aren't you?"

"I'm afraid so, darlin'."

Anna drew a deep, determined breath. "Then the least I can do is fix you a good breakfast to get you started."

She climbed off the bed and hurried from the room, but not before Maguire saw her tears begin to fall.

***

Maguire settled her ruck over her shoulders and shifted until the weight was as comfortable as it was going to get. Without a backward glance, she walked out of the cabin and silently closed the door behind her. The early morning fog settled on the ground, and for one moment she could hear only peaceful silence.

She slid her boonie hat onto her head and began her walk from the temporary quarters to the front house. Women nodded their heads or turned away. There were some, friends of Carrie most likely, who grinned in triumph. To them she flashed an evil smile that sent most of them scurrying out of the way.

As she passed the troll in question, Carrie sent a smirk straight at Maguire. For some reason it amused the Irish woman rather than evoking the intended response. She didn't bother with another look in Carrie's direction, but suddenly her way was blocked.

"I see your true colors are showing. Yellow much?" There was more than a hint of triumph in Carrie's voice.

Maguire slowly looked the woman up and down until Carrie squirmed, then said, as though she was commenting on the weather, "Stay downwind of your target. The stench of your insecurity is a dead giveaway of your presence." Maguire continued in a level tone, "Now, unless you'd like a repeat of our first meeting, get out of my way."

Carrie stepped away.

Maguire went up the stairs and pulled the door open and entered the command building. It was her intention to drop off a list of the essentials she'd taken, but hearing loud voices as she neared the office, she hesitated in the hallway. Luck was not with her, as Prescott spotted her and waved her into the main office. Maguire sighed as she stepped inside and closed the door behind her. When she turned, she saw everyone was staring at her.

"What?"

"How do you know Dr. Elaine Madras?"

"I don't. Should I?"

"She is a satellite engineer who's trapped in Washington state at present."

"Okay. And? Still don't know her."

"Well, she knows you," Prescott added.

Maguire shrugged. "That's not unusual. I've trained and interacted with a lot of people whose names I don't remember."

"She asked for you, specifically," Noble insisted.

Maguire was losing her patience. "Look, I only came to drop off a list of the supplies I am taking with me. I need to be on my way."

"She asked for you by name, asked that you be the one to lead the rescue team," Noble clarified.

"And I repeat, I have never heard of her."

Noble held up a piece of paper. "She was very specific."

"Good for her. We're done here."

"Aren't you even curious about this bizarre message she has sent for you?" Noble shook the paper

Maguire rolled her eyes. "I'm more curious about what time I'm going to get out of here."

"Maguire!" Prescott said sharply. "This is serious. There's something not right. Let Noble read Dr. Madras' message. If it still means nothing to you, then fucking leave, okay? I'll even walk you out the gate."

"Fine. What's the message?"

Noble adjusted her glasses and began to read from the paper. "Message as follows: I am requesting Staff Sergeant Maguire to help me practice the Tango so I can woo my Romeo, Oscar, during my upcoming flight on Delta to my Alpha brother's wedding in India."

Noble looked up from the paper. "She was adamant that I transcribe this message exactly as she dictated, and that I personally hand it to you so that you read it, retain it, and not destroy it until the message becomes clear to you."

Utterly confused, Maguire took the piece of paper as a dull ache began above her right eye. "This means nothing to me. Delta isn't flying anywhere anymore and India has been destroyed. Your scientist is clearly a nutcase, and I'm not going anywhere near her." Maguire shoved the message into a cargo pocket and turned to leave.

"Maguire," Noble said, her patience clearly wearing thin, "there is phonetic code in that message. She's not a delusional woman. She knows everything was destroyed. This means something, something critical."

"I'm sure it does, just not to me." She moved toward the door, then glanced back at Noble. "Good luck with your mission, whatever it turns out to be." To Prescott, she said, "Take care of Anna. I'll haunt you if you let anything happen to her, and you know we Irish can do such things."

She pulled the door open and went out to the porch. As she stopped to readjust her ruck, Prescott joined her.

"Maguire—"

"I'm done, Prescott. I can't say it any clearer than that."

"Do you even know where you're going?"

"I'll know when I get there." She stepped off the porch and proceeded toward the gate.

***

By the time Maguire reached the town, her curiosity about the note had been piqued, but she didn't take it out of her pocket and read it. She suspected it was some kind of trick to get her to stay, although why they would want her to was a mystery to her.

She walked up to Doc's door and knocked. While she waited, she endured some curious looks from passing townies. She guessed it wasn't every day that a soldier arrived in full combat uniform and gear.

Doc opened the door and smiled when he found her standing on the front porch. "Maguire. Come in." He stepped back to let her in. "I've got tea on. Drop your gear anywhere."

Maguire didn't even attempt to argue with him. She shucked out of her rucksack and placed it by the front door, but kept her rifle in hand as she followed him to the kitchen and sat down when he waved towards the chairs at the kitchen table.

"When are you moving to Noble's fortress?" Maguire asked as Doc placed a cup of hot tea in front of her.

"I'm guessing I won't be. Now that you won't be there, Noble won't feel pressured to bring me out."

"When did she decide she was going to allow that?" Maguire's pitch rose with every word.

"She sent word through Ms. Jennings the day you decided

to leave, I guess." Doc reached over and placed his hand gently over Maguire's, and she instantly calmed. "It's okay. Without you there, I think my existence would be pretty miserable anyway."

Maguire sighed and pinched the bridge of her nose. Her headache was getting worse, and she hoped she could ward it off without having to ask Doc for an aspirin.

"Any idea where you're going?" he asked

Maguire smiled. "Prescott asked me the same thing." She shrugged. "I have options. Maybe back to El Paso. I don't know."

"You could stay here in town with me," Doc offered.

"Too close to Noble. I don't trust her. She has an agenda."

"What kind of an agenda?"

"No clue. She even made up some story about a cryptic message to get me to stay."

"That sounds a little James Bond-ish. What kind of message?"

Maguire leaned back and stuck her hand in her pocket, pulling out the crumpled piece of paper between her fingers. "Something silly. She read it to me, and then she said I had to read it myself. Some scientist friend of hers in Washington needs rescuing and supposedly asked for me personally."

"That does actually sound a little invented," Doc said as he squeezed the teabag against the spoon, releasing the liquid into his cup. He held out his hand. "Want me to toss it out for you?"

Maguire flattened the note against the table. "Let me read it to you first. I mean, she didn't even try to have it make any sense." She concentrated on the piece of paper and read aloud, "I am requesting Staff Sergeant Maguire to help me practice the Tango so I can woo my Romeo, Oscar, during my upcoming flight on Delta to my Alpha brother's wedding in India."

She looked up at Doc. "See what I mean? Noble tried to get me to see the phonetics in it as some kind of code." Maguire shook her head.

"Could it be?"

"Seriously, Doc?"

"Maybe before you discount it completely, you should exhaust all possibility that it could be a code."

Maguire looked up at him and grinned. "Are you stalling to get me to stay longer?"

Doc smiled back. "Maybe. Or maybe I'm just a sucker for spy novels." He stood up to throw away his used tea bag. "At least stay for lunch so I know I'm sending you off with a full belly."

Maguire considered for a moment. "Sure, why not. It's not like I have anywhere in particular to be."

Doc returned to the table with a pencil and a blank sheet of paper. "Okay, Watson. Let's get started."

"Watson? Why can't I be Holmes?"

"Because I thought of it first, and if the message does turn out to be significant, that would make me Sherlock," he told her.

"Don't get your hopes up," Maguire said. She scanned the crinkled paper. "Okay, let's see. Might as well start with the phonetics. Write down just the first letter of every word. Tango, Romeo, Oscar, Delta, Alpha, India." She looked up at Doc. "Got it?"

"Yeah. It spells Trodai. You're right. That makes no sense."

"Trodai? Like Troh Day?" Maguire raised an eyebrow.

"Yep. Unless it's in a foreign language or something."

"Let me see that." Doc slid the paper over to her. "Trodai," she said. "Trodai," she repeated. Something prompted her to put a diacritical mark over the i. "*Trodaí*." Her Irish accent read it aloud. "*Trodaí*," she said again, and suddenly it felt as if a curtain fell away from her memory, and she drew in a sharp breath as her headache exploded in a sharp burst.

***

Doc saw Maguire go pale and begin to hyperventilate, and his professional instincts kicked in. "Maguire, listen to me," he said, his voice soothing. "I don't have a paper bag so you're going to have to press one of your nostrils closed and try breathing slowly from deep within your diaphragm out the open nostril."

She didn't appear to be listening. For a moment, she seemed catatonic, and that worried him. For Maguire to be out of control in any manner was disturbing. He left her briefly, while he quickly retrieved his stethoscope and blood pressure cuff. *What in heaven's name just happened?*

***

Trodaí. Gaelic for Warrior. That one word triggered everything for Maguire. How could she have been so deeply psy-opsed that all memory of Operation Jaded Right had been repressed? How could she have lost nearly a year of her life and how could it so suddenly and completely come back now? And why hadn't she been activated *before* the attack?

"Maguire? Hey, come back to me."

Doc's comforting tone eased into her consciousness. She forced herself to focus, to get herself back to the present moment. She followed Doc's instructions to close her eyes and try to concentrate on her breathing, and eventually felt aware and responsive. She looked into his concerned eyes. "Hey, Doc," she said.

He gaped at her. "Are you okay?"

"Define 'okay,'" she said, her soft response sounding more anguished than she'd intended.

He pumped up the blood pressure cuff, let that read, and then listened to her heart and lungs with his stethoscope. "Pulse, respiration, and blood pressure are back to normal." Doc rested the tubing of the instrument around his neck. "What happened?"

"An epiphany?" She didn't know why her voice lilted the last word, which turned the statement into a question.

"The message was code, wasn't it?"

Maguire nodded. "Yes, Sherlock. You called it."

"What does it mean?" When Maguire cleared her throat, Doc asked, "Do you need some water?"

"Do you have any whiskey?"

***

Doc handed Maguire an 8-ounce, clear glass tumbler of

some nameless Kentucky bourbon. It wasn't Irish whiskey but it would have to do. Not even bothering with a meaningless cheer, she took several swallows and tolerated the burning roughness as it went down.

Doc sat opposite her at the kitchen table. "What's going on?"

Maguire knew she needed to process everything first, but she also needed to talk about it. Afterwards, would Doc really think she'd lost it? She suspected that when they first met, he'd thought she was certifiable. Would this prove him right? Was she? She took another drink of the amber liquid and then looked him in the eye. "I think I know what happened that resulted in Day Zero."

"What? You have to tell me, Maguire. We're in this together now."

"Not in *this,* I'm afraid." She sensed his excitement, anticipation, and dread. She drew a deep breath. "Do you know anything about the attacks?"

"The same as you, I suppose. There was no warning. Suddenly everything was just...over. I don't understand how that could happen. We are supposed to have the most sophisticated early warning and prevention systems in the world. How could we not know anything?"

"That's just it, Doc. We did know."

Doc looked at her as though she'd grown a second head. "What? I don't— What are you saying?"

"I'm saying that our government not only knew it was going to happen, they planned it and executed it."

"*Our* government? The USA?"

"I won't go in to exactly how I know, but do you remember the president's chief of staff?"

"Segundo? Yeah, he was as much of a butthead as the president and his administration."

"Actually, I guess that when push came to shove, he wasn't. Most of that was an act. He found out that the president's cabinet, the corporatists, and the extreme religious right were joining together to plot a catastrophic event that would leave two-thirds to three-quarters of the world's population dead or dying."

When Doc could speak, he uttered on word, "Why?"

"Isn't it obvious? So that the power behind it could go underground and re-emerge as the one-world government, building world domination with them as emperors. The fundamentalists would have their 'end times' and be out of the picture."

"How could you know and not do or say anything to stop it?" he asked, shock and disgust clear in his voice.

"I couldn't. I swear I didn't remember anything until about 10 minutes ago. Segundo worked with a few of his like-minded friends to put together and train a top-secret team. It was called Operation Jaded Right. Our mission was to learn what was being planned, who was planning it, how they were going to do it, and how it could be prevented."

"But it wasn't prevented."

"I have to suspect Segundo was either killed in the attacks, or he found out when it was to happen, and he was murdered. They gave us all this intel and instruction and then repressed our memories for plausible deniability in case the team was somehow exposed before we were activated. We went back to our regular lives, subject to a trigger of some sort to set us in motion. It never came." She took a deep breath and released it. "You did mention James Bond."

"Jesus Christ, Maguire." Doc ran his hand through his hair.

"I know, Doc. This is just the short version. I don't have the luxury of time to give you all the details. I've already wasted six precious months not being with the team to stop this before the situation gets even worse."

"Who is this person who sent you the message?"

"I don't know. But I am damned sure going to find out."

***

Noble awakened to a pounding on her door. She weighed the urgency of the knocking with her need for sleep. Regardless of what kind of physical shape she was in, at her age, sex wore her out.

The pounding persisted. Noble looked over at the restless body next to her. "Stay here. I'll see what's going on." She sat up, slipped on boxer shorts and pulled a t-shirt over her head. She padded barefoot across the floor, out of the bedroom and through the office, to the front door. She flipped a hook that latched the door closed. It was more to protect her privacy when she had overnight guests than it was to try and keep anyone out. In fact, she only used the "lock" when she was occupied in the bedroom.

Noble yanked the door open. "This better be—" She stopped dead at the sight of Maguire. The soldier shouldered her way past Noble and set her ruck on the desk. "What the hell are you doing back?" Noble demanded.

"Tell Carrie her night guard shift is piss poor." She nodded toward the bedroom. "Get Prescott up. We need to talk."

***

The Beginning

Coming soon!

The Resistance (Book Two of The Sanctuary Series)

Author Roselle Graskey

Author Cheyne Curry

About the Authors

Roselle Graskey is the author of two published books, October Echoes and Life's Little Edge. She currently lives in Galveston, TX with her long-suffering wife. Roselle is a veteran of the US Army during the Cold War as a Military Police Officer and Desert Storm. When not working her day job she is writing, reading or watching her favorite hockey team. Now, however she has her own Ro room so that she does not drive her long-suffering wife any crazier than usual.

Cheyne Curry is the author of three published books, Renegade, Clandestine and The Tropic of Hunter. She currently lives in the Midwest with her wife, Brenda, and their fur babies, Liam, Mesa and Belladonna Bossy Pants (the CEO of Bossy Pants Books). Cheyne, a former US Army Military Police Officer, was stationed in California and with the Southern European Task Force (SETAF) in Italy. Cheyne also co-writes, co-produces and composes music for short films for 3 Grunts Productions, her media company with Brenda. Cheyne has a background in law enforcement and entertainment security.

The End

OTHER TITLES BY CHEYNE CURRY
PREVIOUSLY PUBLISHED

Clandestine   Tia Ramone is a gritty, self-destructive, ex-CIA operative who seeks absolution in a bottle. Jody Montgomery is a naïve heiress to a vast fortune, married to a man she discovers she really doesn't know. Tia's and Jody's paths cross in a sinister plot they are forced to take part in. With both their lives at stake, can the clandestine meeting that brought them together ultimately be the bond that saves them?

The Tropic of Hunter   Hunter Roberge left Otter Falls, Vermont when she was 18, to get away from a life of scandal and judgment. Sixteen years later she returns to her 'hometown' for the funeral of the one person who condemned her the most: her mother. Being bequeathed the family house is just the first in a long line of mysteries that unravel the fabric of everything Hunter believes to be true. Can the support of a childhood acquaintance keep her on the right track or will she once again fall victim to her mother's hatred?

Renegade   What would you do if one minute you were in the 21st century and the next you were in the 19th? One day you're driving a Mustang and the next day you're riding one? Dirty cop Trace Sheridan faces this dilemma as she moves from a present day mob war to a range war over a hundred years in the past. The year is 1879, when cattle barons, crooked lawmen, saloons, painted ladies, cowboys and Indians ruled the Wild West, and laws were only as strong as the gunman who upheld them. In Sagebrush, the town and the sheriff belong to the Cranes, who take what they want or bad things happen. Trace finds this out firsthand when she ends up on the land of Rachel Young, a struggling ranch woman who won't give in to the merciless cattle baron and his obsessed son. For some unexplainable reason, Rachel trusts the enigmatic Trace who uses 21st century sensibilities to battle 19th century turmoil, while Trace is forced to keep the secret of her origin from the attractive and vulnerable Rachel. Renegade is a story of redemption in its purest form as Trace discovers what truly matters in life and how past really is prologue.

OTHER TITLES WRITTEN BY
ROSELLE GRASKEY:

October Echoes   Sara Pierson is a dedicated FBI agent, living and breathing her job. When a seven year old boy is kidnapped she pledges that the boy will see his mother's face again. She never expects the twists and turns the case provides, complicating things and making her job that much harder. Nora de Burgh is an Irish terrorist, in an American prison, with a long-ago tie to the boy's father. She has vowed to take her revenge - that the man is now a diplomat certainly complicates everything about the case. It's apparent that Nora has information that Sara needs from their first meeting - contacts in the Irish-American underworld, a culture that never forgets their history of hate and pain. Who are the good guys in the world of international politics? It's hard to tell and Sara begins to learn that fact the hard way. In order to find the boy and keep her promise, she must learn to trust a terrorist and along the way she learns that her black and white world has room for shades of gray. From Ireland to America and back again...both women find that the echoes of the past sometimes find the present.

Life's Little Edge   Callan O'Malley embodies everything that should scare Terri Barclay. O'Malley freelances as a gun runner for a biker gang, the dark secrets of her past influencing her present. Thrown together by circumstance and unexpected complications of living in the biker world, the women's lives are turned into chaos. Loyal friends of past and present, add to the mixture which brings the two women closer than they ever thought possible. Terri, however, is hiding her own secrets. Secrets that could very well get her--or O'Malley--killed. Terri must walk a fine line between what she now wants and what she is forced into by her sense of duty. She must redefine her approach on life and love and acknowledge that not everything is as black and white as she once believed. She soon discovers that living on the edge with a woman such as O'Malley can be an exciting yet dangerous place.

The End

COMING SOON:

Permission To Recover (By Cheyne Curry): It's 1977 and Army CID agent, Lieutenant Dale Oakes is awaiting a medical discharge when she is reactivated by her former commanding officer and secret crush, Lieutenant-Colonel Anne Bishaye. Dale is planted into the first, experimental, co-ed OSUT (One Station Unit Training) company. Her assignment is to spend at least 16 weeks to expose who is setting up drill sergeants, giving the battalion a black eye. She and her undercover partner, Lt. Shannon Walker, get caught up in a whirlwind of unintentional intrigue while trying to keep their cover as new recruits and military law enforcement trainees. Dale discovers much more than is ever intended about the case and herself, as well. Can Dale and Shannon solve the mystery before time runs out?

The Resistance (Book Two of the Sanctuary Series by Roselle Graskey and Cheyne Curry)

www.ingramcontent.com/pod-product-compliance
Lightning Source LLC
Chambersburg PA
CBHW060529260626
47161CB00003B/827